Cover Designed by Artscandare

Editors: Jenny Sims & K.F. Starfell Books

Paperback ISBN: 979-8-9893447-4-1

AMY ROSE

CROSSING

SACRED LINES

CONTENT WARNINGS

Religious trauma
Substance abuse
Religious manipulation
Being shamed for clothing choices
Non-consensual groping
Threat of physical harm from a parental figure
Sexually explicit content
Automotive accident while under the influence of
alcohol
Alcoholism
Emotional abuse from a parent Narcissistic parent
Being disowned
Deconstructing religious beliefs
Emotional neglect from a parent
Emotional abuse
Physical abuse/Assault from a parent

CROSSING SACRED LINES

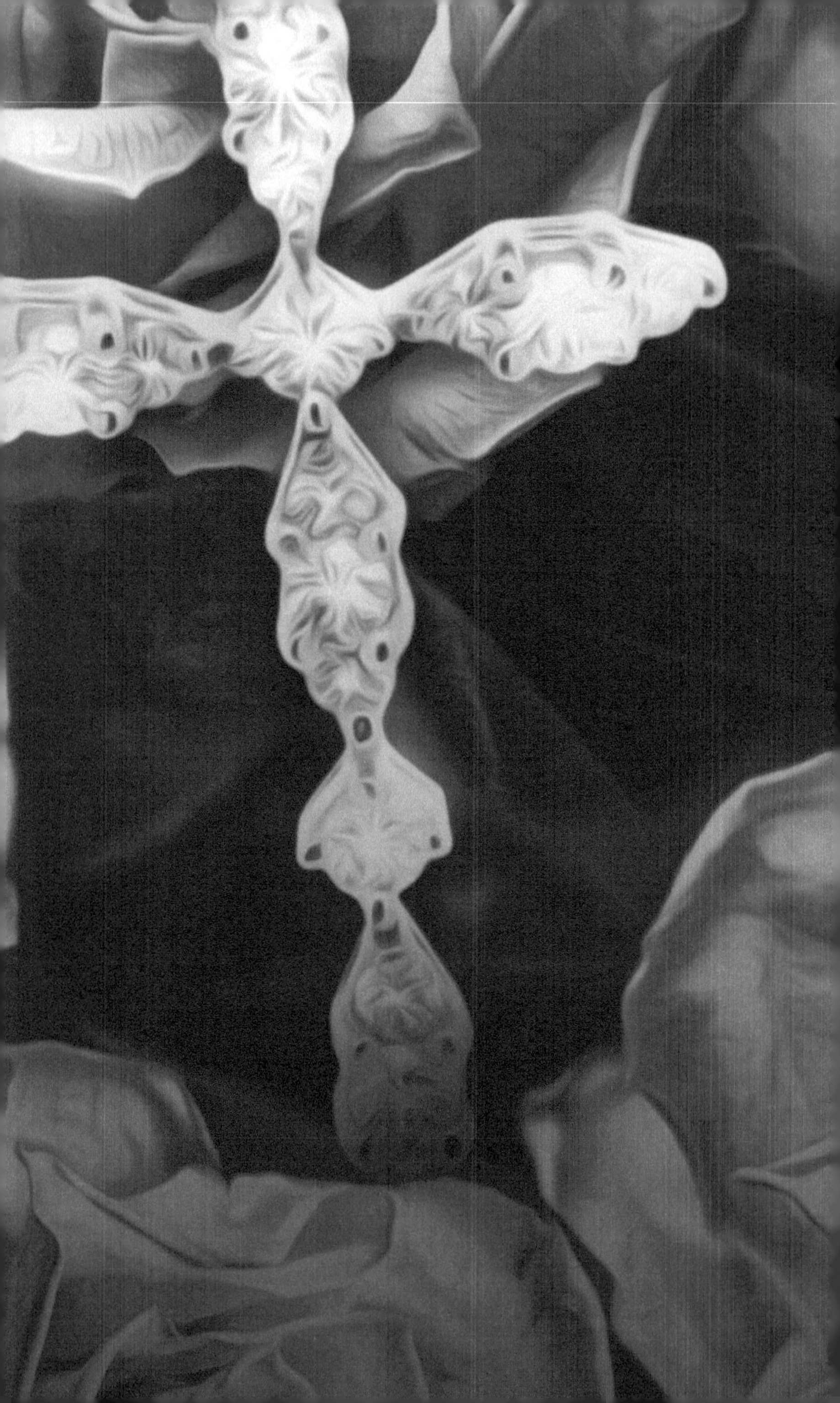

CHAPTER ONE

CURIOSITY, A DOUBLE-EDGED SWORD, OFTEN whispered tales of caution through my father's words.

Growing up within the confines of a deeply religious home, combined with residing in a small town, meant rumors spread like wildfire. A single transgression, even uttering a curse word, would consign one to the pits of hell in the eyes of our community.

Among my family, I remain the quiet one, while my twin brother thrives as the social butterfly and sports enthusiast. My love for solitude and books earned me the title of the family book nerd, and I wasn't exactly looking to change that.

Though I have a few friends, they often gather without me. To be fair, they always ask if I want to join them. More often than not, I prefer to be home, lost in the pages of whatever book held my fascination at the moment. My family and friends constantly remind me that the book will still be there upon my return, but why venture out into the unforgiving heat or bitter cold when I have nowhere pressing to be?

"Elena, get down here, please!" The desire for my own apartment grows stronger with each passing day. Living here has its limits, and I crave independence.

With a sigh, I clasp my silver cross necklace and check my reflection in the mirror. My blond hair, freshly washed and carefully curled, is part of my daily routine. The thought of being labeled unkempt arises if I don't maintain my appearance.

Descending the hardwood stairs, I spot my mom standing near the kitchen archway.

"Yes, Mom?"

"Can you go pick your brother up from his buddy's house?" she asks, arms crossed.

"Is he okay?" I gaze outside the window to witness the sunset peeking through.

"No, he's not feeling well."

"Alright, I'll head out." I grab my purse and car keys, ready to embark on the mission.

I know life isn't as amazing as he expected it to be back when he was in high school. He was a talented quarterback at the time and wanted to go play at a university, but my parents didn't offer to help with tuition, and his grades weren't great enough to win him a substantial scholarship.

To avoid going into debt, Christian just didn't go. He stayed here at home and has been actively looking for a job. Any job. I know my brother is most likely drunk, trying to avoid our strict parents, who have no tolerance for his antics despite his age. Our parents are controlling and treat us as if we are still children. My brother is partying on the other side of town.

He trusts me with his location, knowing I won't tell our parents. I understand his desire to have fun without their interference. He's not actually at his buddy's house, but more like his buddy's parents' beach house.

Driving into the almost dark neighborhood with dimmed streetlights, I flick on my brights to better navigate the surroundings. The multiple-colored lights emanating from a distance confirmed that he's at the beach house, not with his usual group of friends.

As I get out of the car, I'm instantly greeted by a loud party atmosphere with blaring music and people holding red Solo cups. Pushing through the crowd, I make my way to the porch stairs and open the front door. I scan the crowd for my brother, but I lock eyes with his buddy Toby. Standing at an imposing 6'5", he towers over most with an air of undeniable presence. His hair, a rich dark brown, contrasts starkly with his striking ocean blue eyes.

Despite his handsome features, he's notorious for his abrasive demeanor; a man who bends the world to his will, often leaving a trail of exasperation in his wake. His reputation as an unyielding force is well-earned, for he is someone who always —without fail—gets his way.

"Hey, Elena, didn't think you'd come," a deep, raspy voice inquires.

"I'm not here for fun. Where's Christian?" My pulse increases when I see him.

"He's upstairs in my room," he says casually.

Nodding, I make my way toward the stairs. But before I make it to the steps, a hand grasps my arm, stopping me. I turn around to see Toby.

"Wait," he says.

"What?"

"I wouldn't go up there if I were you," he says.

"Let go of me and explain why,"

He lets go and smirks. "Bossy, I like it. He might be with some chick."

"I've seen him like this before."

I turn back around and continue upstairs. I don't see anyone on the upper floor except for a few closed doors and one marked **"Bathroom."** It seems like a creative way to prevent guests from getting lost during these wild house parties. I'm not sure if it works, considering the drunkenness.

I open the first door to the left, but it's empty. Closing it, I move on to the door beside it. But before my hand can reach the doorknob, a repulsive sound from the other side reaches my ears. Scrunching my nose in disgust, I abandon the idea of entering the room and instead make my way back down the stairs.

Toby's waiting at the bottom, arms crossed and a smirk on his face.

"Don't even say it," I warn, annoyed by his potential remarks.

"Say what?" he replies with a hint of sarcasm.

"You know what."

"If I have nothing nice to say, I won't say it. Promise."

Giving him a glare, I walk outside through the open door. I sit on the top step of the porch stairs, awaiting my brother's inevitable appearance.

He's lucky our mom and dad remain oblivious to his activities. Our strict parents used to ground us for a grade lower than an A, and they forced us to concentrate solely on our studies. It made going out with friends difficult.

"Are you alright?" a familiar voice inquires.

It's Toby, which surprises me, since he isn't known for being caring or considerate.

"I'm fine," I say.

He nods, his eyes holding mine for a moment longer than necessary. "Just making sure. You know, parties like this can get out of hand sometimes."

I give a half-hearted smile, not entirely convinced by his explanation. "Yeah, I know. Thanks for the warning."

He seems to hesitate for a moment before speaking again. "You're different from the others who come here. I've seen you around town, and at your house when hanging with Christian, keeping to yourself, buried in books. It's not a bad thing... just different."

I shift uncomfortably under his gaze, not used to being the subject of anyone's attention, especially not Toby's. "I guess I've always been more of a homebody."

Toby leans against the porch railing, his eyes scanning the chaotic scene before us. "You're missing out on life, you know?"

His words hit a nerve, and I sense a pang of defensiveness emerge within me. "Just because I prefer books to parties doesn't mean I'm missing out. I enjoy my quiet time, and I have my own way of experiencing life."

"Oh yeah, and what might that be?" he says, crossing his arms.

"None of your business."

"Fair enough. I suppose everyone has their own way of living."

The laughter, music, and chatter provide a

stark contrast to the stillness I crave. A part of me wonders why Toby bothers hosting these parties.

After a while, my blonde messy haired brother stumbles out of the house, looking disheveled but seemingly in high spirits. I sigh, knowing he will face the consequences of his actions later, but for now, I need to get him home safely.

"Come on, Christian, let's go," I call out to him.

He turns toward my voice and smiles drunkenly.

"Hey, Sis! Having fun at the party?"

"Not really," I reply, offering him a hand to steady himself.

Toby steps forward. "I'll help you get him to your car," he offers.

"Thanks," I say.

We walk my brother to the car, and I get him buckled up in the back seat. As I close the door, I turn to give Toby a nod and he smiles, and I get in the driver's seat.

Life is filled with complexities, and we are all just trying to navigate our way through it.

As I pull into the driveway and help my brother inside, I notice the house is quiet, and the only lights on are the hallway floor lights. I help him up the stairs and guide him to his room. I lean down to sit him on the bed, and he plops back and begins to snore. Glad I was able to complete my mission of helping my brother. I giggle quietly and head straight to my room.

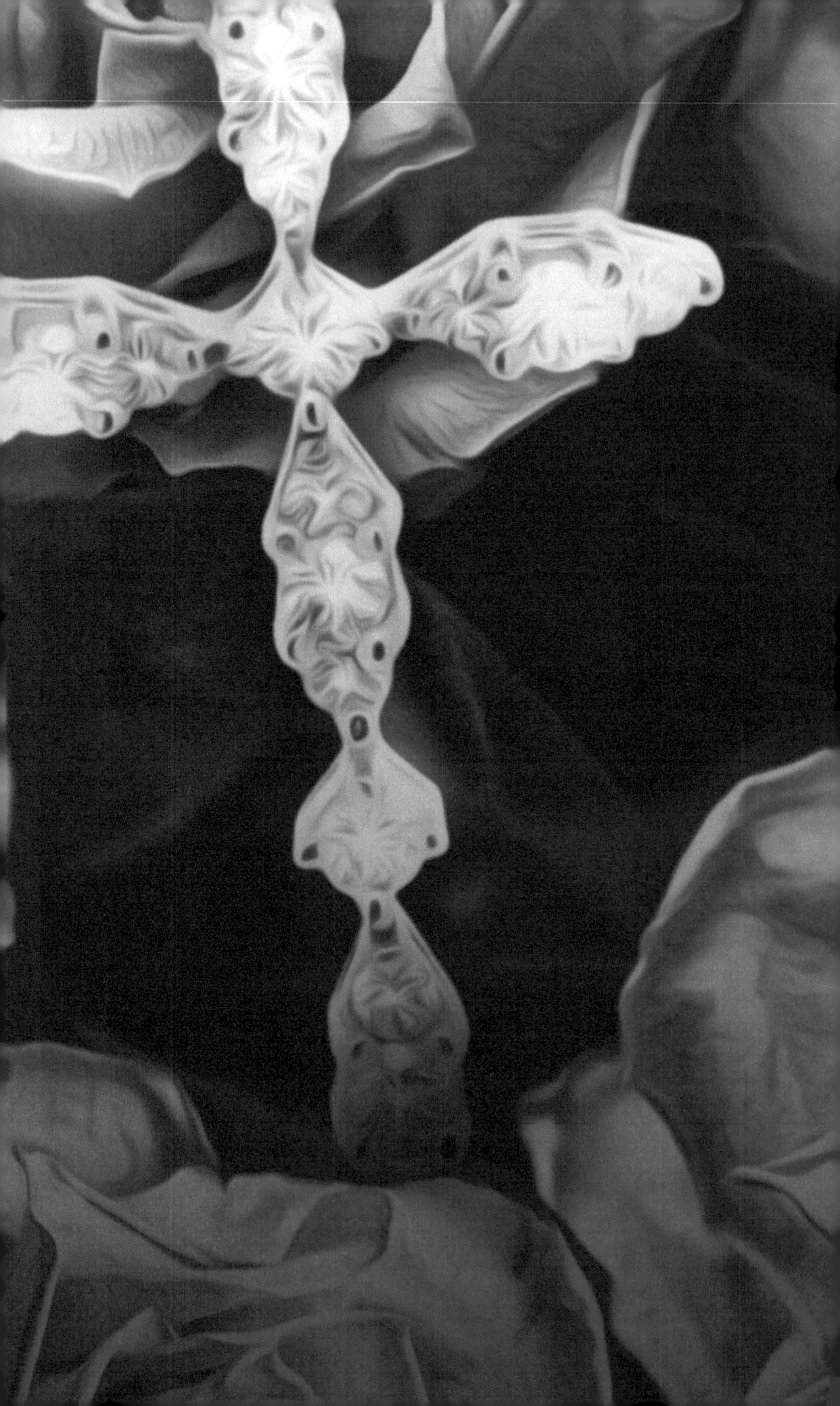

CHAPTER TWO

I'm so glad I'm out of school. I graduated top of my class a year ago.

The days of being grounded for a poor grade are over. The kids in school weren't as innocent as their parents thought, bullying other kids left and right like they owned the place. It was not my cup of tea.

I rush down the stairs, already dressed in a black pair of leggings and a jacket. Ready for my jog to work.

"Bye, sweetie!" my mom hollers.

"See you later!" I yell back.

Hurrying out the door, I walk down the driveway and start my jog on the sidewalk. The cool breeze hits my face, and I breathe in the smell of crisp, burning leaves. Fall is my favorite time of the year.

No one really wears sweaters and jackets in early fall. It's always nice out here in Illinois. It's basically a tank top and short attire until it's 30 degrees and shady outside. But right now, summer dresses, t-shirts, shorts, skirts, anything that suits the summer weather we will wear until it's too cold.

The library is just a few blocks away, so I enjoy walking to work when the weather is nice, like today.

I push open the glass door and head toward the back. My boss, Lindsay, is sitting in her office looking over something on her computer.

"Hi, Elena, would you come here for a second," she says, her voice cheery.

"Hi Lindsay, what's up?"

"It'll be a pretty slow day today, so if you want to go home, it's okay," she offers.

"Oh, uhm." I glance around the library. "I'll just do some inventory for a couple of hours then if that's alright with you?" I ask.

"Of course, a list is waiting for you on your desk." She smiles and looks back at her computer.

"Thank you."

Lindsay is also my mom's best friend—they've known each other since elementary school, over forty years ago. She has always been like a second mom to me. It just so happens her son is Toby. She never stays at the house she owns. She actually lives in her lake house ninety-five percent of the time. Toby never really came over because my parents were boring, so my brother went to his parents' house mostly to hangout with him. I, of course, stayed home and read books.

I head over to my desk and grab the inventory list Lindsay mentioned. As I start counting and checking the library's stock, I can't help but reminisce about the good old days when Lindsay and my mom used to share stories of their adventures and mischief. It's heartwarming to know their friendship has stood the test of time.

I go about my tasks, organizing books and making sure everything is in its proper place. The library is quiet today, with only a few patrons scattered around, lost in the world of books and knowledge. It's at moments like these when I appreciate the tranquility of the library. It provides a welcome escape from the outside world.

As the day progresses, I take a break and walk over to the small café corner within the library. Mrs. Thompson, the kind old lady who runs the café, smiles warmly at me as I approach. She knows my usual order by heart.

"Hi, Elena, dear. The usual pumpkin spice latte today?" she asks, her eyes twinkling.

"Yes, please," I reply with a smile. "You always know just what I need."

Mrs. Thompson hands me the warm cup, and I

take a moment to savor the delightful aroma and the taste of fall in every sip. With my latte in hand, I find a cozy spot near the window and settle down with a book I've been meaning to read. Romance's are my go to's, but I find myself dabbling into mystery these days.

As I'm whisking away in the story, Time flies, and before I know it, it's already late afternoon. I finish up the inventory and decide to head home. Walking back, I pass by the park, where I've spent many afternoons with my friends during my school days. Seeing the children playing happily, I'm glad those days are behind me, but I cherish the memories and the lessons I learned.

Back home, the comforting scent of jasmine greets me before my mom does. She envelops me in a warm embrace, her blue dress billowing softly around her, the fabric draping her form in gentle waves. Sunlight dances through the blonde strands of her hair, now neatly gathered in a high ponytail that sways with her every movement. "How was your day, sweetie?" she inquires, her voice a soothing melody.

"It was good, Mom," I reply, the corners of my mouth lifting into a smile. "Lindsay predicted a quiet day, so I took the opportunity to tackle some inventory and lose myself in a book for a while."

Shit, I just realized I was supposed to be there for only a couple of hours. Oh well.

"Can you check on your brother? He won't leave his room." she pleads.

I nod and head up the stairs, knocking on my brother's bedroom door.

"Hey, Christian? You okay?"

I hear some shuffling around, and the door opens. There stands my brother. Hungover.

After looking down the hall, he grabs my arm and pulls me into the bedroom.

"What the hell!" I spit.

"Sorry, I just don't want to risk Mom and Dad seeing me like this."

"Yeah, I figured!" I sit on his office chair. "What gives?"

"I'm going to need a ride to the store."

"Why can't you just take your car?"

"Because it's at Toby's."

"And why are we shopping?"

"I spilled beer all over my shirt mom got me for our graduation party, I need to replace it before they notice,"

I roll my eyes and cross my arms, standing back up. "Let's go, then."

I stand in the doorway of the clothing store, tapping my foot impatiently as I wait for my brother to finish his shopping. He must have drank a lot of water or something because he doesn't seem hungover. The store is bustling with people, and I can't wait to leave and retreat to the quiet comfort of my books.

As I rest against the doorframe, I sense a soft hand on my mid back. I jump and turn to find Toby standing beside me. My heart skips a beat, unsure how to react to his sudden touch.

"Toby, what are you doing?"

He chuckles softly, not removing his hand. "Just trying to get your attention. You looked like you could use some company while you wait for your brother."

"I'm fine, thank you," I say, taking a step back to create some distance between us.

Toby's smile falters for a moment, but he quickly regains his composure. "Oh, come on, don't be like that," he says, trying to sound charming.

"I don't need company, especially not yours," I say, feeling frustrated.

Toby raises an eyebrow. "Why so cold? I'm just being friendly."

"Friendly? You have a strange way of showing it. You're known for being a flirt and a jerk, and I have no interest in being another one of your conquests."

His smile fades. "You've got me all wrong, Elena."

"Actions speak louder than words," I say.

Toby takes a step closer, his gaze steady on mine. "I get it. I have a reputation, and I understand why you might be wary. But trust me, I'm not into you. You're just Christian's annoying sister."

"Good to know. Now, can you please go?" I snap. Why do those words sting so much? I'm not interested in him or his friendship.

He raises his hands. "Gladly."

With those words, Toby turns and walks away. Christian finally approaches with his shopping bags, but my mind is still preoccupied with my encounter with Toby.

"Was that Toby I saw with you?" he asks.

"Yes."

"Weird, I wonder what he wanted," Christian mumbles under his breath.

I shrug my shoulders, and we walk out of the front exit.

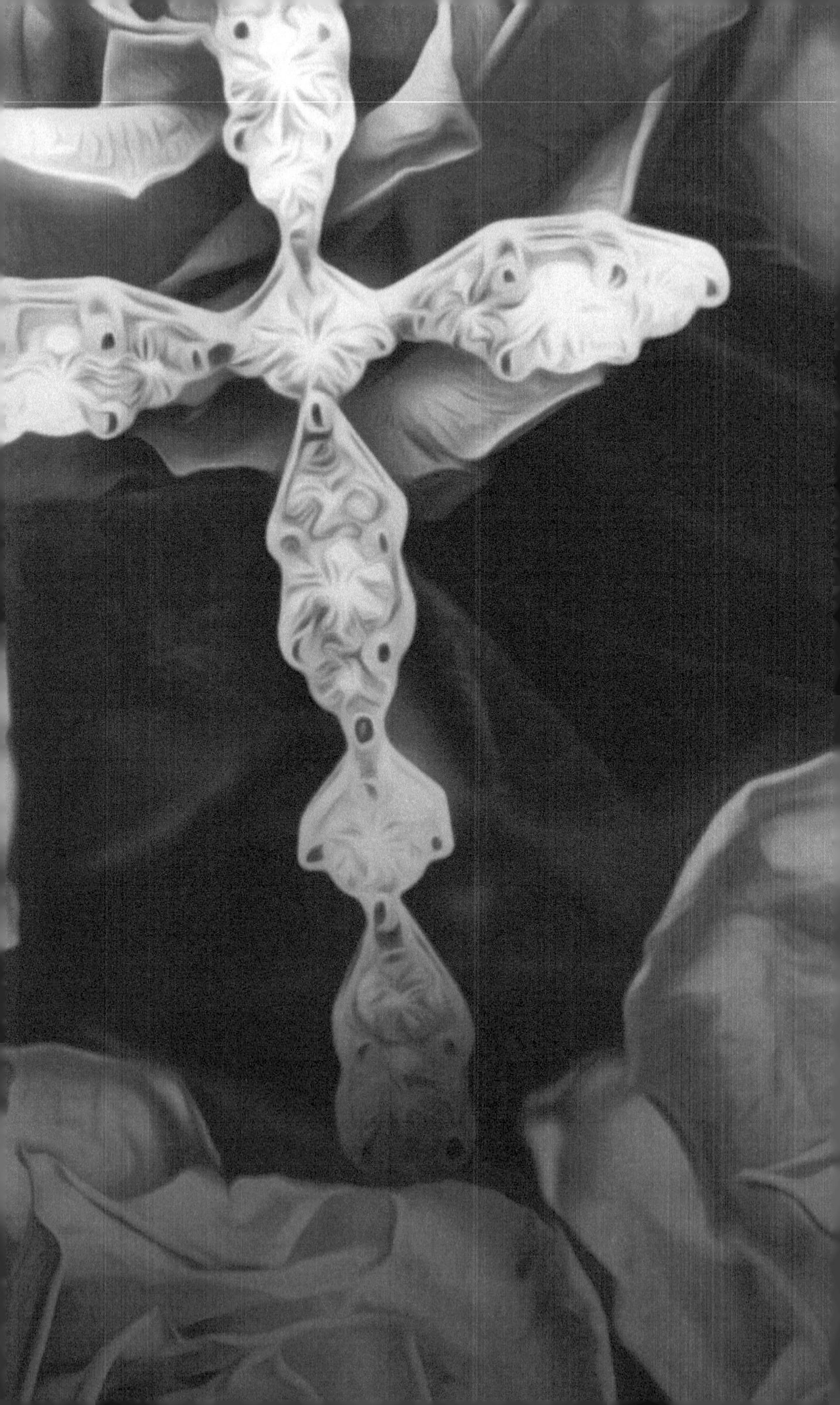

CHAPTER THREE

I scowl in frustration at myself for forgetting my lunch at home. Damn Christian for keeping me up all night with his stupid music. He forgets we have thin walls and are right next to one another. I take a deep breath and step out of the car. A gentle breeze coasts through the air, drawing my hair away from my face and behind my shoulders. I breathe in, and for a second, I'm able to embrace an atmosphere of peace and quiet.

Until the door swings open, and Toby strides out of the library.

"What are you doing here?" My voice comes out sharper and more accusatory than I mean for it too, but the words are already out there. I can't take them back now. It's been a few days since I saw him at the mall.

A laugh breaks from Toby as he stands at the

top of the stairs, peering down at me with a few beads of sweat on the crown of his head. He dusts off his hands, his white T-shirt pulling tight across his chest. "Well, good morning to you, too."

My face burns as a confused expression forms. I've only seen him at the library a handful of times. He doesn't seem like the type to hang out in the library and read, so I can only assume his mom needed him to come by for something. "You didn't answer my question."

"You should ask nicer," Toby replies as a smirk crosses his face.

I remain at the bottom of the stairs for a few moments, my eyes threatening to do another sweep over his body. He's obviously been doing something physical. "Did your mom put you to work?"

Toby shrugs. "Moving boxes of old books to the back. Nothing I can't handle."

I roll my eyes at his cockiness. I don't know if he really thinks that he's all that or if he puts up a front, but it grates on my nerves. "I could've done that."

Toby waves his hand dismissively. "I have to take advantage of every opportunity I can to grace you with my presence."

My face warms up again as I look away from him, shaking my head. He's just doing this to get under my skin. But why? What is his fascination with working me up like this? It must be some sort of sick game to him. "I need to get to work."

Toby takes a step back toward the door, almost blocking me when I reach the top of the stairs. "There's a party at my buddy Austin's house."

I lift an eyebrow at him. "Okay... I'll let Christian know, but I'm sure he already got the memo."

I wish Christian didn't party so much. I don't look down on it in the same way that our parents do, but I just worry about him. He overdoes things so much, and I've heard horror stories about what can happen when people drink too much. At least he calls me to come get him instead of driving drunk. I'm grateful for that, but I just wish he didn't get so wasted to the point of having to call me for a ride.

It's difficult to concentrate on myself when I continuously sense the need to monitor him every time he leaves the house. He's been smart enough to outwit our parents so far, but that won't last. It'll take one mistake for them to find out what he's been up to, and I don't want to see the aftermath of that realization.

Somehow, that chaos will rain down on me too since I've been keeping his secret and helping him.

A chuckle breaks from Toby as he shakes his head. "I was inviting you."

My face screws up in confusion. He's... what? "Huh?"

Toby directs a sharp gaze towards me. "Do I have to spell it out?"

"Why are you inviting me to a party? You know I don't go to those things unless I'm picking up Christian from one," I ask, wondering what kind of game he's playing.

Toby shrugs. "You could have fun. You should give it a chance."

I let out a dry laugh. I mean, sure, part of me has wondered if I'd have fun at a party or not. Some of them I've seen from a distance look a bit too crazy for me, but the thought of having a drink and letting go a little has always been a draw for me.

But the last thing that I need to do is go to a party with Toby, of all people. He'll definitely get me in trouble, and I can't be toeing the line every night like my brother. I don't have the desire to handle my parents' anger in the near future.

"I'm good. Thanks," I say, averting my eyes from him and suppressing the tiny glimmer of disappointment welling up in the recesses of my mind.

Toby tilts his head a little. "Well, if you change your mind, let me know."

"Why would I—?"

Before I can complete my sentence, Toby plucks my phone from my hand. A pleased look forms on his face when he sees that it's still unlocked, and he taps around on my screen.

My blood runs cold as I try to swipe my phone away from him. "What are you doing? Give it back!"

Toby puts his back to me, easily blocking me with his larger, far more muscular body. My chest crashes against his back as I try to reach around him.

"If you wanted to be all up on me, you could've just asked," Toby replies, sending me reeling back to get away from him with a red face. When he turns back to me, he hands me my phone back, looking as pleased and amused as possible. "There."

I snatch my phone away, wrestling with a feeling of sheer embarrassment from his comment. I look down at my phone screen, expecting to see dirty texts sent to everyone in my contacts list. Instead, I see a brand new contact with his name and number put in. "Why would I want your phone number?"

"You'll want it at some point. Might as well give it to you now," Toby replies before pushing open the library door for me. "Have a good day at work, Elena."

I silently fume as I hurry into the library, pitching one more look over my shoulder at him against my own will.

Toby grins like he expected me to do that. He winks before walking off toward his car.

I whip back around and head deeper into the library, doing my best to cool down before his mom sees me. Every interaction we've had lately has been getting weirder and weirder. He's always been the flirty type, but he hasn't set his sights on me until lately. What's the game?

What's different?

I should just feel annoyed, but a twisted part of me deep down feeds off his attention. Maybe it's just because I'm sheltered. Sheltered kids often spiral out of control when they get one taste of real freedom because it sends them reeling.

Will I get to that point? Will it be Toby who unravels me?

I shake my head at myself. No, that will not happen, especially not with him.

"There you are!" Lindsay calls out from inside of her office.

I check the time on my phone and grimace, realizing Toby made me a few minutes late! I stop in the doorway of her office with an apologetic look on my face. "Hey, I'm sorry. I got caught up talking to Toby on his way out."

Lindsay smiles and waves her hand dismissively. "Oh, that's okay. I know just how chatty he can be."

How much does she know about her son? I

don't say that aloud, though. I merely smile and nod. "Christian can be the same way."

"How's he doing? It's been a minute since I last saw him," Lindsay asks.

"He's great," I tell her. Hungover most of the time, but I guess he's happy. "Is there more inventory you'd like me to do?"

"Oh! Yes, I left a note on your desk," Lindsay replies.

I smile politely before walking to my desk, my mind still lingering on my confusing interaction with her son. Will things continue to intensify? Or will Toby lose interest and move on to someone else like he's done countless times before?

All I know is that I can't get close to someone like him. No matter how enticing he is.

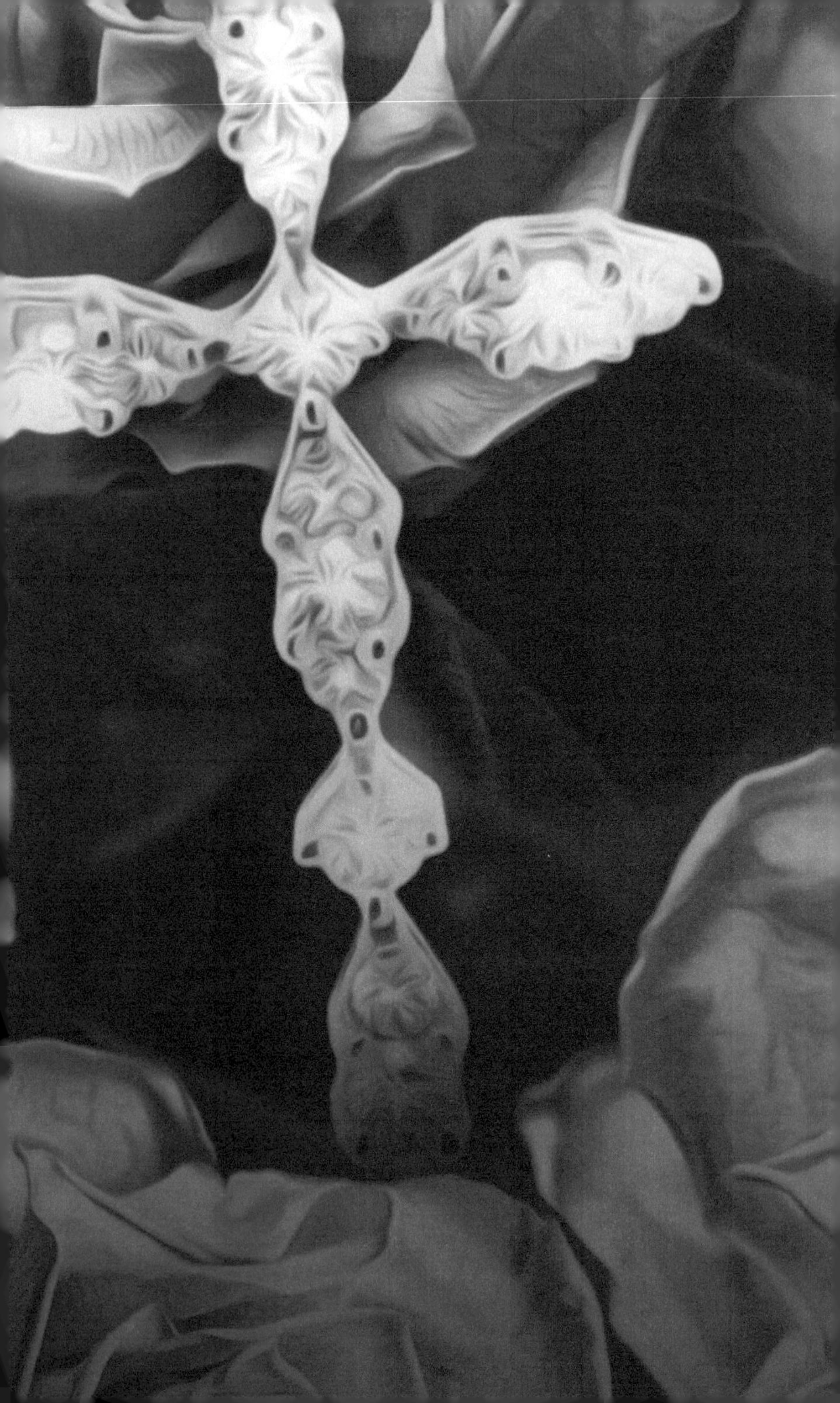

CHAPTER FOUR

"Elena!"

I jolt awake in bed, a strand of hair plopping down over my forehead as a tired, confused daze fills my mind. Did someone just call my name?

"Elena, come here!" mom's voice sounds from down the hallway.

My blood runs cold as I throw my sheets off my body, moving quickly. It sounds like she's by Christian's room, and my mind automatically darts to the possibility that he's been caught.

"Coming!" I call out as I pull on a large sweatshirt over my tank top and white pajama pants.

I hurry into the hallway with a racing heart, expecting to see my mom and my brother out there. Instead, my mom stands outside my brother's room with a slightly worried expression. "Yes, Mom?"

Mom sighs as she gestures into my brother's room. "I think your brother has the stomach flu."

Stomach flu. I have to keep myself from scoffing, because I know this is another scam to cover up the fact that he's vomiting from a hangover. Again! I peek into the room where Christian lies on his side with his back facing us, tucked under the covers like he's on death's doorstep.

"Oh, no. That's terrible," I say, feigning sympathy. How can I have sympathy for Christian when he does this to himself?

Mom nods and pats my upper arm. "It's Saturday, right?" You're off today. Be a dear and keep an eye on him while I'm out running errands."

"Keep an eye on him?" I ask, realizing I'm about to be put on babysitting duty. Again.

She nods. "Make sure he drinks enough water. Maybe bring him the trash can in the bathroom in case he can't make it there in time."

The problem is that I'll actually have to do those things because he's thrown up at least once this morning. I care about my brother, but he is a grown adult!

"Of course. I'll look after him," I tell my mom with a small smile.

"Thank you, honey. Call me if either of you needs anything."

I release a quiet sigh and step into Christian's bedroom, cracking the door behind me because my parents are still weird about closed bedroom doors in the house. I swear I think a part of them still believes we're ten years old. "Stomach flu. Really?"

Christian slowly rolls over to face me, looking a degree paler with dark circles under his eyes. "Close enough. I've been sick all morning."

I stand beside his bed with crossed arms and a glare on my face. "Because you drink more than you can handle!"

Despite me whisper-shouting the words, Christian still grimaces like I shouted in his ears. "I have a headache too."

"You go through this after every party. Maybe you should drink less. Or just not go!" I tell him, feeling my patience become thinner and thinner with him.

He's not a bad guy or a bad brother. He's covered for me multiple times when I went to hang out with friends on nights I was grounded for getting a grade that wasn't an A. But the moment he figured out how to secretly break our parents' rules, it's like he took it as a challenge.

Christian groans and runs his hand over his face, pushing his fingers into his slightly matted, messy hair. "You really need to loosen up, Elena."

I scrunch my face up at him. He sounds like Toby. "No, you need to calm down. Why do you have the urge to get drunk so often? I don't understand."

Christian flashes me a pointed look. "You don't understand anything because you don't try anything."

His words sting a little, making me frown and take a step back from him. It's not like I don't want to try things, but our parents and their rules have loomed over me for my entire life. I don't enjoy getting in trouble, and I'm terrified of getting caught. It paralyzes me. It keeps me from stepping out of line. I haven't snuck out since I saw mom and dad out at a restaurant when I wasn't supposed to be out. I nearly died of fear.

Christian's face softens, and he sighs. He slowly sits up and grimaces, his hand resting on his stomach. "I'm sorry. I know I've been a handful, and I'm really grateful for all you've done for me."

I give him a hard stare for a few seconds before letting my shoulders drop. It's so hard to stay mad at him. It's no secret that it's been difficult being raised by a pastor in a strict household. I've missed out on a lot of experiences growing up because of that.

While we were still in school, school dances, sleepovers, free Sundays, boyfriends. Were *not* allowed. It's still that strict, except I can have sleepovers with my friends now, which is not a sin to do. They just wanted to control every part of my life while I was still underage. I still can't let a curse word slip out, and I can't wear anything too tight or revealing.

All of those boundaries and more have made me mentally claustrophobic.

"Is partying it up that fun?" I ask. It just seems like he goes overboard so much.

Christian shrugs. "It can be. Helps take your mind off things."

"What things?" I reply as I tilt my head at him. What is he trying to escape?

Christian offers me a small smile. "I think I'm going to get some sleep. Don't worry about looking after sick old me. I'll be fine."

Before I can say anything, he rolls back over and falls silent, prompting a frown to cross my face.

"Just let me know if you need anything," I say before walking out of his room. I almost crash right into my dad as he hurries down the hallway. "Oh, sorry."

"How is your brother?" my dad asks as he pauses, adjusting the collar of his white button-down shirt. He's a tall, stocky man with short, blond hair and a resting, gruff face. We all have blond hair and blue eyes, and my dad is sure to describe us as the perfect, faithful family.

If only he knew.

"He's doing okay. He just wants to rest right now," I tell him as I straighten up, feeling a familiar twinge of anxiety whenever my dad's piercing eyes catch mine. My mom can be strict, but she's nowhere near as strict as my dad.

My dad grunts as he nods. "Alright. I need to go to the church. Love you."

After he kisses the top of my head and walks off, I take a deep breath, feeling much more relaxed now that my parents are out of the house. I feel bad for feeling that way because I love them, but they're a big source of my anxiety.

I wander back to my room and sit on my bed, my eyes sweeping over my bare, cream-colored walls. My sheets are pale pink, and my bookshelf is full of books that I bury myself in. Of course, they're appropriate because my parents would faint if they caught me with something... explicit.

Those types of romance books do catch my eye, though, and I've taken a peek or two at some scenes when at the bookstore or library. It's hard to put those books down once I start reading those intense intimate scenes, especially since I have no personal experience with any of those things.

I haven't even kissed anyone yet.

Embarrassment washes over me as I let out a sigh. I do long for things like that, but unless I find a nice Christian boy my parents approve of, it'll probably be awhile before I even get that first kiss.

Let's be real. I'm nineteen! I'm missing out on small experiences because of constant scrutiny. Perhaps I would, if I went to college.

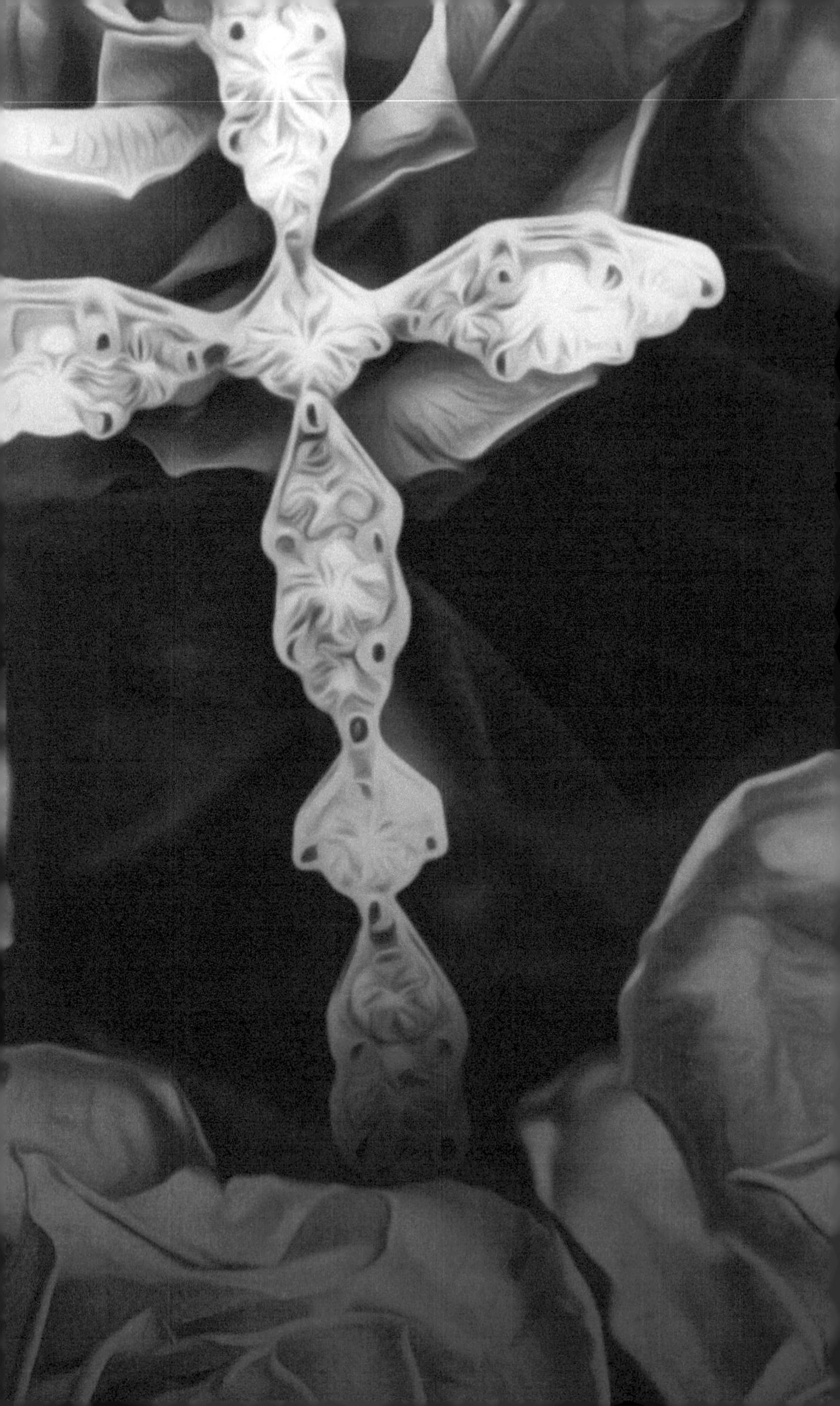

CHAPTER FIVE

The moment I go into the library for my next work shift, I can quickly tell that something is off. Lindsay's worried voice travels all the way from her office as I head that way, a frown forming on my face. What's going on?

"Okay, okay. Just hold tight. I need to pack some things, and then I'll get on the road within the hour," Lindsay says before hanging up the phone.

I slowly approach her doorway. "Is everything okay?"

Lindsay looks up from rapidly typing away on her phone. Her eyes are wide and slightly glistening. "Oh, I didn't see you there. You can come in. I need to talk to you, anyway."

I nod and step into her office, her anxiety rolling off her in waves.

"I just got a call that my mom had a bad fall

and may have broken her leg. My sister lives near her, but she has three kids. She can't be there with Mom all the time," Lindsay explains in a rush as she gathers her things. "I'll probably be gone for a week or two until she's back on her feet."

My eyes widen. She's never been gone longer than a couple of days from work before. Aside from Mrs. Thompson, who works in the cafe area, I'm the only employee. It's a small town, and it's not very busy here. She'll want to be there as long as she's needed. "Oh, I'm really sorry to hear that. Is there anything I can do to help?"

Lindsay offers me a small smile. "Just keep coming in like normal. I told Toby to come by. He'll step in for me while I'm gone."

My heart stops as her words echo in my ears. "Toby is going to run the library?"

Lindsay nods. "Yes, so he'll be able to handle it just fine, especially with your help. If you have any questions, text me, and I'll get back whenever I can."

My lips part to speak, but my shock renders me silent. She's telling me that I'll have to work with Toby for a week, possibly more! No, no. This can't be happening! I worry my parents will make me quit just for working next to a guy they won't like!

"Thank you!" Lindsay says as she rushes past me to leave.

I watch her go, only able to lift my hand in a

weak wave. So much for today being a normal day at work. I hope her mom is okay, but I can't get over the thought of Toby and me working together for hours at a time. Just him and me.

My face warms, and I fight the urge to flee. Lindsay trusts me to continue doing my job, so that nothing falls through the cracks while she's gone. I don't really see Toby as being responsible, but he works for her in the summer. I only started here a few weeks ago and I love it. During the school year, he's a volunteer teacher's aide at the local middle school, which confuses me to no end.

He's responsible and mature enough to help teach children? He actually likes that? I can't see the flirty party boy as a serious worker, but I'm about to see if that side of him exists.

My mind keeps bouncing back to him, so I decide to busy myself with my usual tasks. Nervousness shudders in my chest as I slide the rolling ladder toward the shelving section where I need to stack books. How in the world am I going to get through the next couple of weeks?

I hold a bundle of five books against my chest with one hand, using my free hand to climb up toward the top of the ladder. My motions are automatic since I've done this same task over and over again, sliding books onto the shelf neatly and in the order that they need to be in.

But I'm far more distracted today than usual.

It's bad enough that my brother is trying to drown out his worries with alcohol and partying. Now, I have to deal with Toby almost every day when I go in for work. He'll make my life hell. "There, I said it," I grumble.

I place the last book on the shelf and start moving back down the ladder, having to distribute my weight specifically to keep the ladder from moving around too much. I'm almost down at the bottom when I suddenly hear footsteps behind me, sending a jolt of surprise through me that makes my foot slip off the last rung. With a gasp, I flail a little as I fall backward, my eyes squeezing shut as I prepare for the hard impact with the ground.

But it doesn't come.

Instead, I fall into someone's arms, my back hitting a strong chest. The breath is knocked out of me a little, but it's a far better outcome than hitting the floor. I steady myself before turning around, my eyes widening at the sight of a pleased-looking Toby.

"You good?" Toby asks with a light chuckle.

My chest becomes hot and I scramble out of his arms. I narrow my eyes at him and step back from him. "You caught me off guard." I huff, flattening out my skirt.

"Looks like we'll be working together,

princess," Toby says, amusement glinting in his eyes.

I clench my teeth. "Don't call me that."

"Whatever you say," Toby replies as he crosses his arms, quirking an eyebrow up at me. "You know, I think this kind of makes me your boss."

My cheeks flare up with heat. He can't be serious. "It does not. Your mom said we're working together while she's gone. That means keeping this place running until she gets back, as equals."

He holds my stare for a moment longer, the air charged with unspoken words. Then, with a nonchalant shrug, "It'll be fun." His assurance feels hollow as he turns away, striding toward the employees-only area.

I don't trust him. He may work here during the summer, but I doubt he's ever been put in charge before. If he has, he's certainly convinced his mom that he's more responsible than he probably actually is.

I follow him with a suspicious look on my face, wondering what he's up to. He just got here. Is he already going to mess something up? "What are you doing?"

Toby holds open the back door for me, his eyes meeting mine. "Getting to work."

I raise an eyebrow at him as we step into the back where storage is kept.

He turns and faces me, the side of his mouth turning up. "What?"

I shrug. "Shouldn't you be going with your mom to check on your grandmother?"

His smirk falters. "I would, but my mom needs me here."

That's... pretty selfless.

"Oh, that makes sense," I say, silence following my words. I expected a cockier response, but even his expression remains serious as we peer at each other. I have a solid grasp on his personality, but he occasionally does things that confuse me. What's an act, and what isn't?

The tension that lingers afterward unsettles me a little, but maybe it's because we're all alone in the back of the library. There will be a lot of moments like this.

Eventually, amusement floods back to his face. "My mom texted me a list of things to do, so I'll get started on those. Unless you're dying to chit chat with me."

And he's back.

"I have books to stack," I mutter before turning and walking out of the back room.

The instant the door slams shut, I regain the ability to take deep breaths. Being close to him drives me mad because he somehow knows how to get under my skin, and it's always been that way. He must be more observant than he let on.

All I know is that the next two weeks will be far more complicated than I ever could've predicted when I woke up this morning. There's a change in the air, and I'm nervous to see what it leads to.

And, deep down, maybe a little excited.

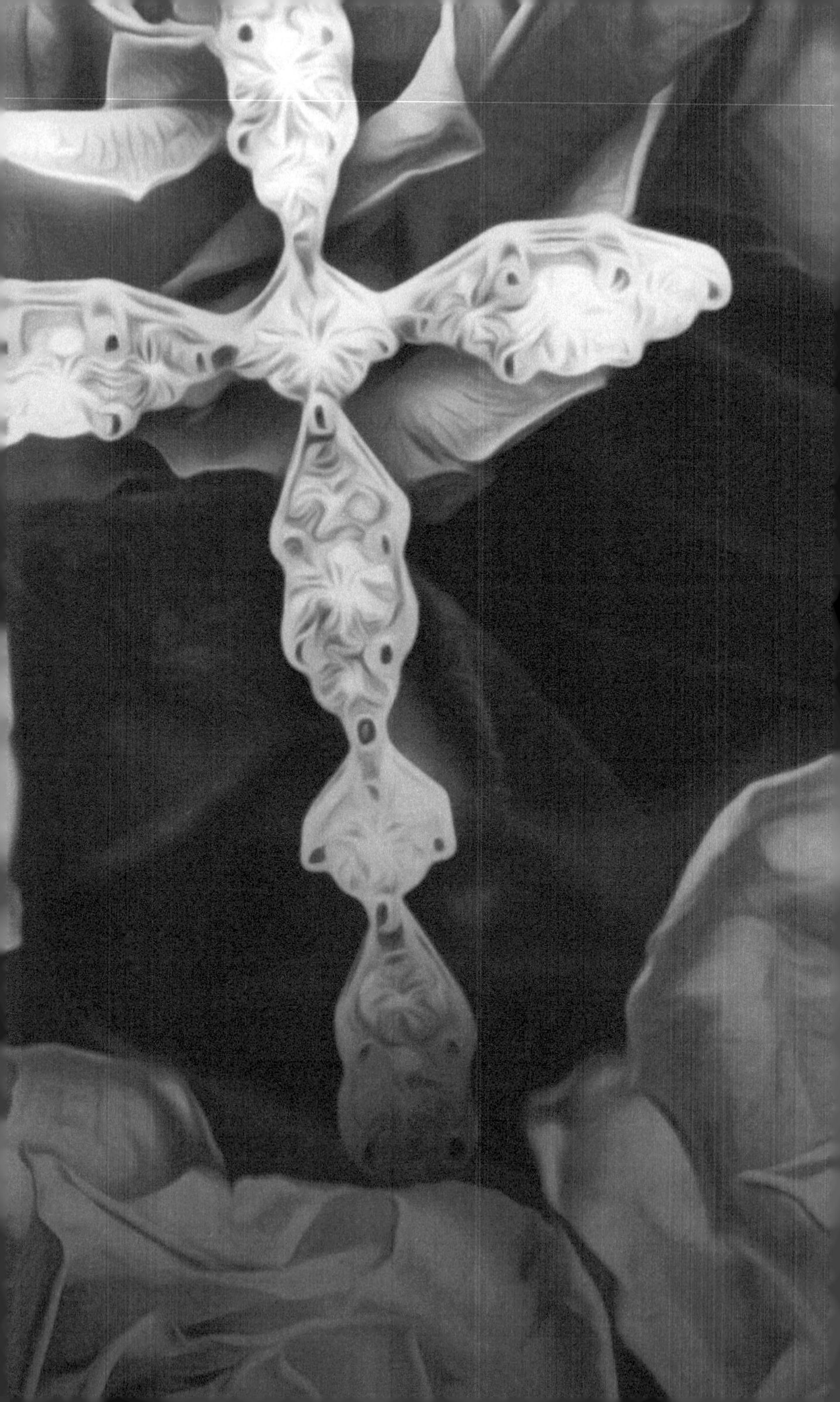

CHAPTER SIX

Working at a library should be one of the most relaxing, non-stressful jobs in the world.

Unless you work with Toby.

"You better have a good reason for dragging me out here on a Saturday," I tell Toby pointedly as we walk behind the library and into an open field.

Early afternoon sunlight beams down on us, making me shield my narrowed eyes. Yesterday, I made the mistake of texting his number to let him know that I'd be a few minutes late to work because I managed to drop grape jelly on my white shirt right before I had to leave. Now, he has my number to contact me whenever.

I didn't expect him to text me early on a Saturday morning, asking if I could meet him at the library for a small project.

"Got something better to do?" Toby replies as

he picks out a key on his keyring to unlock the back door.

"Depends on what you're forcing me to do," I say as I raise an eyebrow at him.

Toby grins and steps inside for a few seconds before hauling a small, old bookshelf out of the building and into the grass. He slaps the top of the light brown wood.

"We're going to paint this a bright color, and it'll be full of free books for kids. Summer reading program and all that jazz."

At first, I say nothing because I'm too surprised to think of something to reply. "Lindsay hasn't mentioned this project to me yet."

Toby steps closer to me, making my heart rate increase. "Because it's my idea."

I can't help it. I let out a little laugh. "Really? You want to paint a bookshelf for kids?"

"Well, yeah. We have a bunch of children's books that were donated. Bright colors will catch their attention, and their parents don't have to worry about shelling out a bunch of money for books they'll just outgrow. Like a Little Free Library, within the library," Toby explains. "Yay? Nay?"

Warmth blooms in my chest as I ponder the idea, visualizing a bunch of kids crowding around the bookshelf and getting to pick out books to read before going back to school. I was that kid growing up. I love books, but I also know they're not the cheapest things nowadays. A free summer reading program for kids is an amazing idea.

"That's... pretty genius," I admit, seeing his face light up. It's not in a cocky way, though. He looks genuinely happy and relieved. "How'd you come up with this?"

"During school, they have these book fairs the kids like going to. Unfortunately, they're costly, especially when the kids also want fancy erasers and holographic bookmarks. I felt bad seeing kids not being able to even buy a book," Toby replies as he shrugs. "It just seems like something all kids should have access to."

I mean, his mom is a librarian. I shouldn't be too surprised that he has this mindset. "Well, I'm down. What color are we painting it?"

Toby clasps his hands together. "I have a few options. Hope you don't mind getting a little *dirty* today."

My face burns hot enough to rival the solar heat of the sun. Oh, boy. Why did he say it like that?

"It's fine if I get paint on these shorts."

"Good," Toby quips before heading back inside to grab the small paint cans he picked up from the store. Red. Green. Blue. Yellow.

I cross my arms as we stare at our options, goosebumps threatening to pop up on the back of my arms as he stands next to me. My eyes briefly flicker over to him, admiring the way his blue T-shirt hugs his biceps as he crosses his arms.

Stop it!

I mentally grimace as I scold myself, forcing my attention back to the project at hand. It's an excellent project, and we need to do it right, which means focusing. "Do we really need to pick a color?"

Toby lifts an eyebrow at me. "Are you thinking of something multicolor?"

I gesture to the three shelves. "We can paint each shelf a different color, and the fourth color can be for the outside."

Toby snaps his fingers and grins. "Nice idea, princess. I knew we'd work well together."

I try my best to keep my face straight and firm, but my lips betray me and curl up in a small smile. If everyone behaves, maybe today won't be so bad. Maybe it'll be a good day, and surprisingly, Toby will be the reason for that.

But I also can't seem to forget all the damning things I've heard about him.

"What about a sign? What should we put on it?"

I cross my arms, attempting to keep myself warm from the fall breeze. I stand there, my mind wandering over a few ideas, but before I could say one, he stands in front of me, hand on his hip.

"How about 'Free books for young minds'?"

I nod. "That's perfect."

Somehow, someway, my negative thoughts and feelings about him are subsiding, and I wonder just how true all those rumors are about him.

I bite my lip as I watch the muscles moving in his arms as he opens the paint cans and stirs them with a wooden stick. He hands me a paintbrush and the can of yellow paint. "You take the top shelf, and I'll take the bottom one. We'll meet in the middle."

I nod and dip my brush into the paint, feeling a surge of adrenaline as I apply the bright yellow color to the wood. I glance at Toby, who is doing the same with the red paint. He looks focused and determined, his tongue sticking out slightly as he concentrates, making my heart flutter. His dark hair falls over his forehead, making him look even more adorable.

I shake my head and try to focus on my task, but I can't help stealing glances at him every now and then. He catches me once and winks at me, making me blush. I quickly look away and pretend to be engrossed in my painting.

We work in silence for a while until I hear him chuckle. I turn to see what's so funny, and I gasp. He has a streak of yellow paint on his cheek, and he's holding his brush like a weapon. "What are you doing?" I ask, alarmed.

He grins wickedly and points his brush at me. "I'm sorry, princess, but this is war."

Before I can react, he flicks his brush and splatters some red paint on my arm. I squeal and try to dodge it, but he's too fast. He flicks again and hits my leg. I glare at him and grab my brush, ready to retaliate. "You asked for it, mister."

I flick my brush and aim for his chest, but he dodges, and the paint lands on his shoulder. He laughs and flicks back, hitting my stomach. I gasp and clutch my belly, feeling the wetness seep through my shirt. He smirks and moves closer, his brush raised. "Surrender, princess. You can't win this."

I shake my head defiantly and flick my brush again, hoping to hit his face. He ducks, and the paint flies over his head, landing on the grass behind him. He takes advantage of my distraction and lunges at me, grabbing my wrist and pinning it to my side. He presses his body against mine, trapping me against the bookshelf. His face is inches from mine. "Gotcha."

I feel his breath on my lips, and my heart skips a beat. I look into his eyes, and I see something. Something that makes me want to lean in and kiss him.

He must see the same thing in my eyes because he lowers his head slowly, his lips parting slightly.

As he leans in, my heart races, and I duck under his arm.

"I'm sorry, we can't. I can't."

"I'm sorry, did I upset you?" he asks.

I look up into his eyes, "No. Uh. I-I've never kissed anyone before," I whisper.

My heart skips a beat as Toby's playful smirk dances on his lips. "You've never been kissed before? Not even once?" he asks, his words revealing my innocence, which feels so exposed at this moment.

I shake my head. "I grew up in a strict environment."

With every step he takes closer, his towering figure casts a sensual shadow over my petite frame. My cheeks heat, but I can't tear my gaze away from his piercing blue eyes.

"May I kiss you?" he whispers, making my body erupt in goose bumps.

He gently caresses my chin, guiding my face upward to meet his. Our lips are close but not touching, and my heart feels like it's about to jump out of my chest. His intense gaze entices me, evoking a sensation similar to a moth drawn to a flame.

He leans in, and our lips meet, his warm and sweet. I instinctively mimic his movements, trying to learn and keep up. Every touch, every brush of our lips sends electric sparks through my body, awakening desires I never knew existed.

My hand lingers on his chest, feeling the rise and fall of his breath. With a sigh, I break the kiss and softly utter, "I've gotta go home." I put the brush down and I grab my purse and head back to my car.

While driving away from the library, I touch my lips, a slight smile escaping.

What did I just do?

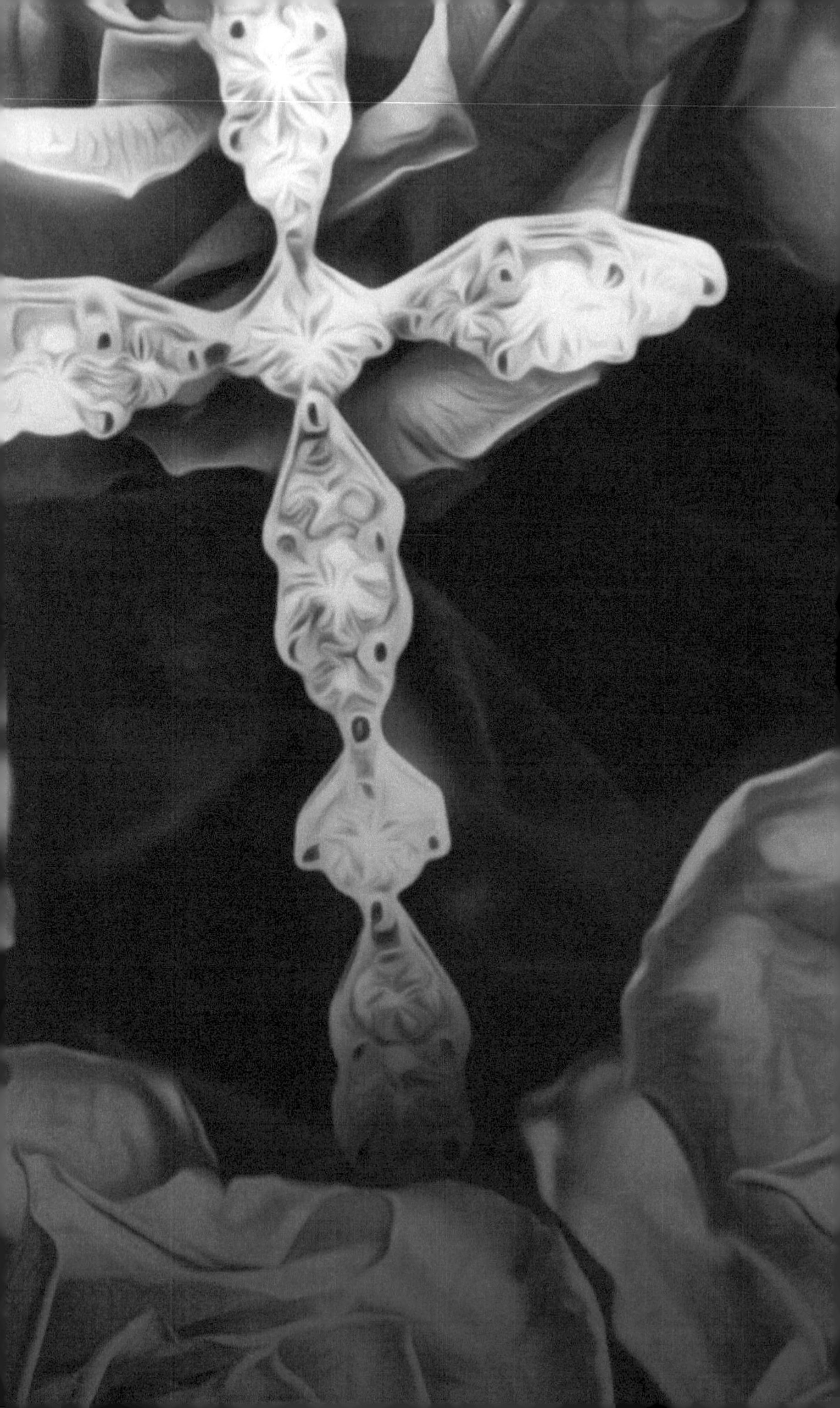

CHAPTER SEVEN

A s I sit in the front pew of the church the next day, my mind is a whirlwind of emotions. The kiss with Toby still lingers on my lips, and I can't shake the warmth and excitement it brought. But guilt gnaws at me, threatening to consume my every thought.

Between my mom and Christian, I fidget nervously. The cross on my necklace feels heavy, a constant reminder of my broken promise to God. The sermon begins, and my father's voice fills the sanctuary. He speaks of sin, and quoting. Each word feels like a direct arrow aimed at my heart.

"Are you okay?" Christian leans over, concern etched on his face.

I look at him. "I'm fine," I hiss, my voice sharper than intended. I didn't mean to snap, but

I'm afraid my mom might overhear. I can't let anyone know what I've done, not even my brother.

His brow furrows, but he doesn't press further. He turns his attention back to our father as he continues to preach. I tighten my hands into fists in my lap, forcing myself to stop fidgeting with my cross. All the while, I'm still battling the same thoughts of guilt and confusion. Is the kiss really so bad? I've been taught that it is, but it felt so right.

When the sermon finally ends, the congregation disperses, chatting and laughing. I excuse myself and slip into the bathroom. Alone, I gather my thoughts. How can I reconcile my faith with this newfound longing?

I take a breath. I'll be fine. I just need to control myself.

But deep down, I know my heart is torn between two worlds—the sacred and the forbidden.

Hours later, at home, I scroll through my phone, see a couple of posts from Emily and Rose, and tap like on them. I miss them. I should call them soon. They are more outgoing and fun than little ole me who's a homebody.

I open up our group chat.

ME

Hey, movie night next weekend?

"Elena, dinner's ready!" my dad calls me from downstairs.

I put my phone aside and hurry down the stairs. Plates and food are already set at the dining table, just like every breakfast and dinner. I take a seat. Chicken and potatoes and green beans tonight. Yum.

"So, good service today, right?" my mom asks.

I nod as I chew my food. I feel a ping of guilt and my appetite grows smaller. My blood chills, cold as ice. I can't let them find out about that kiss. I'd be shunned for as long as I live and after.

"Yes, just like every Sunday," Christian says.

"Well, kids, I was wondering, how would you feel if I brought the church home?" my dad asks.

I'm not a kid. "Don't we already?" I ask.

"I mean, like, having service at the house."

"No, I think that'd be odd," Christian replies, taking a drink of his water. We weren't allowed to have soda or other caffeinated drinks growing up and we're still not allowed to have it in the house. Little do they know Christian drinks the devil's juice on a weekly basis.

"This way, we can do fun crafts and have a get-together after a service instead of having to travel to another area," my mom pipes in.

"I mean, I guess. But why not use the backyard area of the church?"

"We are building a parking lot there for all the people moving into town,"

"Can we think about it?" I ask.

"No, the decision has already been made," my dad says sternly. He's using the tone you don't want to argue with. Then why ask?

"Oh, okay," I say, picking my dinner.

"I got a text this afternoon from Lindsey with some pictures of that project you and Toby were working on. Is that why you came home looking a mess yesterday?" mom asks.

I nod, "Yeah, uh, it's for the children's books,"

"Oh, well, just be careful not to get paint in your hair,"

"Yes mom,"

After dinner, I retreat to my room.

I sit on my bed, contemplating my next move. I've gotta confide in someone.

As I stare at the ceiling, my phone buzzes with a message notification. It's Emily, asking if everything is okay. I hesitate for a moment before typing a reply.

ME

I'm struggling, Em, I did something I shouldn't have, and I don't know how to reconcile it with my faith.

Almost instantly, she responds.

EMILY

We all make mistakes, Elena. It's how we learn and grow.

ME

Thank you

I put my phone down, then change into my pajamas and doze off.

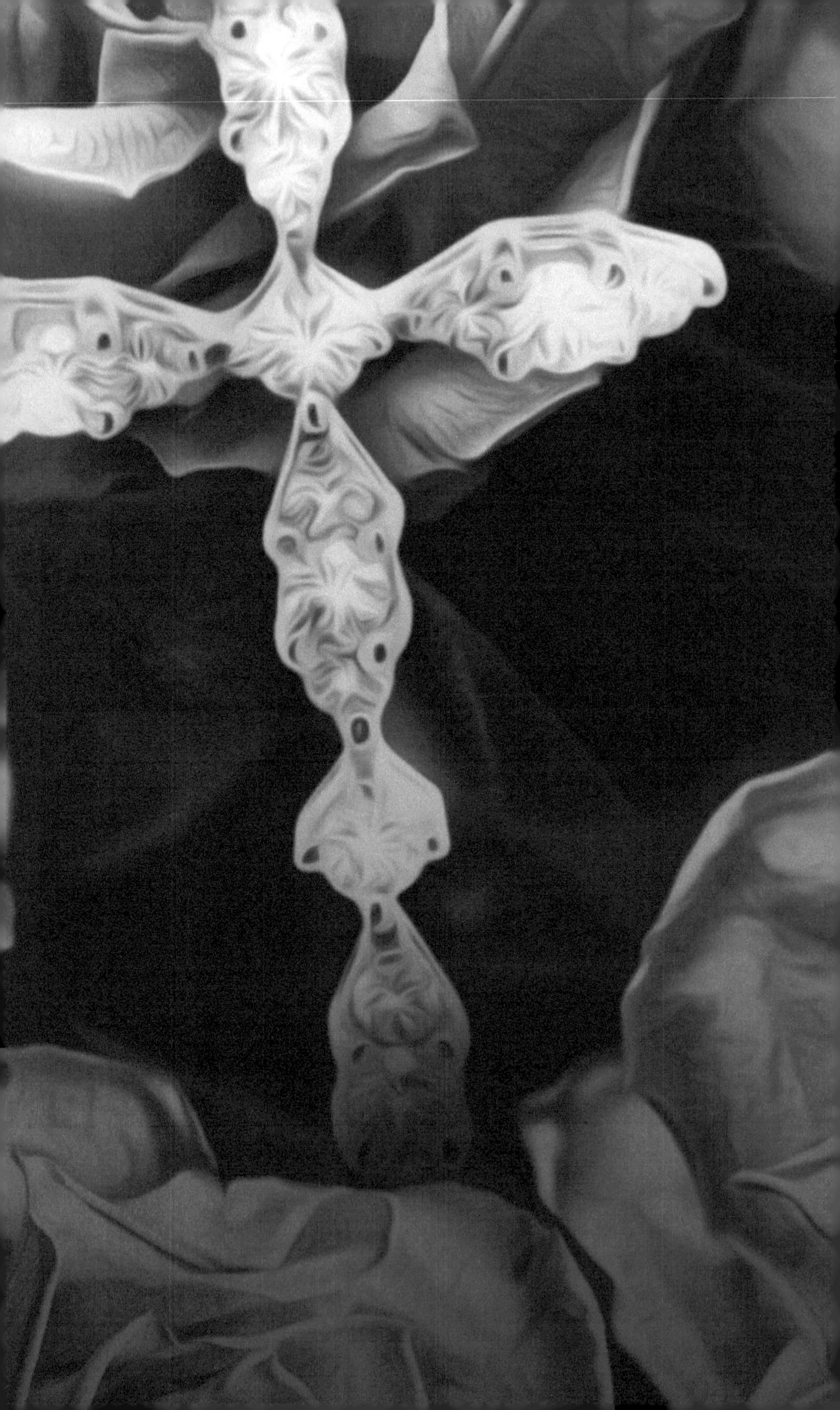

CHAPTER EIGHT

I DRAG MYSELF TO WORK THE NEXT MORNING, feeling like a zombie. I'm honestly considering texting Toby and telling him I'm sick, but that's too obvious. He'll know I'm trying to avoid him, and I can't hide from him forever. Not after what happened on Saturday. Our kiss. My first kiss.

I still can't believe it. How his lips felt on mine, how his arms wrapped around me, how his breath mingled with mine. It was the most amazing and terrifying moment of my life. And I hate myself for it.

I made a promise to God. A promise to stay pure until marriage. A promise that I broke with Toby. And now I don't know what to do. How can I face him again? How can I face myself?

I'm about to leave for work when Christian

stops me in the hallway. "Hey, Sis. What's going on with you?" he asks, blocking my way.

"Nothing. Why?" I say, trying to sound casual.

"You're acting weird. You barely ate anything at breakfast, you didn't say a word to me or Dad, and you look like you haven't slept in days. Are you okay?"

I force a smile and nod. "I'm fine. Just stressed about work, that's all."

"Work? What's so stressful about working at the library?"

"Well, Lindsay is gone, you know. She's out of town for a week. So I have to do everything by myself. It's a lot of pressure."

He doesn't know about Toby and me. He doesn't know about our kiss. And I want to keep it that way.

He gives me a look before reaching to hug me and a kiss on the cheek and tells me to take care of myself.

"I'm going to be late." I say.

"I love you, Sis. You know you can talk to me about anything, right?"

I nod, feeling a pang of guilt. I love him too, but I can't talk to him about this.

I rush to work, hoping to avoid Toby as much as possible. But as soon as I enter the library, I see him. He's helping a girl who looks to be around my age. She has long blond hair, blue eyes, and a slim figure. She's wearing a tight red dress and high heels, and she's leaning over the counter, batting her eyelashes at him. Ah, the usual with him.

She's flirting with him. Blatantly.

I can't help but sense a spark of jealousy that swiftly transitions into more guilt. Why am I feeling jealous? Toby isn't mine, and I don't want him to be mine. I can't. He's not the kind of guy I should be with. He's not a believer. He's not a virgin. He's not the one God has planned for me.

But then why does he make me feel things that no one else does?

I shake my head and try to ignore them. I walk past them and head to the back room, where I usually store the books. I hope Toby doesn't see me, but of course he does.

"Elena! Hey, there you are!" he calls out, leaving the girl and walking toward me.

His smile causes a sensation of warmth on my face. His presence makes me feel things I've never felt before. He's as adorable as ever, his dimples ever so charming. He's wearing a black T-shirt and jeans, and he looks good. So good.

"Hi, Toby," I say, barely looking at him.

He leans down and whispers in my ear, "I thought about our kiss all weekend long. Did you?"

I move away from him, feeling flustered.

"Toby, listen. There won't be another kiss. I'm

sorry, but I can't do this. I made a promise to God. And I have to keep it."

He looks at me, confused and hurt. "A promise to God? What are you talking about?"

I take a deep breath and try to explain.

"I'm a Christian, Toby. You know that. And I believe intimacy is a sacred gift that should only be shared between a husband and a wife. And that includes kissing. Kissing is an intimacy that leads to temptation and sin. And I don't want to sin. I want to honor God with my body and my life. Do you understand?"

He stares at me for a moment. Wide eyes.

I wish I could just kiss him again and forget everything else.

But I can't.

He runs his hand through his hair and sighs.

"Elena, why is a kiss so wrong? It's just a kiss. It means nothing. It's just a way of showing affection, of having fun, of feeling good. What's so bad about that?"

I find myself lost for words. I've heard explanations before from my dad, from my pastor, from my Bible study group. But the words are lost to me as I gaze up into Toby's eyes. I feel the same urge to kiss him as before, but I know I can't. I know I shouldn't.

But before I can say anything, someone else walks into the library. It's Mrs. Jones, the old lady who always comes to read the newspapers. She greets us with a smile and asks for Toby's help.

He looks at me, then at her, then back at me. He gives me a sad smile and says, "I'll be right back."

He walks away, leaving me alone. I feel a confusing mixture of relief and disappointment with myself. I busy myself with doing some dusting. I try to avoid his eyes, but I can't. I catch him looking at me a few times, and I know he's not giving up. I know he's going to talk to me again, to convince me to change my mind, to kiss him again.

And I know that this is going to be one of the biggest temptations I've ever faced.

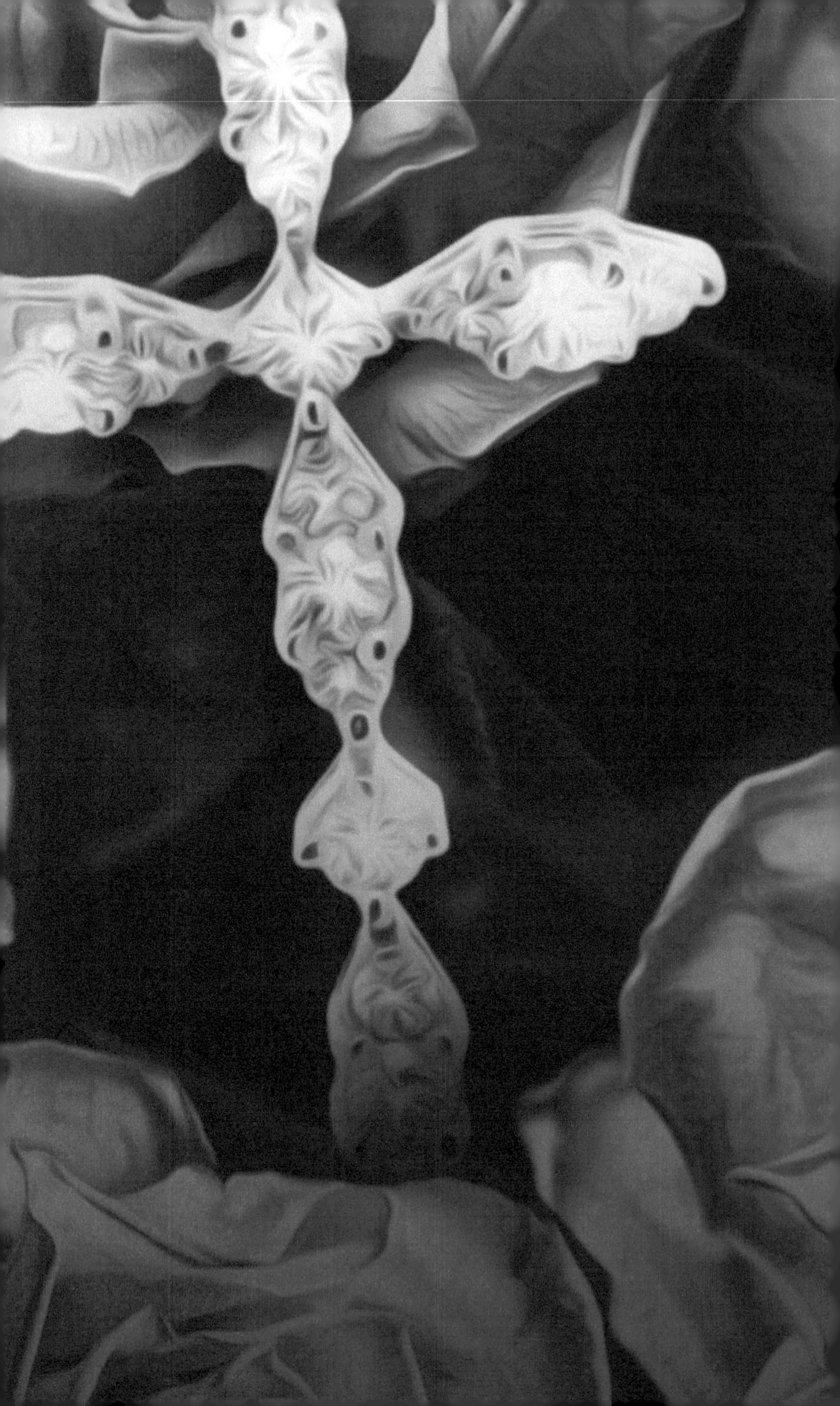

CHAPTER NINE

I'm glad to see Emily, Jenny, and Rose waiting for me at the cafe inside the mall. I would never miss Emily's birthday. Every year we meet in this spot.

"Hey, Elena! You look great!" Emily greets me with a hug. She's wearing a cute floral dress and a matching necklace. She's always had a knack for fashion.

"Thanks, Em. You too. Happy Birthday!" I smile and hug her back.

"Thank you love,"

"Hi, Elena!" Jenny and Rose say at the same time. They're twins, but they have different styles. Jenny is more girly, with long blond hair and pink lipstick. Rose is more edgy, with short black hair and a nose ring.

"Hi, guys!" I say as I hug them both. They are my oldest friends.

We sit at a table and order our drinks. The cafe is cozy and quiet, perfect for catching up.

"So how have you been, Elena?" Jenny asks. "We haven't seen you in ages."

"I've been okay, I guess." I shrug. "Just busy with work."

"How's work going?" Rose asks.

"I work at the library with Toby," I say casually, hoping they won't make a big deal out of it.

"Toby? As in Toby Morgan?" Emily gasps. "The town's hottest player?"

Of course, Emily likes to make it a big deal when it comes to boys.

I feel my cheeks heat. "Yeah, him."

"Oh, Elena. You're not falling for him, are you?" Jenny asks with concern.

"No, of course not." I lie. "We're just friends."

"Friends with *benefits*?" Rose winks.

"No!" I protest. "We're just coworkers. Nothing more." I can't tell them the truth. Not right now.

They don't look convinced as they exchange glances and giggle.

"Come on, Elena. You can tell us," Emily says. "We're your best friends. We won't judge you."

I sigh. I know they mean well, but they may not

understand. They've all had boyfriends, and they are happy. Jenny and Rose have even moved in with their boyfriends and are excited about the future.

They don't know what it was like to be under the strict eyes of my religious parents. Their parents are also religious, but not in the same way as mine. Less strict, which I envy.

I feel a tug of sadness as I wish I could join in on their excitement.

I look at them and force a smile. "There's nothing to tell, guys. Really. Toby and I are just friends. He's nice, but he's not my type. You know that."

They don't seem to buy it, but they drop the subject and start talking about their boyfriends, their plans, their dreams. I listen and nod, but I feel like an outsider.

Jenny drags me through the aisles like a tornado in stilettos. She is a fashion evangelist.

"Come on, Elena!" Jenny's eyes sparkle. "You can't live your whole life in those beige cocoons."

I glance down at my sensible sweater and ankle-length skirt. My parents' religious convictions have woven the fabric of my wardrobe. Modesty is my song, and I sing it well.

But today, surrounded by racks of lace and denim, I feel like a captive bird glimpsing the open sky. Jenny thrusts a hanger at me—a skirt that defied gravity and reason. Its hemline flirted with scandal, daring to reveal more than my knees.

"Try it on," Jenny urges. "Just once. For the thrill."

In the fitting room, I hesitate. As I shimmy into it, my heart races. The fabric clings to my thighs like a secret lover's touch. I twirl, feeling the colors blur into a kaleidoscope of possibilities.

When I emerge, Jenny's jaw drops. "I knew you had hips! You look like a goddess!"

The other girls gather around. "Hot damn, church girl is a baddie!" Emily smacks my butt and I roll my eyes with a laugh.

"Hey now, I'm not no 'baddie,'"

"I know it's my birthday, but I am buying this for you." She walks to the register before I can protest.

We carry on walking around the mall for the next hour drinking coffee, shopping for clothes, and even talking about the newest movies coming out. I love these girls.

Sitting on my bed, I touch the silky edge of the skirt and doubt gnaws at me. What if my parents see this? Or worse, see me wearing this? Their God-fearing eyes would widen, and they'd clutch crosses. Hellfire would rain down upon our modest home. But if they found out what I've done with Toby? Oh, I'd be in the pits of hell already.

Is it acceptable to wear it at the church picnic? Heck no. The heavens may open up, showing me a displeased God. At Least that is how my parents would put it. Maybe I'll just keep the skirt hidden for a while. Maybe I'll consider it after I move out. *Maybe.* I hide it in the deepest corner of my closet.

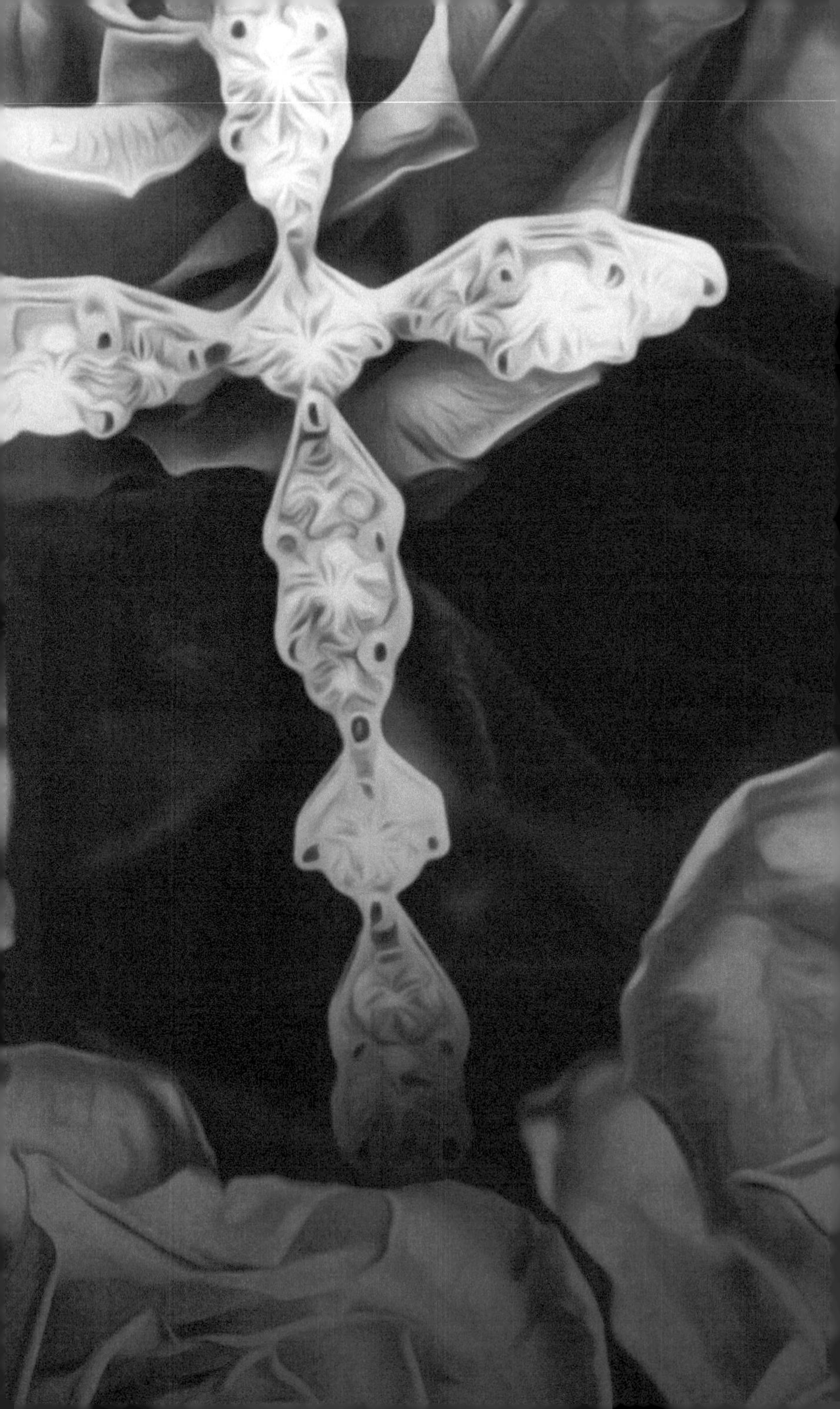

CHAPTER TEN

Every nerve in my body becomes electrified from the goosebumps as he kisses me. My heart pounds as I deepen the kiss, not having a care in the world because of the overwhelming sensations he brings out in me. His hands run all over my body, making me slip out a moan. I can feel the smirk on his mouth as he presses his lips against my upper neck, right under my jawline.

He slips a hand under my shirt, taking it off me. He trails a finger toward my cleavage as we stare into each other's eyes. Wrapping an arm around my upper waist, he unclasps my bra.

I look down as it falls to my feet, but he places his finger under my chin, nuzzling my head back up, where we meet eye to eye again. He lays me down on the bed, and as he's beginning to unbutton my jeans, I close my eyes, allowing myself to relax more into his touch. But right before the good part comes, my eyes flutter open.

My skin is hot, and my hair is messy from tossing and turning. I feel shame rolling over me because I'm still physically turned on, but I can't help my dreams. I sit up and look down, praying for guidance and strength to battle my desires, before getting out of bed and taking a cold shower.

I ignore Christian's curious eyes when I hurry back to my room to get ready for my day at work. He still knows something is up with me.

I look through my closet for something to wear. Most of my clothes are fairly modest. No short shorts. No crop tops. I put on jeans and find a strappy tank top that I often wear over white shirts or undershirts for layering. I put the tank top on, which shows my shoulders and a hint of cleavage. I like how it looks and admire myself in the standing mirror in my room.

Suddenly, my mom barges into my room without knocking, as she's done so many times before. I cover myself, but my mom is quick to chastise me about dressing provocatively.

"You are asking for attention with that shirt on!"

"Mom, I haven't put my blouse on over it yet! Plus, what happened to only God can judge?"

"Honey, I have to protect you from creeps in this world as much as I can."

"Well, your comments don't make me feel safe."

"Oh, whatever. Can you head over to the store after work? Your dad can't make it and neither can I," she asks with a hand on her hip.

"Why can't Christian?" I ask.

"Because. He's going to a friend's helping work on a project."

I highly doubt that.

This is one of many reasons I've been saving up for my apartment—privacy and I feel like I can't breathe under their roof. I let out a frustrated sigh once she leaves my room and put on a blouse before heading to work.

"Hey, good morning! You look.... different today. Is that a new blouse?" he asks, his voice warm and friendly. Toby's cheerful greeting pierces through the fog of my morning. I glance up from my desk, my eyes meeting his.

His hair is tousled, and there's a hint of curiosity in his expression. His eyes linger on my outfit.

I suppress the urge to roll my eyes. "What do you care? Just let me work," I snap, my tone sharper than I intended. But Toby doesn't back down; he's persistent, like a dog with a bone.

"Whoa, sorry. I was just trying to be nice. What's wrong with you?" His brows furrow, concern etching lines on his forehead. I can almost hear the gears turning in his head, trying to figure out what set me off.

"I feel like I can't breathe in that house." The words tumble out before I can stop them. It's true— I suffocate in the walls of my childhood home. The memories cling to every corner like cobwebs I can't brush away.

Toby leans against the edge of my desk, his gaze steady. "Wow, that sounds rough. I'm sorry you have to deal with that." His empathy catches me off guard. Maybe he's not as clueless as I thought.

"Yeah, well, it's not like you understand." I cross my arms, leaning back into my chair. "You have cool parents who let you do whatever you want. You have your own car, your own place, your own life." The words spill out, raw and unfiltered. I'm suffocated by my parents. Now when I look at him, I can't get the feeling of his dream versions lips off my mind.

He straightens, his expression serious. "Hey, it's not all roses and rainbows, you know. I have my own problems too." His voice softens. "But I get it. You need some space."

"I didn't mean to snap," I admit, my voice

quieter now. "I'm just frustrated. My parents treat me like a child, and I'm a grown woman. Just a couple more months, and I can move out." The thought of freedom the taste of it lingers on my tongue. Toby nods, understanding passing between us. "Hang in there, Elena," he says softly. "You're stronger than you realize." He winks and walks to the back office.

And for a moment, I almost believe him. Almost. I kind of feel bad for snapping. It was uncalled for.

A young lady walks up, laying a book on the desk. "I'd like to check this book out please,"

"Sure thing." I smile.

While I'm working, I steal glances at Toby from the service desk. He's like a magnet for kids, drawing them in with a gravitational pull I can't quite fathom. His patience, the way he crouches down to their level—it's striking. When he finishes helping a young girl, choose a book from our free bookshelf, he saunters over to me. He brushes my shoulder and his touch lingers as he assists with paperwork, and I seize the opportunity to ask the question that's been gnawing at me.

"Why did you start working at the school?" I blurt out, my curiosity piqued.

Toby's eyes soften, revealing a vulnerability I hadn't expected. "I grew up close to teachers and coaches," he confesses. "They were my guides, my cheerleaders. They saw something in me, something I didn't always see in myself. Contrary to popular belief, I liked school—the structure and the learning. I excelled, and that fire led me here. But then life happened. Social circles, distractions, and the relentless whisper of impostor syndrome. I'm only a few years away from full certification, but it feels like an eternity."

As he talks, I can see the passion in his eyes— the same fire that fuels my love for books. And something shifts within me. My edges soften when he's near, like pages worn by countless readers. Toby still digs under my skin, but there's a sincerity to his struggle. He's trying to be better, to defy the labels slapped on him.

As I continue stocking books, the front entrance bell chimes. "Toby, can you get that? I'm a bit occupied."

"Yeah!" I hear him shuffle toward the front.

"Hey, man, what's up? I feel we haven't seen each other for a minute," a male says to Toby. I pause what I'm doing and listen in, being a bit nosy.

"Yeah, I know. Hey, I'm dropping by to tell you

there's a secret rave going on tonight. Invite only. You in?"

"Hell yeah, man. What time?"

"Starts at nine."

"Okay, see you then!" Toby says. The bell chimes again. The guy must have left.

"Hey, Elena," he says, his voice a smooth echo in the quiet aisle as he walks into the row I'm in.

"Yeah?" My response is automatic, but my heart skips a beat, betraying my calm exterior.

"There's a rave tonight. I think you should come," he suggests, his eyes holding a mischievous glint that sends a familiar thrill down my spine.

"Sounds like it's invite-only," I say, trying to focus on stocking the shelves, but the memory of that dream—the one where his hands weren't just skimming over book spines—creeps into my mind, heating my cheeks.

"Well, you're invited then. You have no excuse now." His grin is infectious, and I can't help but return it, even as I fight the flush spreading across my face.

I sigh, pausing what I'm doing to face him. "I don't know, Toby. My parents expect me to be home at a certain time every night." The words are a weak defense, and we both know it.

He walks closer to me, the space between us charged with unspoken words and lingering glances from dreams I dare not admit. He leans casually against the bookshelf. "Come on, maybe a friend can cover for you?"

I draw in a shaky breath, his scent mingling with the musty smell of books. It's disarming, how a simple conversation can feel so intimate.

"I'll think about it." My voice is a whisper, drowned out by the sudden rush of my pulse in my ears, echoing the same rhythm that haunted me in my sleep—fast, insistent, and dangerously close to crossing sacred lines."

I spend the rest of the day avoiding Toby as much as I can, trying to clear thoughts of that dream from my head while debating whether I was dumb enough to accept his invitation.

Hours go by and the clock shows it's only thirty minutes until the rave starts. I'm still unsure if I should go. It's not my vibe nor do I hang out with those types of people.

It sounds kind of fun, and Toby will be there, but I'm also at risk of being caught.

I hear a light thud and catch Christian on his way out.

"Hey, are you going to that rave?" I ask.

"Uh, yeah, how did you know about it?"

"Well, Toby's covering for his mom at the library, and I overheard the conversation about it. Can I tag along?" I ask. Even though I was already invited, I didn't want my brother getting pissy about being asked to go.

He looks at me with a furrowed brow. "Okay, but you'll probably have to drive us home. It'll be easier for you to already be there since I was probably going to call you anyway."

I nod and hurry to my bedroom to change into my new skirt. I also switch to a nice blouse that shows my cleavage a bit more. Our parents are out for the evening, so I should be okay wearing this. I just hope they don't come home early.

"I'm surprised you own a skirt that short." He laughs as we head into the car.

"Just trying something new."

"I'm just glad you're actually getting out for once."

"Same."

We drive to the rave, and I can't help but feel a pang of guilt. Is going to a party a broken promise? Is having fun okay? I'll just be sure not to drink anything and try not to be around Toby when Christian is very close by.

We park, and I can feel the thumping bass reverberate through the soles of my shoes before we even enter the building. It's a place on the outskirts of town. As I follow Christian inside, the darkness swallows us whole, punctuated only by the erratic heartbeat of strobe lights that cast silhouettes.

I let it pull me toward the dance floor, where the world is nothing but sound and motion.

Around me, tables are filled with alcohol and mixers. My heart hammers against my ribs. Is this what it means to feel alive? The noise is over-whelming. This place should send me running, yet here I am, anchored in by the very thing that terri-fies me.

"Come on, let's go drink a round of shots," Toby offers.

"Oh, I'm good. You two can go do that, though."

"But you're already here, come on," he says.

If I can conjure the courage to be here, I can deal with one shot of alcohol. It may help loosen me up too.

The burn of my throat after taking a shot makes me gag, I don't feel great about drinking alcohol. While Christian is chatting up a guy he knows, Toby laughs and leans close to me and whispers, "You look good in that skirt."

My traitorous heart flutters in response to his warm breath in my ear. "Hey, I'll be right back," he says.

"Okay," I say as I watch him walk off, only to realize that my brother has wandered off too, leaving me alone. *Oh man, I shouldn't have come here. Maybe it was a bad idea. Yeah, I think it was.* I look over at the table full of alcohol and take another shot for some confidence. I stumble along the edge of the dance floor, listening to the loud, pounding music and watching bodies writhe and sway to the beat. It's almost entrancing, and I nearly run right into a guy who steps right in front of me.

"Damn, want to dance?" A man I don't even know asks me.

"N-no, thank you." I look at him, but I can barely make out his features.

He grabs my hips, pulling me closer as I try to break free from his grip. My pulse races like a sprint as he slips his hand up the back of my skirt.

"I-I said no, please stop." I try to pull away, but his grip on my hips tightens.

Suddenly, the guy is shoved away from me. I turn to see Toby, who's red in the face and noticeably angry. "Back off and do not touch her again."

"Who are you? Her little boyfriend?" he mocks.

Toby grabs the man's collar. "Leave this party now before I beat your fucking ass," he spits in the guy's face.

"Elena, come here," Christian says, grabbing my hand and ushering me behind him.

"You got a problem, dude?" he asks the man.

"No, but a little skirt means open for business, like a slut." The man says.

I open my mouth in shock because I've never been called that before. Toby punches him in the face, and the guy falls down to the ground. I grab Christian by the shoulders, hiding my eyes from it.

I expected Christian to stand up for me, but not Toby. I don't like violence.

"Come on, Elena, we need to go home," Christian says.

I nod and grab his hand, looking back at Toby. He looks at me and gives a small smile.

As soon as we get home, I crawl into bed, trying not to wonder what would have happened if Toby hadn't stopped that guy?

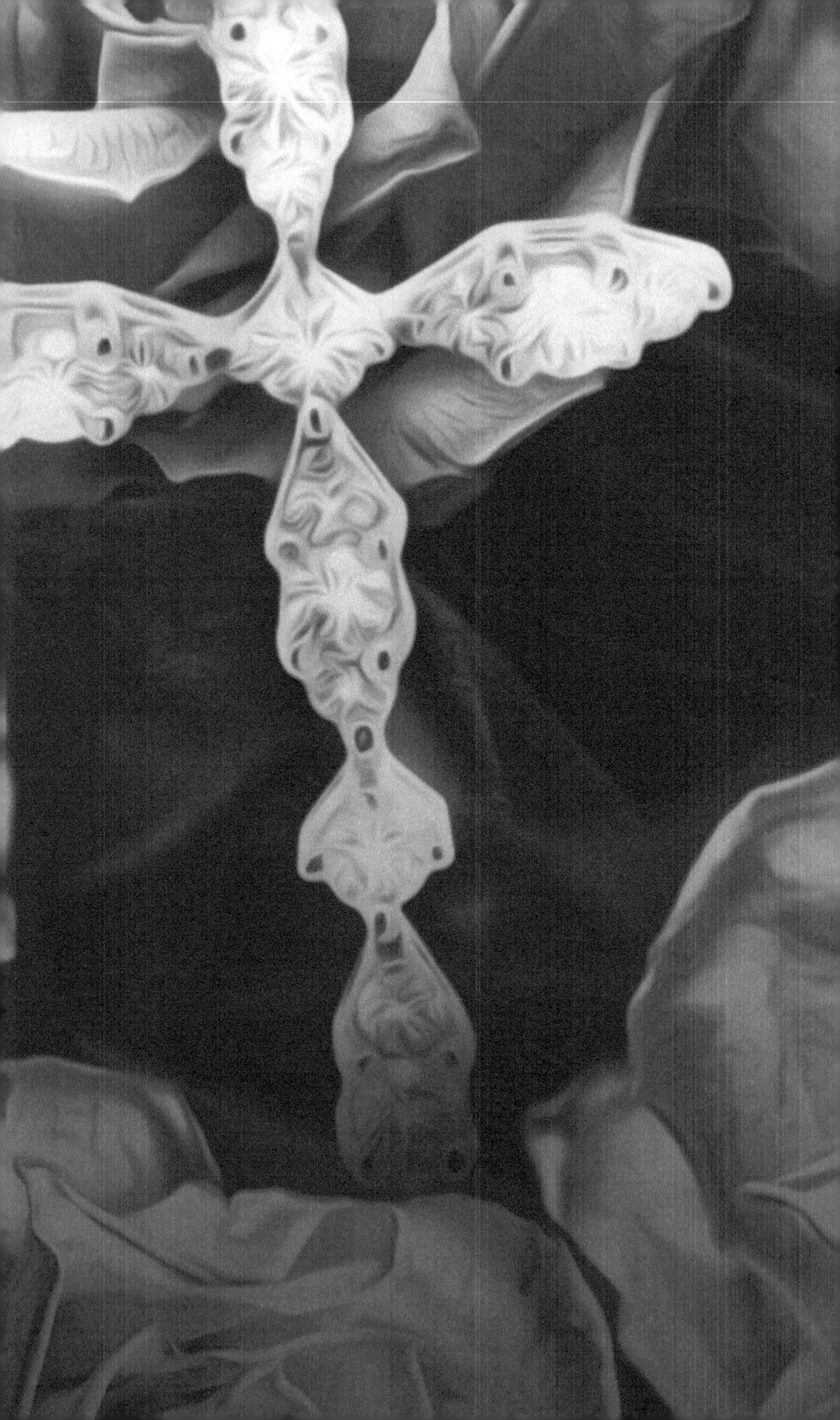

CHAPTER ELEVEN

The library hums with the scent of old paper and the soft shuffle of footsteps. I vow to keep my mind on work, to bury myself in the world of books, and escape the chaos of my heart following the events of the rave last night.

The fresh arrivals rest on my desk, their spines flawless and full of potential. I flip through their pages, lost in tales of distant lands and forbidden love. However, the words quickly become hazy and my mind drifts to Toby—the man who has started to fill my dreams.

When the bell above the entrance rings, I snap back to reality. Toby stands there as if summoned by my thoughts, his dark hair falling across his forehead.

"Need help?" His voice is a velvet whisper.

"Yes, please."

We carry the books to the back corner, away from prying eyes. As he reaches up to place a book on a shelf, his other hand grazes my back.

"Thanks," I mumble, my heart fluttering.

I shouldn't become another one of his playthings. If I'm going to push boundaries, I should at least do it with someone who truly cares about me.

Him protecting me the other night has made me feel something more for him.

"You're so beautiful," he whispers in my ear.

He pulls me into him and I allow it. He kisses my neck from behind, his hands gliding over my body. I close my eyes and lose myself in his touch. He plays with my cross necklace, "You shouldn't let faith get in the way of what you want," he says.

Those words snap me out of my daze, and I push him away with a glare.

"You don't know anything about my relationship with God, and you're just using me to get what you want. You don't care about me."

Before he can say anything, I leave the aisle and spend the rest of my shift, trying desperately to avoid him. I'm frustrated and confused, wondering why I'm having to face this challenge of my faith and feeling unsure if I'm strong enough to defeat it. I fear what may happen If I keep giving in.

From what I've heard from my dad, God will turn his back on me if I turn my back on him, and

I'm scared of the consequences. It's been instilled in me since I was young.

When it's finally time to go home, I get out of the library as fast as possible, tears filling my eyes as I drive. I hurry inside and shut my bedroom door and lay on the bed, curling into a ball and crying to myself, feeling lost when it comes to my life.

I feel barred from what I want, and I don't know the right move to make. I hear my bedroom door open and see it's Christian. He sits on the edge and places a comforting hand on my back.

"I'm struggling with my faith," I admit.

"Do you want to talk about it?"

"Not really," I shake my head.

He sighs, placing his hand on my knee. "I struggle all the time. While I don't have any firm answers for you, faith is a personal journey. Just block out the noise coming from other people, including our parents, okay?"

I wipe the tears from my face and hug him. "Thank you." I sense he's weighed down by something too. "Are you okay?"

"Yeah, why do you ask?"

"Because when the guy touched me, I could see your face growing red." I feel ashamed, disgusted by what happened.

He takes my hand in his. "I should be asking you that question. Don't be hard on yourself, you did nothing wrong nor did you tempt that guy, he shouldn't have touched you,"

"I love you, brother," I whisper.

"I love you too." He stands up and walks out of the bedroom.

I hope things will make more sense and life becomes easier soon.

My phone buzzes a few times, causing me to wake from my deep slumber. Confused, I check and see that Toby's texting me, telling me that he's outside my house. He couldn't sleep and wanted to talk to me. I sigh, considering telling him to go home, but my curiosity gets the better of me.

I put my phone down, throw on a robe, and slowly sneak out of the house. Thankfully, the floors don't creak, so I don't have to worry about waking anyone up. I see he's parked across the street in his car, and I get in the passenger seat.

"Why are you here? I could get in a lot of trouble for this." I look around.

"I couldn't sleep because of what I said earlier. I didn't mean to disrespect you and your faith."

I smile at his apology, "I've been trying to strengthen my faith, and my dad's words about sin have scared me into avoiding anything he sees as a sin at all costs."

"You know, I do believe something is out there, even though I'm not religious. I don't fully understand where you're coming from, but I won't push you, especially if you aren't comfortable," he says. I can tell he's being genuine, but I'm still doubtful.

"I fear that you're using me, just like you've done to other girls."

"I admit I've been a player. Clearly, I've been lost and lonely, and I didn't want to get attached again after my first heartbreak. But I'm not trying to use you." He takes a breath, looking into my eyes. "I've been genuinely attracted to you since I first met you through Christian."

Warmth rises to my cheeks as soon as he says those words.

"Can we go for a short drive?" he asks.

I look up at the house and the time on the dashboard. "Yes, but we can't be long," I say.

He drives us through the downtown area, where there are so many building lights but hardly anyone around. "Do you want something more than just working at the library?" he asks.

"I mean, I've always wanted to work around books, but my dream idea is far from being achieved."

"What is that dream?"

"It's probably never going to happen, but opening my own bookstore."

"You should go for it. Don't doubt yourself," he says.

"I have to move out first before I can make that leap."

His encouragement motivates me to start thinking about it more. He drives us back to my house and parks down the street in the dark.

"I had a nice time tonight. Thank you." I can feel tension building between us.

"Can I kiss you?"

The fact that he, a do-what-I-want guy, asks for permission sends a thrill through me, making my heart stumble over its rhythm. He rests his hand on the back of my neck gently, caressing my cheek with his thumb. I lean in, and the moment our lips touch, it's like igniting a spark in a room full of fireworks. Our kiss deepens, and a bold desire unfurls within me, urging me to climb onto his lap and erase any space between us.

My heart is pounding against the confines of my chest, each beat syncing with the rise and fall of my hitched breaths. A wave of heat spreads through me, a fire that only grows as I deepen our kiss, losing myself in the taste of him, the feel of him.

Abruptly, he pulls away, leaving a cold absence where his warmth once was. "Have a good night, princess," he says, his voice a low melody that lingers in the air.

I bite my lip to contain the smile that threatens to spill over. It's a smile of secrets, of shared moments, of a night that's etched into my memory.

Then I sneak back into the house and into my room. I drift off to sleep, thinking of his lips on mine.

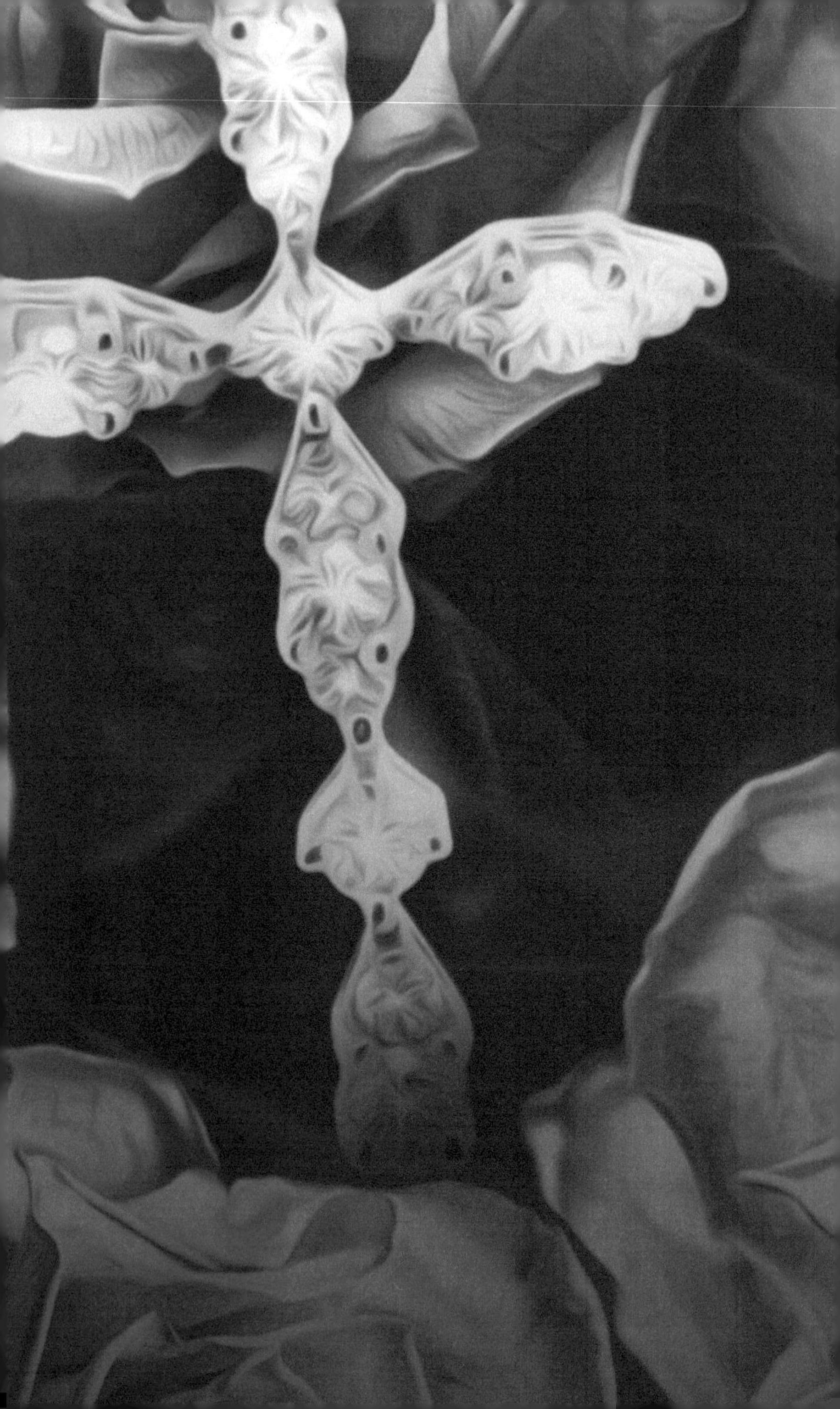

CHAPTER TWELVE

It's Sunday morning, and I find Christian terribly hungover. He doesn't drink every night, but maybe 3-4 times a week, he'll get very intoxicated.

But he knows better than to get drunk on Saturday nights when we have church the next morning. He can barely string a sentence together. "I don't care anymore. I don't want to go to church, and I'm tired of being stuck in the house."

I sigh, knowing he's struggling a lot with drinking as his outlet.

"I'll make up an excuse for you, okay, but you've got to get a grip on yourself. I won't always be around to cover for you."

The desire to get my own place increases stronger and stronger. And I'm just about there financially.

"Hey Mom, Dad, Christian is sick and can't attend service today," I say once I reach the front door.

"Gosh, I wonder what's up with him? He's been getting sick more often."

"He's not putting God first, that's why," my dad says.

"I'm sure that God is forgiving and understanding." I say.

"Elena, Christian will regret not putting in more time with the Lord."

With a sigh, I nod and keep my not-so-nice words to myself. I can't stand how negative and heavy-handed my dad is, especially when it comes to religion. I don't picture God being so cruel and unforgiving, but my dad has always painted God in such a threatening light. As my dad likes to say, "He's very loving, but can be very scary."

I'm beginning to feel a bit of distance between myself and the version of God that my dad preaches, and grows closer to a different version, one that feels more like the true God. A God who accepts and loves me for who I am.

As we step inside the church, I frown when I don't feel as connected as usual to God during service. I feel separated from the people around me and find myself wanting to be with Toby, who accepts me for who I am. Flaws and all. At the end of the service, I stand to make my way back outside but before I could reach the doors, my mom calls for me.

"Yes?" I ask.

A boy my age stands next to her. I've seen him here a few times.

"This is Nathan. You two should get to know one another. It'd be good for you to be with a nice Christian boy like him," she says bluntly.

"Oh, uh…" I don't really know what to say. I never thought my mom would try to push me toward being with anyone.

"Would you like to go out to lunch?" he asks me. He's got nice brown eyes, that's for sure. I can't say no to him in front of my mom. The last thing I want to do is spend time with another guy outside of Toby, but maybe this is what I should do. Maybe this is a sign from God that I should allow more faith into my life.

"Sure, Nathan, I'd love to."

A couple of days go by, and it's nearly noon, so I need to clock out before I'm late for the lunch date with Nathan. I've been working fine alongside Toby, but we've not been flirty or intimate since yesterday in the car. I'm not sure what's going on, but I can't let myself get too attached... I need to repent tonight.

"Can you help me stock the rest of these books in the back before you leave?" he asks.

"Yeah." I place my clipboard down and follow him.

"So what's needed—" Before I could finish, he presses me against the shelves and kisses me. I kiss him back, and I don't stop his arms from wrapping around my waist. It's our third kiss.

I pull away. "What was that for?" I couldn't stop my smile from coming through. The kiss was deep. we're both out of breath.

"No reason." He winks.

I sit across from Nathan, but my thoughts are a thousand miles away. Toby—a man who haunts my dreams—has woven himself into every crevice of my mind. Nathan's words, meant as praise, scrape against my soul like sandpaper.

"You're not like other girls," he says, and I force a smile. But what does that even mean? That I'm not frivolous, not chasing fleeting desires? That I've adhered to the rules, the rigid lines drawn by my upbringing?

I used to wear my well-behaved Christian girl badge with pride. Modesty, obedience—it was my armor. But now, as Nathan chatters about mundane things, I realize I've missed out on life. The thrill of rebellion, the taste of freedom—it's all foreign to me.

The restaurant's soft lighting casts shadows on Nathan's face. I enjoy this place, they have incredible burgers. Nathan seems to be a good man, kind and genuine. But there's no spark, no fire. As the lunch drags on, I force myself through the motions, like a marionette dancing to someone else's tune.

"Thank you for a lovely lunch. You're a great guy, but I'm sorry. I'm just not interested."

His face drops slightly.

"May I walk you to the door?" He asks.

"Sure," I say.

As we walk up the stairs of my porch, he takes my hand and kisses it. "Have a good day, Elena." He says. My heart melts. Why is he so sweet?

He's a good catch. But not the right catch for me.

I walk inside my house, only to face my mother's disapproving gaze.

"I can't be with him, Mom. There's no spark."

"Give him another chance. Your best years are slipping away," she warns. "Soon you'll be left with regrets."

Her words sting. I retreat to my room, the walls closing in. How did I become this obedient vessel, drifting through life without purpose?

Toby's face flashes before me—the boy who challenges conventions, who makes my pulse race.

I want more. More than this scripted existence, more than the judgmental whispers. Even if it means my faith wavers, even if it means breaking free from the cocoon they've spun around me.

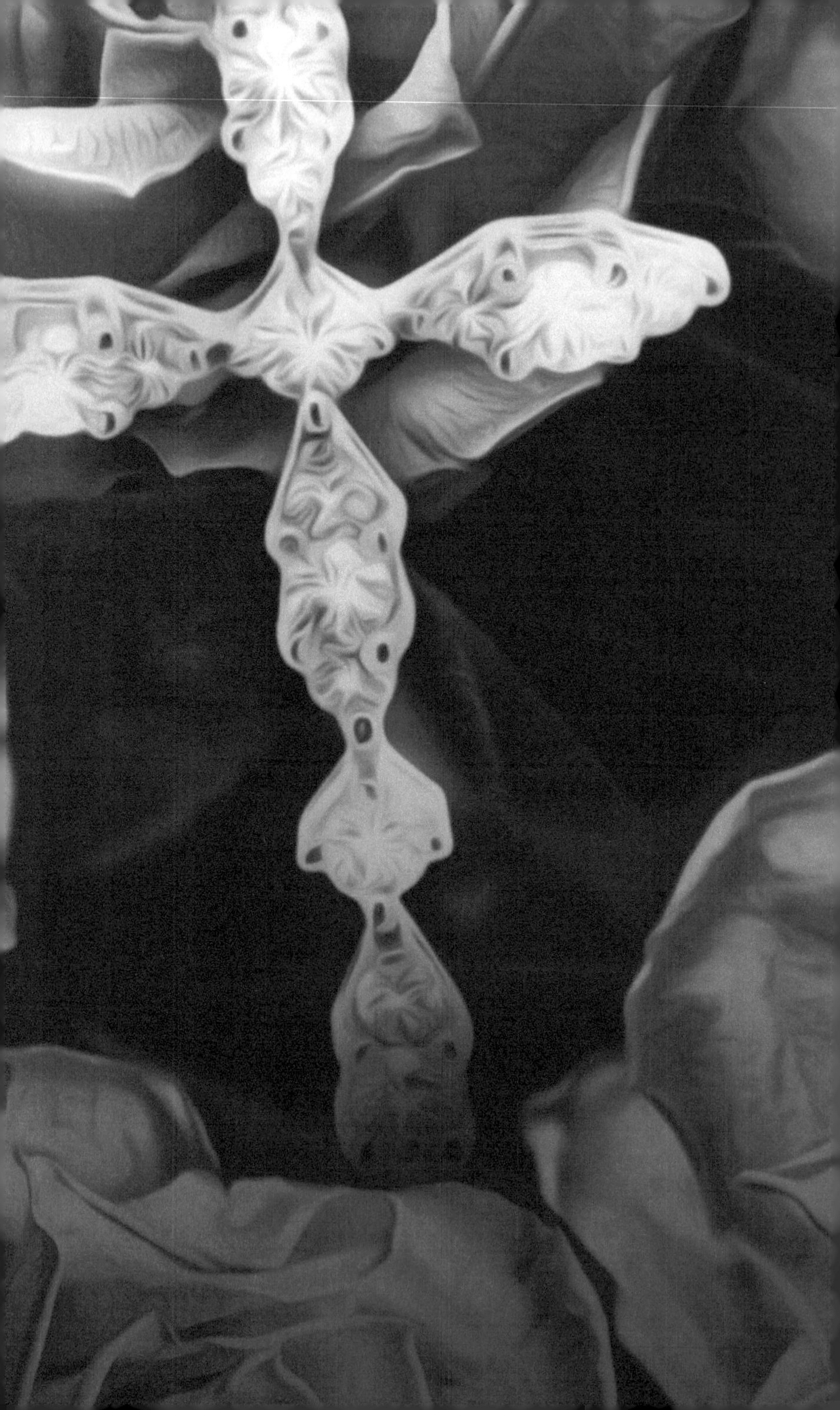

CHAPTER THIRTEEN

Later on in the night, I'm scrolling through my phone and looking through social media when I receive a text from Toby.

My lips curve into a smile, and I feel a stir in my chest when I think about my feelings for him. It's like one moment I'm loving kissing and working side by side with him, but then I'm pissed because he makes little remarks about my religion, but I don't really know what to think right now. I can't help how I feel. With each passing day, I am falling head over heels for the guy.

ME

> It didn't go well, and it was my
> first actual date.

TOBY

> **I'm going to take you on a
> proper date. A good first date.**

I laugh. He's gotta be joking.

ME

> Sure, whatever you say,

I finish scanning a couple of books for a customer. "Have a good rest of your day!" I say. The girl nods and walks out of the library.

"So, ready for our date tonight?" Toby asks, standing next to me at the counter.

"What? I figured you were joking."

"Oh no, I wasn't. I want to take you out for dinner."

A warmth spreads through my cheeks. Something about him just fades the negative feelings about him I had before.

"Okay, but I can't just leave. I'll see if a friend can cover for me. My parents and Christian can *not* know."

"Okay, I've gotta leave early today, but I'll be back to pick you up."

I nod and watch him walk out the door, while I'm left trying to figure out how to get away with going out tonight. I grab my phone and tap Mom in my contacts, sending her a quick text.

ME

Hey Mom, I'm going out with Jenny tonight for a movie, so I won't be attending dinner tonight, that okay?

MOM

Sure, sweetie, just call me if you need anything.

I tap open Jenny's name.

ME

Hey, can you cover for me? Going out with a boy... if my mom calls...

Sweat forms on my forehead as thirty minutes go by and Jenny hasn't responded. I let out a shaky breath and send Rose the same text. Not even a minute later, my phone dings.

ROSE

Uh, yes, I've got you!

We can't be seen in public together, and I'm glad to have friends willing to cover for me.

I spend the rest of the day anxiously awaiting the end of my shift. I'm busily organizing the last of the books for the day when the entrance bell pings and I turn to see Toby walking back into the library, holding a bouquet of white roses.

"Oh, for me?" I smile, giving a small laugh.

"Yes, for you, princess. Let's go," he says as he hands me the roses and offers me his arm. I loop mine through his, and we head to his truck.

We drive for about twenty minutes, but all I see are cornfields and a perfect sunset view.

I go to open the door, but before I do, he stops me. "Wait."

I let go of the handle, and he steps out of the truck and walks to my side, opening the door for me.

"Come on." He offers his hand. I take it, and he closes the door behind me, grabbing a blanket and picnic basket from the back of the truck. As he lays out the blanket on the tailgate, smoothing it out, I can't help but watch his movements. He seems so sweet. I can't believe he's doing this for me.

He offers his hand again, and I take it, and he helps me up on the tailgate. I sit in the back next to him.

"So, what did you pack?" I ask.

"Hungry, aye?" he jokes, opening the basket and pulling out strawberries, grapes, what seems to be Italian sub sandwiches, and a bottle of champagne."

"Are you watching me eat my lunches at work?"

"You're the only one I know who eats Subway like four times a week," he says.

"No, I don't, more like once a week. They are amazing."

We both laugh, and as we eat our food, a comfortable silence surrounds me. He's a flirt, a non-Christian boy, someone my parents would disown after seeing me with. But the things he's done in his past don't matter. What matters is how he is now. No matter what my dad's views are, I have to believe God knows what he's planning for me. He's made this moment for me. Whether it's a lesson to learn or the right path, I have to do what my heart guides me toward.

"Sunset is beautiful," I say.

"Not as beautiful as you." He smirks at me.

I laugh loudly. "Oh stop, I'm sure you say that to every woman you see."

"I've never watched the sunset with others, actually."

"Oh, I'm sorry. I shouldn't have assumed."

"No, it's okay. I understand I have a reputation, but if I'm being straight with you, I haven't had a girlfriend since the tenth grade after I caught my ex cheating on me with someone who was supposed to be her cousin."

"What? Her cousin? What the?"

"Oh, it wasn't her cousin. She just said that to be with him whenever she wanted without being questioned."

"I'm sorry, Toby. That's awful," I say as I eat the last grape.

"Hey, I wanted that one."

"You've gotta pay attention, silly."

He nods and stands, jumping over the side of the truck. He opens the door, turning the car on and radio. A slow song turns on.

Oh boy, what is he doing?

"Care to dance?" he asks.

My lips curve as I see his hand reach out to me.

I stand and walk over to the edge of the tailgate. "Uh, I don't know how..."

He walks closer, lifting me from the ground. We dance in the field, feeling our souls connect. Each step frees me from old, rigid beliefs, replacing them with a sense of freedom.

"Just follow my lead, princess,"

My lips curve as I see his hand reach out to me.

Blushing, I bite my lower lip. "Okay, yes," for too long I've lived in fear. "I'd love to."

God no longer seems like a distant overseer but a part of everything around us. I realize that God's true nature is not in loud commands but in quiet connections and the gentle tug towards kindness, understanding, and love.

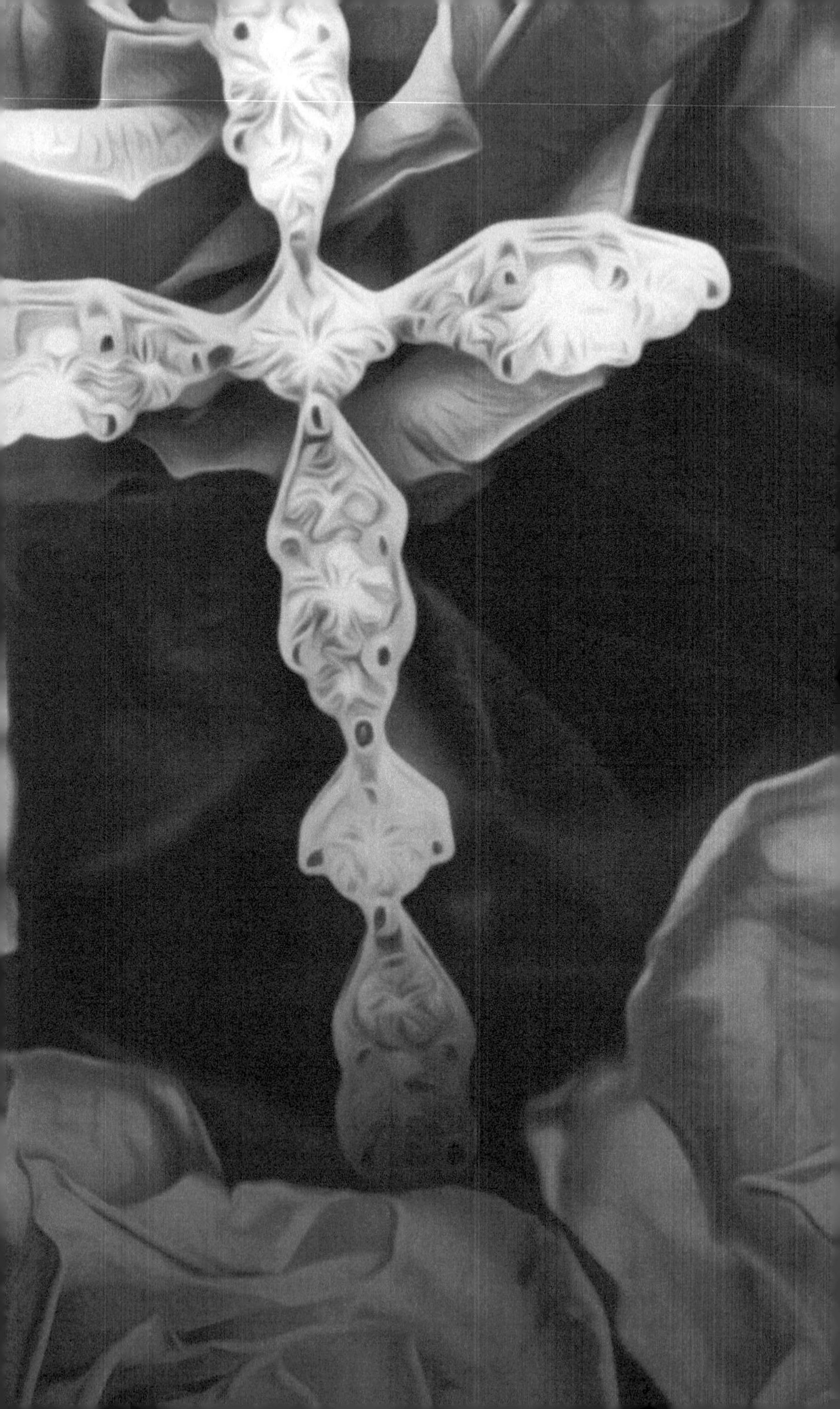

CHAPTER FOURTEEN

The piercing sound of my father's enraged voice echoes through the hallway, shaking the very foundation of our home. "Christian! Get up!" he bellows, pounding on a door as if trying to break through the walls themselves. My heart races, and a chilling uncertainty grips me.

In a hurry, I fling aside the covers and wrap myself in a robe, and rush outside my bedroom to confront the storm brewing within our family. "What's wrong? Why are you yelling?" I demand, my voice trembling.

His eyes blaze with anger. "Your brother has stolen money from the church savings account."

The words hang in the air, an accusation that feels like a betrayal. "That doesn't sound like Christian," I protest.

"We caught him in the act, and I won't tolerate

it," my father responds angrily. "If he wants to become a thief, he is free to move out."

"Dad, have you even thought about why he would do it?" I plead.

"There's no excuse to steal! It's not about being a Christian right now; it's about being a good person and not being an idiot!" he snaps back, dismissing any possibility of understanding.

"Dad! Your son, my brother, has been having a hard time lately," I yell, tears welling in my eyes. "Maybe if you sat down and talked with him and spent more time with him, you'd see that!" I yell again.

"Don't yell at me! I am your father! You're in my house!" he roars, the authority in his voice cutting through the air.

I couldn't handle his demons any longer. "I'm sorry, Dad, but you aren't in the right here, and neither is Christian for stealing, if he even stole—which I am still not convinced he did until I hear it from him. I'm not choosing sides. If you want a stress-free household, quit causing stress by being so goddamn strict!" I widen my eyes, realizing what I just said.

His rage intensifies, and he storms toward me, pushing me against the wall and pointing his finger in my face. I squint my eyes.. He's never been this way before. "You are a disrespectful brat! Say

God's name in vain one more time, and you are out of this house for good!"

I meet his gaze, and I can feel the blood rushing into my cheeks. I run up the stairs to get ready for work and hurry out of the house after.

All I could think was, *Where's Mom?*

It's been a few hours since the fight this morning, and I'm trying to lose myself in my work.

Toby approaches the front desk, concern etching his face. "Elena, are you okay?" he asks gently, his eyes searching mine.

I shake my head, blinking back tears. "Not really. It's like my entire world is falling apart." I sniffle.

He takes my hand. "I'm here for you, Elena. Whatever you need."

I wipe a tear falling down my cheek. "Thank you, Toby. It means a lot."

Toby continues to hold my hand.

"Do you want to talk about it?"

"No. Yes. Maybe." I try to breathe, but my chest constricts. The next thing I know I'm telling him about my morning and the run in with my dad. I feel the hot trail of tears running down my face as

I confess, speaking back, something I know is never allowed.

"Just know you can come to me, okay? I'm going down to the basement to grab more shelves."

"What? Why?"

"Three shelves on the tall bookshelf near the front door need to be replaced. They've become loose."

I nod. "Okay, just call for me when you need help."

"Will do, princess." He winks, walking to the back.

I smile as he walks away. My phone dings and I look at it, a text from my brother.

CHRISTIAN

Are you okay?

ME

I will be. You?

I go through the online inventory and let my brain wander off about everything that's gone on for the last couple of weeks. This summer is completely different. I'm being pulled into a path I never thought I'd step foot on. My phone dings again and I look at it.

CHRISTIAN

Same.

Toby and Christian have been best friends since we were in the 9th grade in high school. They knew of each other because of mom and Lindsay being best friends, but I didn't hang out with anyone much, not even my own group of people. My dad would kill me if he caught me talking to him in a way he would see as 'bad' for me. He knows him well enough, of course, to have such thoughts about him. But he will never approve of any guy who is not a Christian.

Every boy I had a crush on, my dad would tell me crushes are not a thing, that if it's meant to be, it'll happen on his terms. And when I see how happy my friends are, and now after me and Toby kissed and went on a date, my views are shifting. Feeling so guilty at first over a kiss... I'm beginning to believe a kiss is not something God will disown me for, but definitely something my dad would.

"Hey, Elena!" I hear Toby holler from the basement. I snap from my thoughts and turn to walk down the stairs. The library's basement is beautifully furnished with white tile flooring throughout the entire area and shelves filled with multiple genres of books all over the walls, even aisles of bookshelves, and warm lighting throughout every corner of the basement.

I notice Toby sitting on one of the reading chairs. We often use the basement for weekly reading events for students of all ages.

"What do you need help with?" I ask.

"My desires," he says with a wink.

My cheeks warm up a bit. "Come on, Toby, seriously."

"Oh, I'll come. Just give me something to use."

"Toby!" I laugh.

"Okay, okay, seriously, can you grab the mop from the back corner of the closet? I can't get through to reach it."

"Could have started with that!" But I'm really enjoying those comments of his...

Oh, stop it, Elena.

I head toward the closet and see the mop way back in the corner. Clearly, a small person can get through here, and he's too bulky, like a football player, to fit.

I feel a hand over my left thigh, grazing over my butt.

I rotate rapidly, my flowing blond hair whirling in front of me. I start losing strength in my body, almost stumbling backward, but he reacts quickly, placing his arm around me to maintain my balance yet also pulling me forward.

As I direct my gaze into his eyes, he meets it with his own. All the knowledge I have gained in church throughout the years dissipates, while my longing for him intensifies in this very moment. He runs his tongue over his lip, and without any second thoughts, I proceed to kiss him. He lifts me into his arms, and I wrap my legs around his waist. He sets me on a table, and as our kiss deepens, he procceds to slide his hand up just underneath my bra.

My breath quickens, and he pulls away from the kiss, pushing my hair to one side. He kisses my neck, starting right underneath my ear, and a moan escapes my lips. My eyes widen, and I place my hands on his chest and push him away.

"Wait." I let out a breath.

"What's wrong?" he asks, his dark hair a mess from my hands gripping it.

"It's just, I like you, but the more we kiss, the more I want you, and I'm not sure if I'm ready to more,"

"I understand," he says with a smile. We break apart and go our separate ways. That smile makes me feel at ease.

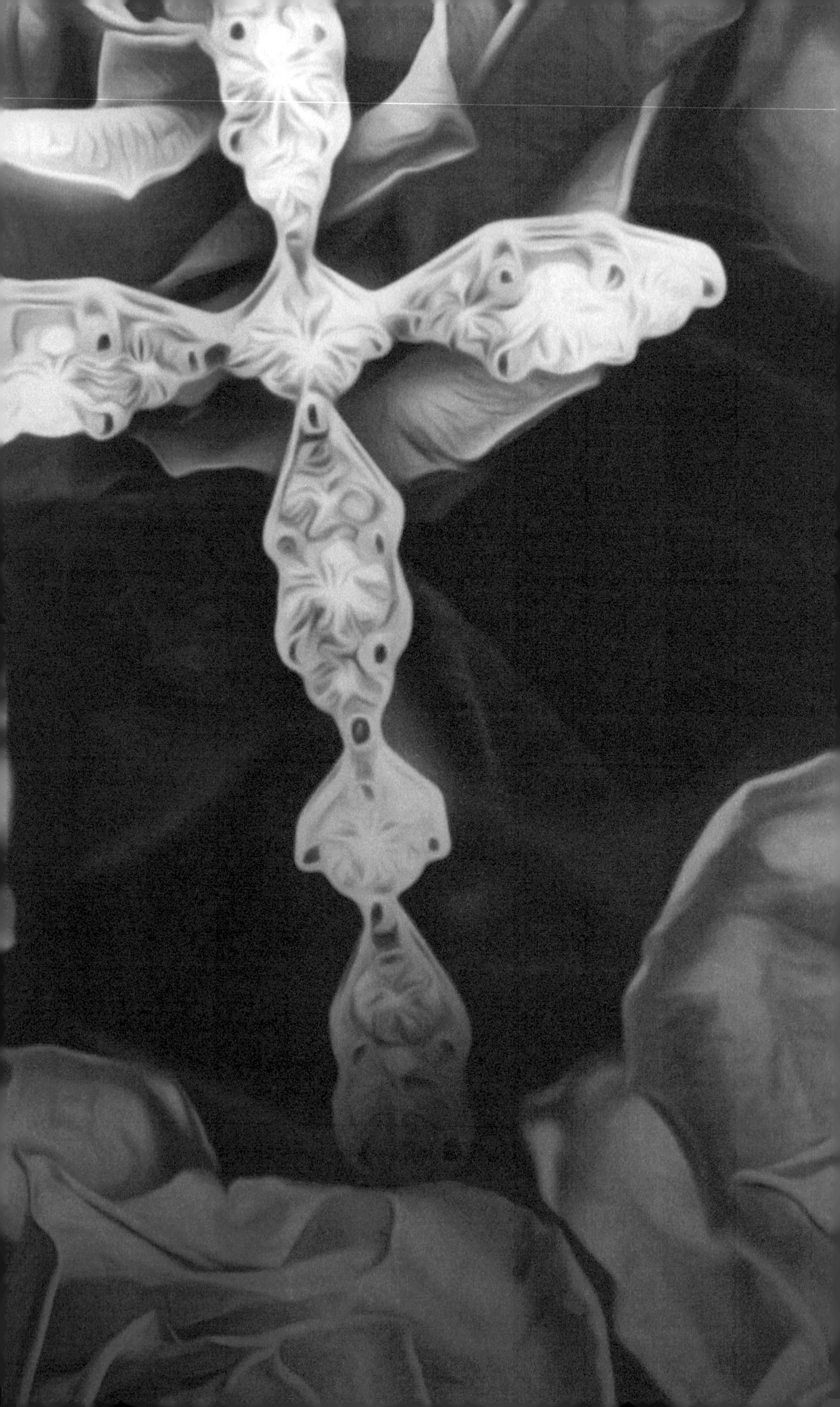

CHAPTER FIFTEEN

As I organize another stack of returns, I can't stop thinking about the heated argument from earlier this morning. Dad has never acted out of line like that. Sure, he's strict, and I understand why he's angry with Christian, but I couldn't hold my tongue anymore. I had to say something. I don't know where Mom was this morning, and I haven't called her yet. I look at the time on my phone and see it's about three in the afternoon. My body is trembling still from the argument.

Toby's still somewhere in the basement doing god knows what. I bite my lip, remembering our heated make-out session down there. We've kissed before, but not like that. The way I turned to face him felt like a slow-motion scene in the movie.

It was leading to more, but I had to stop myself. I'm loyal to God. But I'm human, and I can't help the way I feel. Should I go down there with him? Maybe not. Oh, I can't help myself. I walk toward the basement and head down the stairs to see Toby writing on a big piece of paper.

"What are you doing?" I ask, my interest piqued.

"Drawing out a new layout design for the basement. Mom called; she wants new contractors to hire and redo it."

"What? But I love how it looks. It's very nice and cozy!"

"It is. I won't forget our little make-out session down on that table; that's for sure." He laughs.

"Hey now." I giggle. Warmth rushes to my cheeks. I'm so glad the lights are dimmed right now.

"It's true, though. That table will be removed when it comes time to renovate."

"Damn, I do like that table, though. It's the perfect height for me when I'm going through new books."

"I bet it is, shorty," he jokes, smirking.

I push his arm slightly, laughing with him.

"I think I'm going to head out early. I need to see if Mom is home. This morning was insane."

"Everything okay? Do you need a ride?"

"Yeah, I'm fine. But no, the last thing I need is my dad freaking out over nothing."

"See you tomorrow?"

"Yes."

I see my mom's car in the driveway, but it wasn't there this morning. I open the front door and hear my parents arguing in the living room.

"Psst!" I hear Christian whisper from upstairs.

"What's going on?" I ask as I walk up the stairs.

"I didn't steal the money, and I told them that. Someone is framing me."

"Who would frame you?" I ask.

"Dad."

"*Dad?* No way."

"Yes way, I couldn't sleep the other night, and when I headed to the bathroom, I overheard him on the phone with someone about the church money and him wanting to pull some out."

"I don't understand. Our family has enough money, so why would he take it from the church?"

He shrugs. "I told Mom once she got home, and that's why they're arguing."

"Let's just go hide out in our rooms. I'd like to tune them out for the rest of the afternoon," I say.

"He's not hitting on you, is he?"

Oh crud, does he know something? "Who?"

"Toby."

"No, that'd be weird," I lied straight through my teeth. Forgive me, Lord.

"Okay, you just let me know if he does, and I'll have words with him!"

If he has words for him over flirting, I'm scared to know what he'd do after he found out about our kissing and date night.

I leave my brother and head to the bathroom. In the shower, the warm water flows onto my skin nicely, relaxing me from all the stresses in my mind. I finish and get out, wrapping a towel around my body when I hear a loud crash downstairs. What the heck?

I quickly put my robe on and hurry down the stairs to see my mom in tears and glass shattered on the tile floor.

"What in the world?"

"Elena, go back to your room!" my dad spits.

"What? No! Mom, why are you crying?" I ask as I walk up to her.

"Don't worry about it, sweetie! Just do as your father says."

"Mom! I'm heading out with some friends, is that okay?" Christian asks.

"Yes, just be home by eleven," she whispers.

"Can I come with you?" I ask.

He shrugs. "Sure." He grabs his keys, and I hurry upstairs to change into something decent before heading out with him.

There's a shift in the family. I'm unsure what exactly is going on, but all I need right now is my brother, my rock.

"I hope you know we aren't just going to a friend's," he says.

"I figured, whose house are we partying at?"

"Toby's parents' house, the last place you picked me up from."

"Oh, okay," I whisper.

"Is that okay with you?" he asks.

"Yes, that's fine. Why wouldn't it be?"

"Nothing, just wasn't sure. I know you don't care for my friends much because of them not being in your crowd."

"Yeah, big book nerd here." I laugh.

"We may look alike, but that doesn't mean we have the same interests!"

"That's true!"

We pull up into the driveway, and I hear music blaring from the windows.

Every step I take closer to the steps to the door, my heart seems to pound faster and faster. He isn't expecting me, so it's going to get really awkward.

I hope Christian doesn't notice.

"Hey, guys!" Toby greets us with a smile, but as soon as he sees me, his smile turns more into a smirk. He didn't expect me tonight.

"Hey, man, nice party," Christian says and walks off somewhere into the apartment.

Toby watches as he walks off before looking back at me. "So what brings you here?" he asks.

"Family drama. I just needed to get out of the house."

I walk inside the place and try my best to keep some space between us. Christian is here, and I don't really want him thinking about things.

I navigate through the crowd, I catch glimpses of familiar faces and overhear snippets of conversations, but my mind is preoccupied with the impending encounter. Toby follows closely, his curiosity evident in the occasional glances he throws my way.

I find a corner where the music isn't too overwhelming and lean against the wall, stealing furtive glances around the room. Christian is nowhere in sight, which brings a fleeting sense of relief. Maybe I can avoid any awkward confrontations after all.

Toby appears beside me, handing me a drink from a nearby table. "You okay?" he asks, his voice laced with concern.

I nod, taking a sip to buy myself some time. I squint my eyes at how bitter-tasting it was.

"Yeah, just trying to decompress," I reply, forcing a casual tone.

"Listen, I know things are a bit tense with Christian here," he says quietly, "but I was thinking... Maybe we could hang out later this week?"

I blink in surprise, looking around to make sure Christian isn't nearby.

"Oh," I say, struggling to find the right words. "I mean, yeah, that sounds nice."

He studies me for a moment as if debating whether to press further, but he ultimately lets it go with a shrug. "Great, just know I'm here if you need anything," he offers before wandering off to mingle with other guests.

I want him more than I've ever wanted anything else. I wanted him to say and push for answers, or drag me away somewhere to make out again...

"What was that about?" Christian walks up, asking me.

"Oh, uh, he could tell I was tense and offered a drink." I lie.

"Do you want to head back home?" he asks softly. It's clear he doesn't want to leave—the night is still young, and the party calls to him like a siren —but at this moment, his concern is for me.

"No, not really."

"Okay, just let me know if you change your mind, okay?"

I nod. He walks off to talk to some blonde. He obviously didn't need much convincing to stay longer.

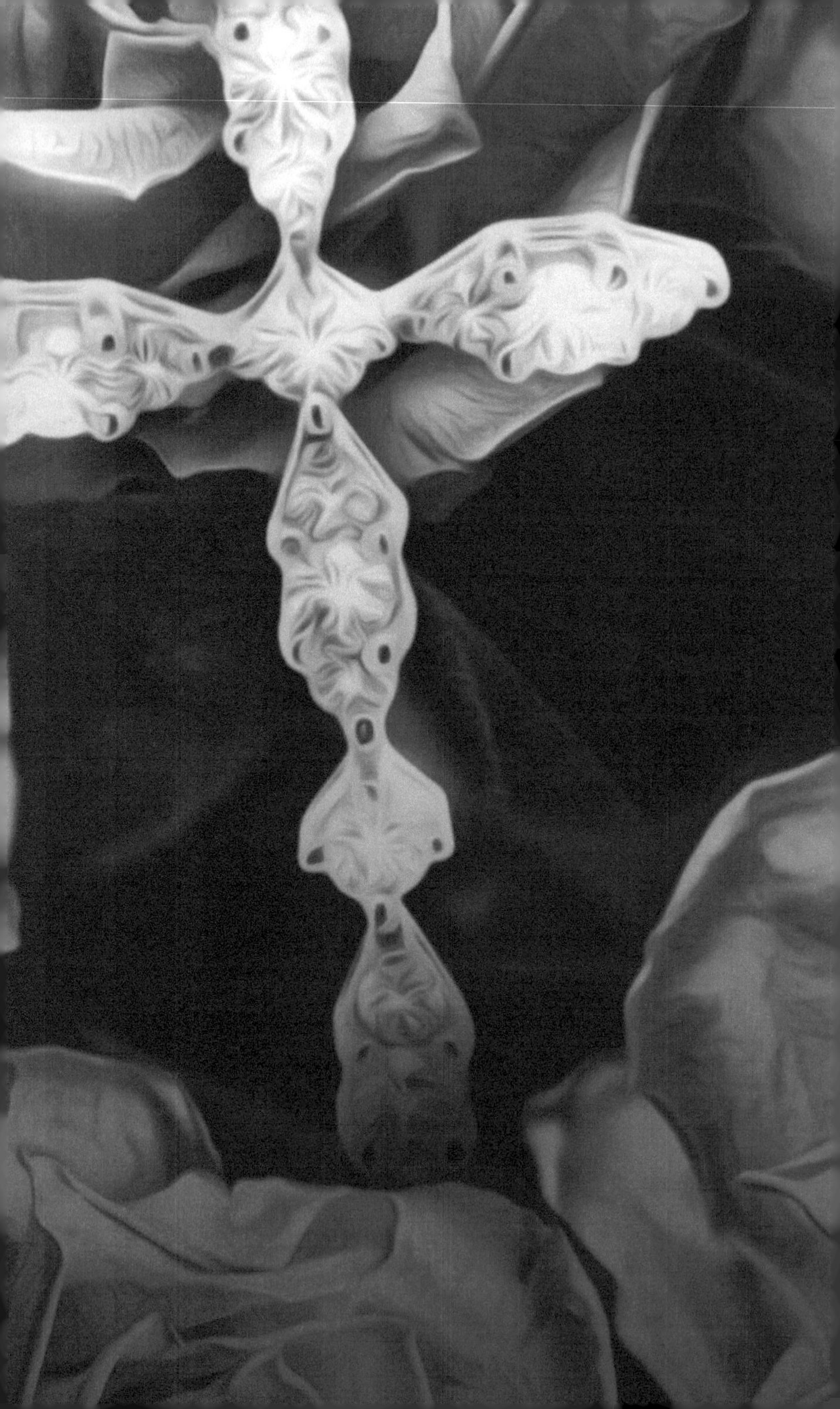

CHAPTER SIXTEEN

The clock on the dashboard ticks away the seconds as I navigate through the streets toward Toby's place. It's been a few days since the party, a few days since our parents have been continuously fighting. I decided to stay longer at work and hang out until my curfew hours, but I lied and told my parents I'm a bit behind on work and just need the extra hours. But really, it just gives me a chance to spend some time with Toby.

I park the car and sit for a moment, contemplating whether I should go through with it. Doubts creep in, and the familiar comfort of my routine calls out to me like a siren song. But deep down, I know I can't keep avoiding the inevitable. If I want a life of my own, free from the strings my parents have woven around me, I have to take risks.

I step out of the car and make my way to Toby's

front door. After a hesitant knock, the door swings open, revealing Toby's warm smile. His eyes light up, and I can't help but feel a surge of reassurance. Maybe this risk is worth it. I've never been alone in a house with a boy aside from my brother, but Toby makes me feel at ease with that smile.

As I enter, a sense of relief washes over me. Toby's place is a stark contrast to the chaos I often find at home. It's organized and clean like mine, but has a welcoming atmosphere. I let out a soft chuckle, realizing that even his living space reflects the calm I crave.

Toby leads me to a corner where his impressive vinyl collection stands proudly. He runs his fingers over the records. He carefully selects a vinyl and places it on the turntable.

The room fills with the soft crackle of the needle finding its groove, and a soft melody begins to play. Toby's eyes lock with mine as he extends his hand, inviting me to join him in the moment's dance. I hesitate, my shyness threatening to hold me back.

"Come on," he teases.

"I thought we were going to watch something and eat," I say.

"We are, but come on, have a little fun," he insists.

I glance down at his outstretched hand, unsure. After a moment, I shrug, my curiosity winning over my reservations. "Okay, but I don't dance," I warn, my cheeks flushing.

"Slow dancing is easy. Just follow my lead," Toby reassures me, his smile warm and inviting.

Taking a tentative step, I place my hand in his. The vinyl spins, and we begin to move together in the small space between the records and the cozy furniture. The world outside seems to fade away as Toby leads me with a gentle sway, the soft music enveloping us like a comforting embrace.

The feeling of his hands on me drives me crazy, and I do my best not to look at his lips.

Meanwhile, he's looking at mine. When the song comes to an end, we look into each other's eyes. As he runs his fingers through my hair, I feel my heart race with anticipation. He lifts me up and carries me to his bed, gently laying me down. He then kneels beside me.

"Have you ever been *touched* before?" he asks me, his voice gentle and sweet.

I cock my head to the side. "What do you mean?"

"Sexually,"

I shake my head, unable to form words as I am lost in the moment.

"Would you like to be?" I nod eagerly, feeling a surge of excitement coursing through me.

His fingers trace a tantalizing path up my back, causing my body to arch towards him. The fabric of my shirt gives way to his touch and I feel his breath on my skin as he leans closer. With each kiss, my desire grows stronger and I surrender myself to pleasure and curiosity.

He takes it slow, exploring every inch of my body with his lips and hands. "You look so good, princess," he whispers against my skin as his finger grazes over the fabric of my now-damp panties. My hips instinctively lift towards him, begging for more of his touch.

"May I?" He asks, gently tugging on the edge of my underwear. I nod.

As he slides them off my legs, I spread them open without hesitation. His eyes roam over my naked form.

"You've got such a beautiful body," he says, making me blush under his gaze.

But before I can fully take in the compliment, he lowers himself between my legs and glides his tongue over my lips. A tingling feeling runs through me as he teases and explores every inch of me with his mouth. His moans only intensify the pleasure and I feel myself losing control.

Suddenly, he pulls away and slides a finger inside me, causing me to gasp loudly. I grip his hair tightly as he continues to thrust his finger inside me.

He laughs into my skin, sending vibrations through me that only add to the sensation. My body quivers and shakes, a wave of warmth spreading from my core.

A loud moan escapes my lips as he stops and I sit up, breathless and flushed with exhilaration. A laugh escapes me, and I couldn't stop. Why am I laughing?

"Did you enjoy yourself, princess?" His voice is laced with smug satisfaction as he wipes his mouth with the back of his hand, leaving behind a trail of my own arousal. He leaves the room for a moment, only to come back with a wet rag.

"I did, but what are you doing with that?"

"Cleaning you up,"

"Oh?"

He kneels down, spreading my legs for me, and wipes everything clean. After he's done, he grabs my panties and helps me put them on while I'm still laying down. He lays down next to me, pulling the blanket over us.

"I'm glad I was able to help you, I really enjoyed it," he smiles, looking into my eyes.

"It felt really good," I say.

"That's probably why you were laughing," he says.

"I don't understand?"

"You relieved any and all tension when you orgasmed. Sometimes laughing is part of it,"

I hide my face into his chest, and he chuckles.

"What kind of movie do you want to watch?"

"Something... romantic,"

My heart still races from the intense pleasure I just experienced. I lean up to peck his cheek before nestling back into his strong arms. With each of his warm breaths against my skin, I can feel myself relaxing more. His fingers idly trace patterns on my back, soothing and calming me down.

I'm still in a haze from the intensity of everything as I drive home after the movie. *What could I've done to him?* I'm hardly able to believe I gave in. I'm starting to realize just how much I've missed out on.

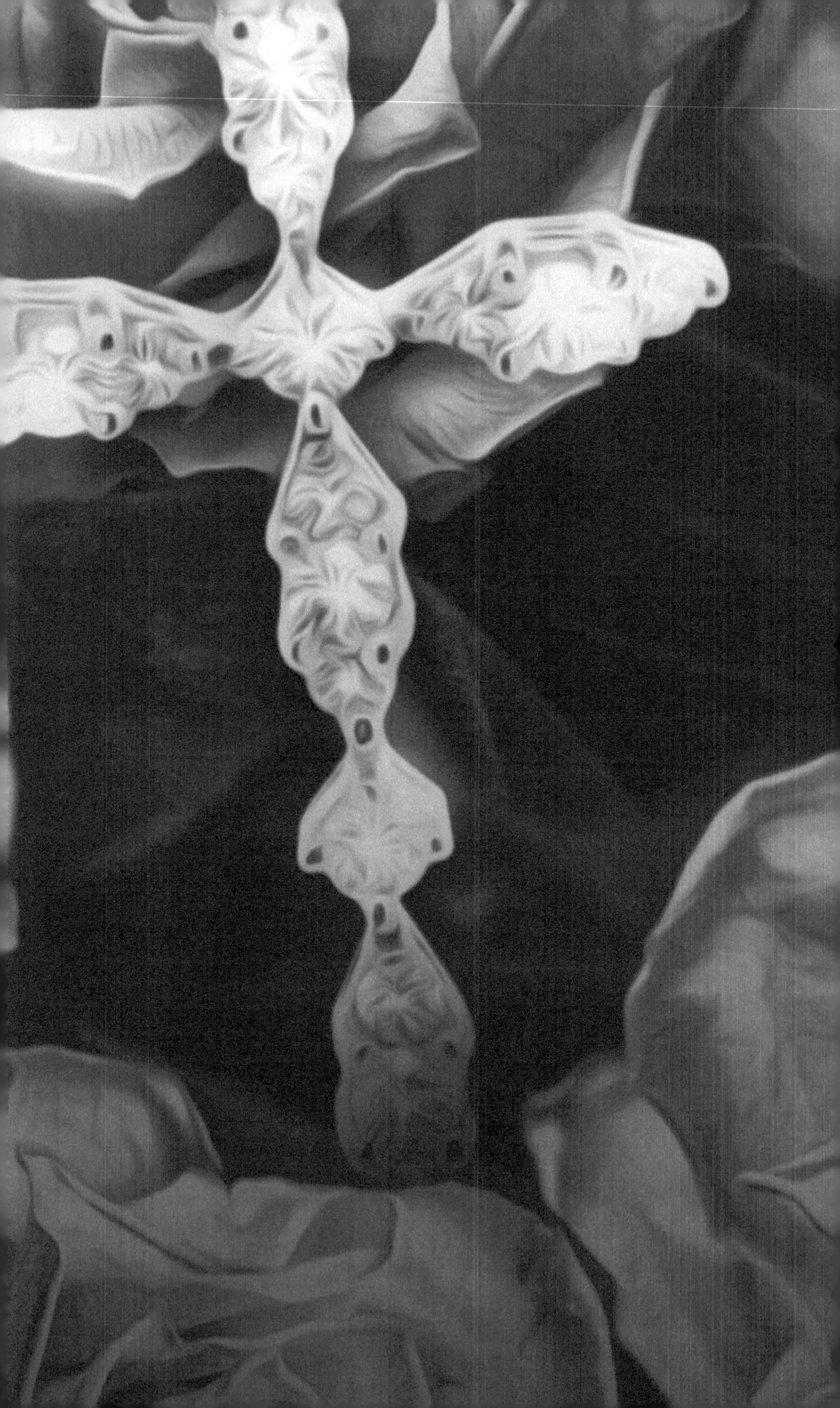

CHAPTER SEVENTEEN

A few days go by, and whenever I see Toby at work, I can't help but think of his hungry eyes looking up at me from between my legs. Saturday is the slowest day of the week for me. Our parents are out for the day visiting friends, and Christian is sleeping in and probably won't get up until later. I sit at the kitchen table, drinking a glass of orange juice. I grab my phone, I want to check on Lindsay and see how she's doing.

I can't stop thinking of Toby. Something about him just makes me crave him, all of him. I set my now empty cup in the sink and get ready to leave the house and head toward Toby's place.

I can't shake the image of Toby from my mind. Each thought of him pulls me closer until I find myself standing at his door. My heart races with a mix of worry and something else as I knock. The door opens, and there he is, looking every bit the rebel, including the cut under his eye and the split lip.

"Oh, Toby, you're hurt!" I gasp, my voice a mix of alarm and care.

He just smirks that infuriatingly charming smirk. "It's nothing. I won the fight. That's what matters," he says with a dismissive wave.

I frown, my worry turning into frustration. "What happened?"

"The guy at the party the other day said some things about you after we ran into each other at the gas station. We got into it again," he says.

I frown, my worry turning into frustration. "You didn't have to fight for me," I say, even though a part of me flutters at the thought.

But he was unrepentant, his eyes burning with a fierce intensity. "The guy deserved it for the way he touched you," he says, and I hear the jealousy in his voice, feel it in the air between us.

I like that he is jealous, more than I probably should. "Let me help you with those cuts," I offer, hoping to ease the tension. "You can help me with something in return. Deal?"

He steps back, allowing me space to enter. "Deal," he agrees.

Stepping into the dimly lit apartment, I close the door behind me, the sound echoing a definitive click. I motion for him to sit on the worn-out couch. "Where's your medicine cabinet?"

"Bathroom, top right cabinet next to the mirror," he says. I grab it, coming back into the living room.

"Here," I said, returning with a first-aid kit. "This might sting a little."

He just shrugs, a half smile playing on his lips. "I can handle it."

As I dab at the cut under his eye with antiseptic, I can feel his gaze on me, intense and unwavering. "Why do you always have to play the hero?" I ask, trying to keep my voice steady.

"Because you deserve someone who'll fight for you," he replies, his voice low and serious.

I meet his eyes, and for a moment, the world seems to stand still. "I don't want you getting hurt because of me," I whisper.

He reaches up, his hand gently covering mine, stopping my ministrations. "Elena, I'd go through a hundred fights if it meant keeping you safe."

My heart skips a beat. "Toby..."

He leans in, his forehead resting against mine. "No more talking," he murmurs. "You wanted to play nurse, so do your job."

I can't help but laugh, the tension breaking as I continue to tend to his wounds. There is a comfort in this, a silent acknowledgment of the bond between us. And as I finish patching him up, I know that this is just the beginning of something deeper, something real.

As I finish cleaning up his wound, he takes my forearm and begins kissing the inside of my wrist, making me shudder. I put the wound supplies on the coffee table and focus on him.

"I can't stop thinking about the last time you were here."

My cheeks warm. "Y-yeah that was my first," I pause looking into his eyes, "Orgasm," I whisper.

"Have you never masturbated before?"

I can feel my face becoming hotter. "No, because I've been told it's a sin."

"There should be nothing wrong with learning what feels good to you, especially if you ever expect to have sex in the future," he says.

"That's a fair point, but my sex education is health class back in school, and it has mostly consisted of being told to stay abstinent, and though I know what some things are, I've not taken part in anything. Not until that moment with you. Plus, I wouldn't even know where to start."

"How about I guide you?"

I fidget with my thumbs, "I don't know how I

feel about being the only one here touching myself?"

He chuckles. "I'll join if you'd like."

He makes me feel comfortable and tends to bring out a different side of me, and I love it. I bite my lip, looking him up and down. "Sure."

"Lie on that end of the couch, and I'll lie on the other end, okay?"

I nod, and we move into our spots.

"Take off your clothes, and wet a bit of your index fingers using your mouth, and begin rubbing your nipples. Both nipples." He orders with a smile.

I do as he says. I slowly lift off my shirt, and unclasp my bra exposing my nipples which harden as I do so. I then take off my pants and underwear. He proceeds to take his clothes off. *Am I crazy for doing this?* I stare at his already hard self when he takes off his boxers.

I've never seen a naked man, his legs are muscular, as if he works out often. The more his hand strokes his cock, the larger it gets. I'm transfixed by how sexy it is and my mind is clouded with a hot, hazy fog.

"Never seen a man naked before?"

I shake my head no.

"Do you like what you see?" he asks.

"Yes,"

"Is there another thing you can show me?" I

ask, my gaze raking over his body, drinking him in, and crawling over to him.

"Yes, wrap your lips around the head of my cock and slide it in as far as you're comfortable with. Bob your head up and down." His eyes burn with desire.

I can tell he wants me to touch him badly by his hard breathing. My tongue swirls around the head of his swollen cock, and a moan escapes his lips. "Good girl, that's perfect, keep doing that."

I keep going until I feel a warm liquid flow through my mouth. Unsure exactly what to do with it, I swallow and slowly sit up to face him. His eyes widen. "I'm sorry. Did I do something wrong? Was I not supposed to swallow?" I begin to hyper-ventilate,

"Oh, no. Far from wrong, princess." He covers himself back up and leans in, kissing my lips, "That was an incredible blow job, but let me return the favor," he whispers. He leans me back, kisses my neck, and strokes my breasts. As he swirls his tongue around my nipple, my phone goes off. Oh crap.

"Wait, stop," I say.

I panic, thinking maybe Christian knows I'm here.

"Hello?" I answer.

"Hey, Sis, can you bring me back an energy

drink whenever you're done with what you're doing?"

"Yeah, I will."

"Thanks," he says and hangs up. My face feels on fire. I put my phone back down and get dressed.

"Toby, I really need to go," I say with a sad smile.

With a cheeky smile, "I'll pay you back soon, I promise," he winks. He escorts me to the front door and I hurry home.

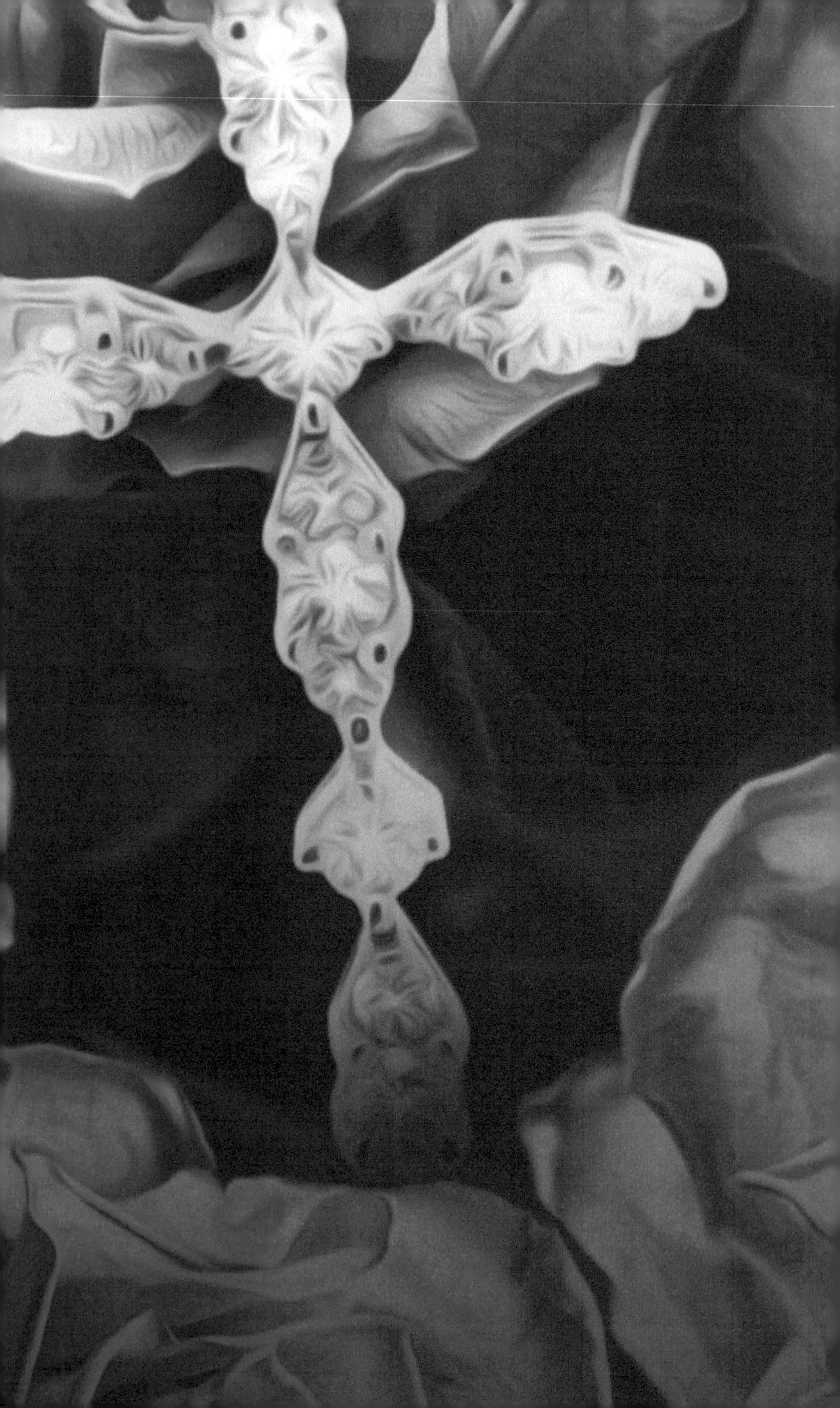

CHAPTER EIGHTEEN

I listen to my father's words as he speaks about the Bible and mentions something about thieving and why it's not okay, and I tune him out, knowing his words are full of shit.

Sorry Lord, I don't mean to curse. I'm just frustrated by my dad's actions.

Blaming my brother for something he didn't do is bullcrap. I'll never understand why he would point the finger at Christian when it was him the entire time taking money from church.

My mom put every cent of it back and locked my dad from the account until things calm down, and he's being dragged to therapy apparently now. No one knows what's going on, which is shocking but not entirely surprising because when it comes to my family drama, not a peep is made outside the walls of the home we live in. But anyone else's drama? That's all over town in two minutes, it seems. Christian sits next to me, eyes closed with earbuds in. He's clearly not happy with our dad either, and it shows.

"You need to take those out before we both get in trouble," I whisper.

"Shut up," he whispers back.

I'm not sure about all the details. Frankly, I don't care anymore. I roll my eyes and tune the rest of the morning.

The moment I lie down on my bed and look at the ceiling, tears begin to form. I've done things with a boy who has been as sin engraved in my mind for as long as I can remember. I don't feel entirely guilty, as I believe God will love me no matter what. But I still broke a promise to Him, and to my dad and that is something to be upset about.

My thoughts are interrupted by a knock on my bedroom door.

"Come in!"

My door creaks open and it's my mom, a sad look on her face.

"What's wrong sweetpea? I heard crying," she asks as she closes my door behind her.

I can't tell her the truth, she would punish me in ways I don't want to think about.

"Can I ask you something?" I wipe the tears from my face as she sits down on the foot of my bed.

"Of course," she says.

"When you met Dad, how did you know you were in love with him?"

She lets out a heavy sigh, taking a moment before answering me.

"Well, we were on our third date at the local theater watching an old black-and-white film. It was one of those classic love stories where you could predict the ending after the first ten minutes, but that didn't matter. Your dad... he had this way of seeing the beauty in the predictable, finding joy in the simple things. Halfway through the movie, he reaches for my hand, and it just felt right. Like two puzzle pieces clicking together. I look over at him, and he was already looking at me, with that goofy grin of his. And at that moment, I just knew. It wasn't about the butterflies or the racing heart; it was the calmness, the certainty that he was my person. That's when I knew I was in love with him." She stops talking and faces me, "Why do you ask?"

"No reason," I lie straight through my teeth.

"I just know that you guys have been fighting a lot and wanted you to think about a happy moment." I just made that up, but honestly do want her to think more happily.

"Well, you can always come to me if you meet someone."

I did. But because he's not a full believer you'll kick me out before I can say a word.

"Thanks Mom, I'm sorry it didn't work out with Nathan, I just didn't feel right with him."

"I understand, I just want you to be happy." She pauses, her eyes distant yet warm, as if reliving the memory right there with me. "Love isn't always about grand gestures or passionate declarations. Sometimes, it's in the quiet moments, the understanding glances, the shared smiles over something as mundane as an old movie. That's what your father and I have. And it's wonderful."

I nod.

"Is us fighting causing you to be upset honey?" She caresses my chin.

"Yeah,"

"It'll be okay sweetie, everyone goes through rough patches. You'll understand one day," she stands up and heads toward the door, "Dinner will be ready in an hour,"

"Thanks."

She starts to leave but pauses at the door. Turning back, "Remember, honey, when a man makes you feel safe, loved, and happy, that's how you know he's the one." With a smile, she closes the door behind her.

Well, that sums it up. I'm in love with Toby.

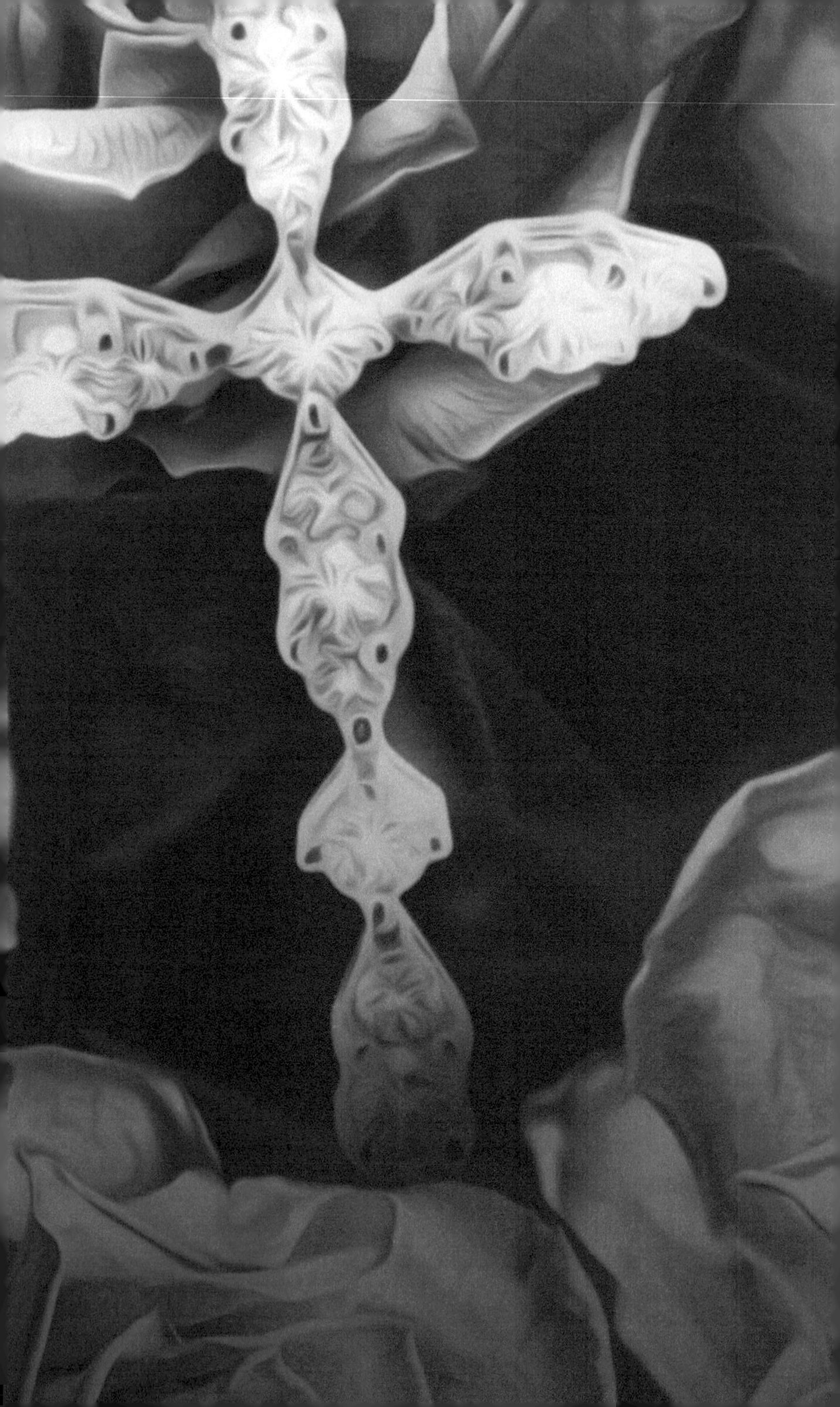

CHAPTER NINETEEN

The library is crowded with school buses full of kids. It's field trip day for them and because Toby works at the school, he's handling them mostly. I like kids but I just don't want to deal with them at the moment.

"What do you think? Is your mom going to like the new bookshelf we painted?" I ask him with my arms crossed while looking at the kids scanning over the children's book section.

Toby replies with a chuckle, "She's all about the bottom line, but I think she'll appreciate the effort. It adds a nice touch to the place, don't you think?"

I nod, my gaze lingering on the vibrant colors we chose for the bookshelf, hoping it would inspire the kids to read more. "Yeah, it does. It's more... lively now."

Toby's eyes meet mine, and there's a hint of something more than just agreement in his look.

"Your grandma doing okay? It's been a couple weeks and no update from your mom,"

"She is doing better, mom will be there for another week though,"

I nod.

"How about we add a little excitement to our evening? I was thinking, if you're free tonight, maybe we could go out for dinner?"

I can feel a smile spreading across my face, and I'm already nodding before I even speak. "I'd like that."

He grins, his eyes lighting up. "Great! It's a date, then."

"It is," I reply, feeling a warm flutter in my stomach. As the kids' laughter echoes around us, I realize that despite the chaos, this library—and this moment with Toby—feels just like where I'm supposed to be. I find him very attractive, and not just because of his looks. Watching him with the kids and seeing how good he is with them amazes me.

The Italian restaurant is cozy and inviting. I look around, making sure no one I know is here to recognize me. We sit and a server comes over with menus.

"What would you like to drink?" he asks.

Toby orders a soda, and I get water. We talk and laugh, sharing stories while we wait for our food.

When dinner arrives, Toby takes my hand. "I'm glad we're here together," he says.

I smile, feeling happy. "Me too," I reply. It's a simple but perfect evening.

About twenty minutes go by, and our food finally arrives. We dig in. "Wow!" I say as I taste the spaghetti sauce.

"Good huh?" he asks.

I nod in agreement.

As we finish our main course, the server returns with a smile. "Did you save room for dessert?" he asks, presenting a tray of tempting options. There's tiramisu, gelato, and a classic panna cotta.

Toby looks at me, raising an eyebrow in a silent question. I nod, and we decide to share the tiramisu. It's the perfect sweet ending to our meal.

"So want to head to my place tonight?" He asks me as we head out of the restaurant.

Looking at the time on my phone, I nod.

"Uh, yeah, let me just text Jenny to see if she can cover for me."

He nods, and I send her a swift text.

He opens the truck door for me, and I step in.

As soon as we get settled into his apartment, I wonder what I am doing sneaking around. It's out of character for me. I've heard stories where children of strict parents often rebel against them and although I'm not a child, I still feel like I'm rebelling.

Rebelling against my parents and the Lord.

Lord, I know you're listening, I don't know what path you are guiding me on right now, but I trust you.

"So how did you like the food?" he asks as he hands me a glass of wine.

"It was really good. I love spaghetti, but that meal was amazing."

"Better than home?"

"Nothing beats a home-cooked meal." I laugh.

"True that. I don't think I've had an actual home-cooked meal in months," he admits.

"What? Really? I'll need to make you something,"

"Oh, so the book nerd knows how to cook?" He smirks.

"Barely, I know a meal, and that's it."

"I'll be the judge of that,"

My phone pings, I look at a reply from Jenny.

JENNY

For all night?

I purse my lips.

ME

Yes.

I put my phone down, looking back at Toby. "Looks like you have me for the night."

"Oh yeah?" he winks and I smile.

As the evening wears on. The conversation turns to music, and Toby's face lights up as he talks about his favorite bands. "You have to listen to this one," he insists, pulling up a song on his phone.

The music fills the room, a gentle acoustic melody that seems to resonate with the mood. We sit in comfortable silence, letting the music speak for us.

Eventually, the song ends, and Toby turns to me, "I'm really glad you're here," he says softly. "It feels right, you know?"

I nod, because it does feel right. For all my worries about rebellion and expectations, being here with Toby feels like a choice I'm making for myself, and it's a good one.

I lean my head onto his shoulder, and he begins to run his fingers over my arm, goosebumps rise making me shudder slightly.

I have truly grown to care for him, and I hope

that he truly cares for me and that this isn't some sort of ploy.

Looking up at him, he leans in kissing me softly. It's sweet and gentle. My heart beats faster and I lean up adjusting myself onto his lap. He lifts me, standing on his feet and walks us to his bedroom while we're deep in our kiss.

With a gentle touch, he moves his fingers beneath my shirt, and I respond by lifting my arms, granting him the ability to remove it. My body radiates with warmth as he hovers over me, with one swift movement he unclips my bra, lays me back kissing me again, before lowering his lips down my jawline slowly making his way down my neck. A moan escapes my lips, and my body erupts in goose bumps right as he licks my nipples, moving from one breast to the other sucking both, back and forth.

He lowers down sliding off my leggings, tossing them to the floor alongside my shirt, and kisses my inner thighs. Arching my back from the pleasure of his tongue teasing me right on the outside of my panties, I can already feel that I'm growing wet. He slides my underwear off, gliding his tongue right on the edge of my inner lips before making his way to my clit.

"That feels so ... oh my God!" I yell. He continues staying in the spot. While he goes down on me, I feel the sensation of his wet fingers sensually stroking my nipples. My body is overwhelmed by the feeling, making my nerves ignite like fireworks. I move my hips in rhythm with his tongue, tilting my head back. My hands begin to ache from tightening my grip on the sheets. I've never pleasured myself, nor have I ever been touched before until I met him

I close my eyes, relaxing every muscle in my body but that only creates more intense pleasure.

A tingling feeling pulses through causing my body to shake, creating more sensitivity and throbbing in my clit.

"Please, don't stop!" I urgently grasp his head, pushing his face deeper, feeling his grip on my thighs tighten. I rock my hips back and forth, slightly positioning myself up with my elbows and cry out throwing my head back.

A sudden rush of liquid flows out of me, leaving my body calm and shivering.

After he takes his mouth off my clit, he wipes his mouth. "You're definitely a screamer and a squirter," he smirks.

"Is that bad?" I ask.

"No, far from it, means I did my job right."

"I want more of you," I whisper.

"Are you sure?" he asks.

"Yes."

He takes my hand, kissing it before looking into

my eyes. A warmth spreads through my cheeks as he does so.

As he inches closer, I feel his soft lips pressing against mine, I can taste his kiss on my lips, a mixture of sweetness and the lingering flavor of the mint he must have had earlier.

As he climbs on top of me, my breath quickens and becomes louder. The sight of his muscular arms sends a surge of arousal through my body that I never anticipated.

If I truly care about him, and he truly cares about me, how can giving myself over to him be so wrong? The nagging guilt that's always in the back of my mind goes silent.

"Are you positive this is what you want? I'm okay with waiting longer. I know how much your first time means to you." Such a gentleman. My first impressions of him were wrong.

"Do you care about me? Will you take care of me? That's all I need to know."

"I promise," he whispers, sealing his words with a kiss.

"Do you have condoms?"

"I do," he opens the drawer from the nightstand and grabs one. He walks back to me, and slides the condom on. He carries himself confidently, very sexy. My heart begins to race. Desire grows inside me, making my stomach flutter. He's so hot.

He climbs onto me, looking into my eyes before

leaning down to kiss me. My heart races, matching the rhythm of my breathing.

"Are you sure?" he asks me.

I caress my hand over his cheek, looking down at his lips, to his eyes, "Yes Toby, I am,"

He positions himself on top of me, stilling his hips for a moment, and I can feel the hardness of him against my entrance. His eyes never leave mine as he kisses me sensually. Slowly, he starts to press inward, stretching me open.

It's not painful but it is uncomfortable; I gasp at the feeling and my body tightens slightly. He doesn't rush or force anything.

"Are you okay?" he asks, hovering over me, kissing my cheek.

"Yes," I whisper.

"Shh," he says softly, "let me take care of you."

His thick cock fills me up perfectly, stretching me out in all the right places. His grip on my hands is firm yet gentle as he takes control of our rhythm, pulling me against him with each downward thrust.

The friction between us sends shockwaves of pleasure through my body that make my toes curl in.

I feel myself opening up for him.

Conflicting emotions swirl within me as I question the morality of surrendering to this desire. Yet, in this moment, the nagging guilt that typically resides in the recesses of my mind falls silent. If our feelings for each other are genuine, is it truly wrong to give myself to him?

He must have noticed something was on my mind because he immediately kisses me, which in turn distracts my thoughts and redirects my focus to the present moment.

"Are you feeling good, prin-"

I moan loudly, interrupting him. He smirks and continues to thrust slowly.

"Faster, please!'

"Whatever you say, princess," he thrusts faster and my moans grow louder. I lose myself, eyes rolling in the back of my head. The worries and judgments from the world fade into the background.

The bed squeaks beneath us as we move together; the headboard bangs against the wall.

His gentle touches send electric waves of pleasure through my body, causing me to shiver. I can feel the warmth of his breath on my neck as he kisses my neck and jawline.

He takes my hands and locks them with his, pulling them above my head.

"Don't stop," I beg.

"I won't," he whispers, his deep voice only intensifies the pleasure.

I feel myself getting closer and closer to the edge, every nerve ending alive with pleasure. Just when I think I can't take it anymore, he slows down slightly before picking up the pace again—driving me wild. My body tenses up momentarily before releasing onto him. He follows closely behind, crying out my name. When he's done, he pulls out and kisses me slowly.

"I love you," I blurt out.

He looks at me with a huge smile on his face, "I love you, too."

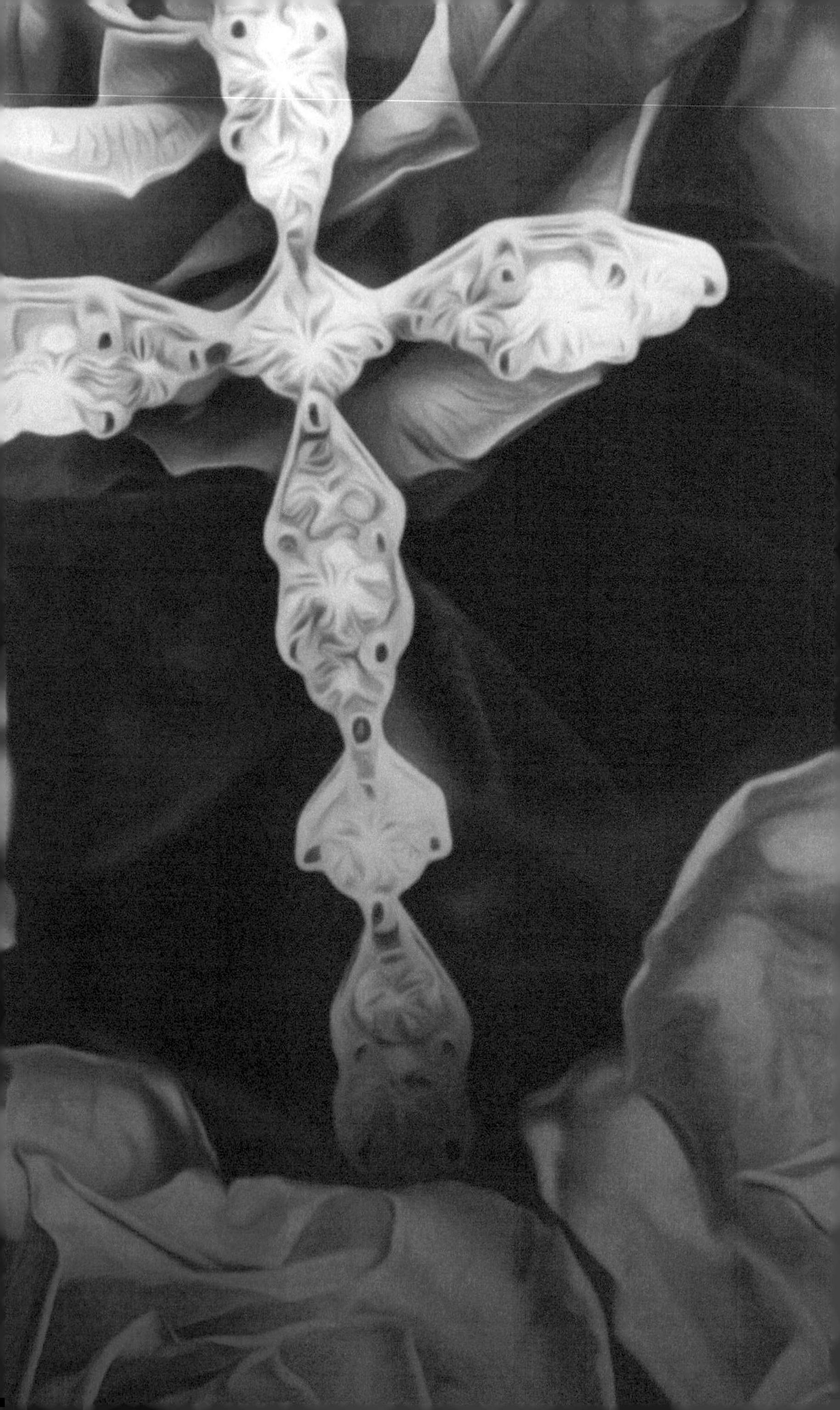

CHAPTER TWENTY

The morning sun streams through the window, casting a warm glow across Toby's bedroom and promising a day as radiant as the feelings bubbling inside me. I lay in bed for a moment longer, savoring the remnants of last night's dream—or was it a dream? No, it was real. Toby and I, together, sharing moments so intimate and tender that they feel like whispers from a different world.

As I get ready for work, my mind replays every laugh, every touch, every look he gave me. Toby isn't the person others warned me about; he is kind, genuine, and passionate. With him, I feel a connection that runs deeper than anything I've ever known. Yet amid this euphoria, a twinge of guilt gnaws at me. I made a promise to God, a vow I have broken. But then, isn't love part of His grand design? I cling to the hope that this is meant to be, that Toby and I are part of a larger plan. I need a sign, some divine guidance to reassure me.

I walk into the living room to see Toby making pancakes, shirtless. I stare at him for a bit, watching him dance along with some tunes as he cooks. "Good morning," I say.

He jumps, turning around to see me, "Hi beautiful," he says, turning back to flip a pancake before walking toward me. He leans in for a kiss, and walks back.

"Coffee?"

"Yes please," I say and sit on the couch.

Breakfast with my family is a performance these days. But this? This is real. With my family, I play the part of the Elena they know, the one whose life hasn't been irrevocably altered by a single night. I chat and smile, while the melody of my heart plays a joyful tune that only I can perceive. I can fully be myself, and more open with Toby.

The walk to work drags on. My nerves are through the roof. Would Toby regret last night? I frown at the thought. I couldn't bear it if he did; it meant everything to me.

Stepping into the office, I brace myself for his presence, but instead, I find Lindsay. She is back, her smile as bright as the news she shares—her mother is healing well. Relief and sadness collide within me. Toby's temporary role is over, and with it, our stolen moments at work.

Then he appears, his eyes finding mine across the room. "Elena, can we talk?" Toby's voice is tentative but hopeful.

I nod, following him to a quiet corner. "I've been thinking," he starts, "about going back to school, getting my teaching license."

My heart leaps, "Toby, that's wonderful!"

He grins, "Yeah? You think so?"

"I know so," I say, my voice a whisper, aware of his mother's watchful gaze not far from us.

Toby's voice breaks the silence, "About last night... are you okay with it? With us?"

His concern only deepens the affection I feel for him. "Yes, Toby, more than okay. It was perfect because it was with you," I assure him, my heart in my words.

"Random question, but do you plan on looking for apartments soon?"

That is a random question.

"Yeah, eventually, why do you ask?"

"No reason. Let's leave at lunch?"

"Uh." I look up at the time before looking back into his eyes. "Sure."

The day is a carousel of doors and hallways, each apartment a different horse to ride, and with Toby by my side, the city feels like a landscape of possibilities. But as we tour the units, a knot of anxiety tightens in my stomach. The reality of living alone, of being truly independent, is daunting. The last thing I want is to retreat to the safety of my childhood home, admitting defeat, but the discomfort of the unknown is scary.

Toby seems to sense my unease. "You've got this, Elena," he says. "You're ready for this step. It's going to be good for you."

Toby's gaze lingers on me, "I want to take you out tonight."

The invitation sends a thrill through me, but I hesitate. "If my parents or Christian or someone from the church see's us, things are going to go south,"

He stepped closer, his hands finding mine. "I don't care about what others think. I want you to be mine, Elena. I want us to be together."

His words are a balm to my soul.

"It's just hard, you know?" I sigh. "I've been in this bubble for so long I'm struggling to see how to get out of it,"

"I'm with you, on your side always,"

My phone lights up, shattering the moment and I see that it's Christian.

CHRISTIAN:

I've been in an accident, I need help.

Panic surges through me. I show Toby the text and we exchange a look and without a word, we are on the way.

As Toby and I arrive at the scene, I notice a small dent in the front of Christian's car, but he's clearly intoxicated. The car is skewed awkwardly against the fence, the front bumper crumpled like a piece of paper. I'm just glad he's the only one in the accident. He's leaned against the car, his form slack, eyes unfocused, and his clothes disheveled.

"Elena," he slurs as we approach, the smell of alcohol strong in the air, "I tried calling you... to pick me up."

"Are you drunk?" I ask, my voice trembling with a mix of worry and anger.

He looks at me, his eyes bloodshot and glassy, struggling to focus.

My face grows hot as anger boils inside me, my fists clenching at my sides.

"Christian! You could've killed someone or yourself driving like this!" I yell, the words bursting out of me.

His voice rises to meet mine. "Why'd you bring him?" He jabs a finger toward Toby.

Toby steps forward, his voice firm. "You shouldn't have driven."

Christian's eyes narrows. "Why are you two together?" When neither of us could find the words, realization dawns on his face. "No wonder you've been acting strange," he spits out.

In a flash of anger, he swings at Toby, who avoids the blow. I grab Christian's arm, pulling him toward my car. "We need to get you home," I said, my voice strained.

Toby nods. "I'll take care of the car, don't worry."

The drive home is silent. We sneak inside, and he gives me a look that could freeze boiling water before collapsing onto his bed.

A light snore escapes him and I tiptoe out of the bedroom, hurrying to mine. I lay in bed and watch T.V for the rest of the day, skipping dinner as well. I close my eyes, letting out a deep sigh.

My phone dings, waking me. It's nearing eleven at night. I see it's Christian messaging me.

CHRISTIAN

> How could you lie to me? I
> thought we were honest with each
> other.

I sigh and put my phone back down, and walk out of my bedroom to his.

I knock on his door, "Come in!"

I twist the knob, pushing the door open. "Christian." I say firmly. "We need to talk." He looks up, eyes sharp. "What about?"

"It's about secrets," I admit, stepping inside. "I'm sorry for hiding my relationship with Toby,"

He's visibly upset. "You lied to me, Elena."

I meet his gaze, unwavering. "I know, and I'm sorry. But you're in trouble too. Your drinking problem — it's dangerous."

He turns away, defensive. "I don't have a problem."

I sigh, feeling the weight of our situation. "You do, Christian. And we need to get you help,"

Silence fills the room. He looks away, conflicted, and I see a glimpse of the brother I once knew.

"Please," I whisper. "Let's fix this, together."

He's quiet, then nods. "I'm depressed, Elena. I have no job, nothing to look forward to,"

I sit beside him, "Drinking isn't going to solve your problems, it's just going to make you feel worse,"

He sighs, looking down at his hands before looking up at me.

"But when I drink, I forget. I don't hear Dad yelling at me. I don't feel the pressure to be someone I am not. I don't think about my aimless life. It's the only time my mind is quiet. What am I supposed to do?"

I think about the heavy drinking, the partying and the amount of times I've had to save him. Now he is telling me he drinks to forget? To drown out the noise? I'm worried that he's starting to get addicted to alcohol.

"AA meetings, we can start there."

Shaking his head, "Nope, what if those people go to our church?"

"Therapist then?"

"Sounds better."

"How long have you and Toby been seeing each other?" He looks at me with his brows raised.

"Not long, but if I'm going to be honest... I'm falling in love with him, Christian." I feel my face warm up.

"You know the kind of guy he is."

"I know the type of guy he was, but he's been nothing but kind and caring to me."

He nods. There was silence for a few minutes. A comfortable silence.

"I'm sorry for keeping it from you."

"Don't be, I understand. I'm just glad he's not treating you like dog shit."

"Me too."

My phone pings and I take it out of my pocket to see a message from Toby that Christian's car is ready.

"Ready to get your car?" I ask.

"Yes."

We arrive at Toby's apartment. Christian's car looks as if it's brand new. Stepping out the car, we walk up to the door and knock.

"This is weird," Christian says.

"Shut up."

The door opens, and there stands Toby in the doorway, no shirt and just basketball shorts and shoes. My eyes widen.

"Thanks for the car," Christian says while Toby hands him the keys. "And yes, I know everything."

I look at Toby and bite on my bottom lip, eyes still wide open, and he has the same look as well.

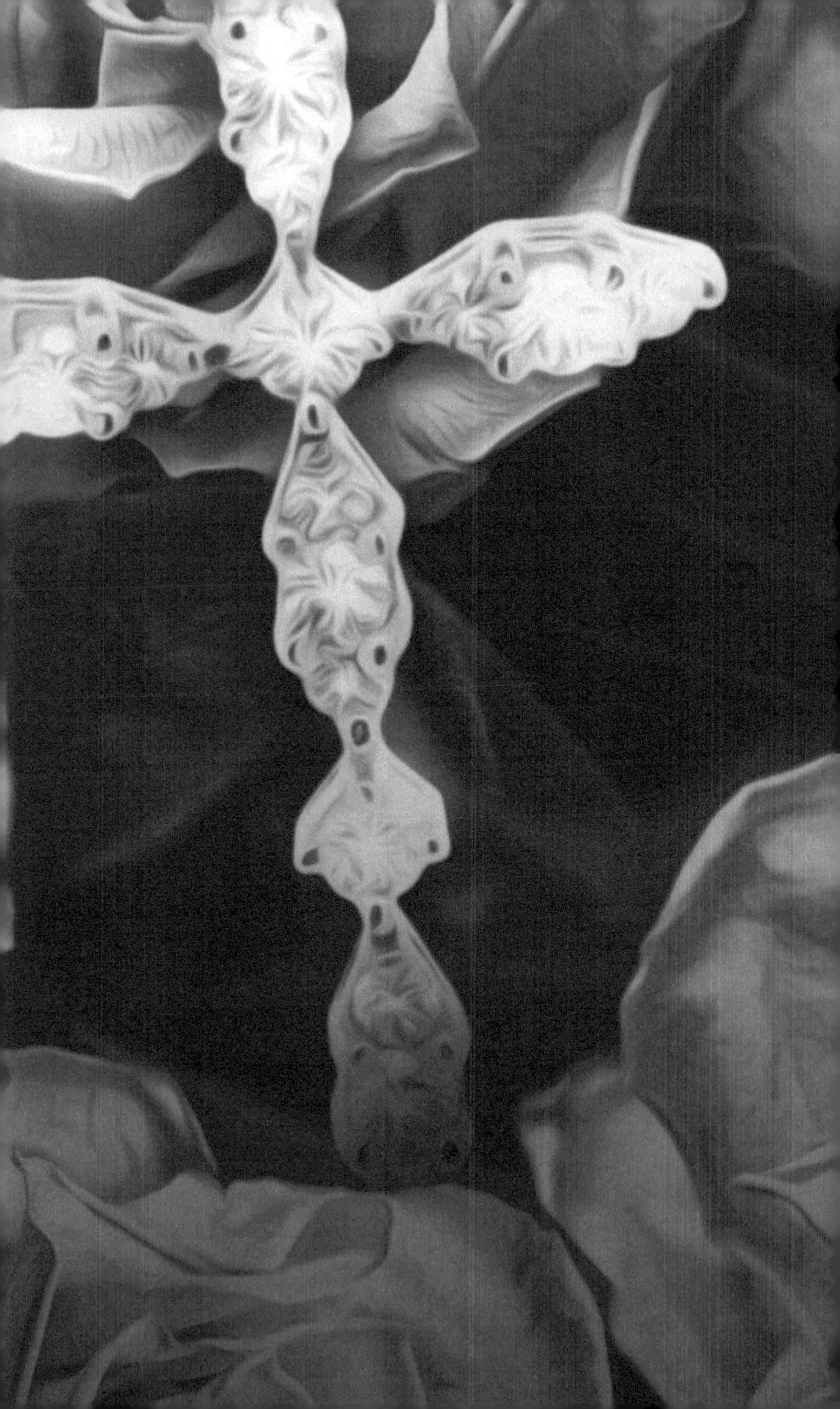

CHAPTER TWENTY-ONE

SATURDAY is here, nothing much going on aside from maybe hanging out with Toby or my brother; would both be weird? Probably.

I pick up a book from my shelf. A romantasy.

My parents weren't too keen on books that weren't Christianity related so I hid my collection under my bed for years.

I set my clock for thirty minutes and begin to read. Deep into chapter five, my phone pings loudly, snapping me from my pages. I take a look to see a message from Jenny asking to hang out. I think about it for a moment before replying with a yes. I need to try to say yes more. I need to live beyond the pages of my books.

The sun is warm on my skin. I'm wearing one of Jenny's bikinis, feeling a bit daring in something that's not my usual one-piece.

The pool is indoor but the walls are screened in with mesh windows, bringing in a slight cool breeze from the fall weather.

Rose is gushing about her boyfriend, convinced he's going to propose. He's tan, cute, funny, and goes to art school, which is amazing for her. I'm half listening, half lost in my thoughts when my phone buzzes. I look down at my phone to see that it's Toby,

TOBY

Come over tonight?

A smile tugs at my lips as I text back.

ME

I'm already looking forward to it.

"Oh, Elena, why are you smiling so much?" Rose asks.

"Nothing," I smile and place my phone back down.

"Is it Toby?" Jenny asks with a joking tone.

I bite my lip, nodding slowly.

"Oh!" the girls say out loud.

"Have you guys been seeing each other sneakily?" Jenny asks.

I let out a shaky sigh, "Yes."

"Ah! That's exciting!"

"But you can't tell anyone! Only Christian knows, but if my parents find out, they will kill me!"

Jenny places her hand on my shoulder, "We've got you, boo!"

I love being able to share moments like this with my friends. I need to spend more time with them, get my head out of books, and get into the real world more.

"He wants to hang out tonight," I say.

"Oh, does he? Well, then, you need to get going!" Jenny says.

"Girls, it's not even seven yet." I say.

"So? Go get dressed and head out!" Rose exclaims.

I shake my head, laughing. "Okay, okay!"

I stand and walk back into the house and begin to get dressed in my usual clothes when Jenny stops me.

"No, no, you need something a little more sexy." Jenny looks at me up and down.

"Like what?" I ask.

She sorts through her closet and brings out a

gorgeous blue skin tight short sleeved dress with ruffled ends.

"Like this." she says.

"Are you sure?" I grab it from her hands and look it over. It's gorgeous, for sure.

"Positive. He won't be able to keep his hands off you!"

I change into the outfit and look in the mirror.

"Girls!" Jenny shouts.

They come rushing in the house and take a look. "Jaw-dropping! When's the wedding?" Emily asks.

I laugh. "Stop it!"

"Oh, we're just teasing. It's so good to see you so happy!" Jenny laughs.

I knock softly. I hope my appearance is better than what I believe. I'm not completely confident about how I would appear in blue since I rarely wear that color, or even sundresses for that matter.

The door swings open, and Toby stands there with wet hair, droplets glistening in the light.

With a gentle touch on my hand, he spins me around, whispering, "You look breathtaking."

"Well, thank you," I say, giving a smile.

"I sense that dress doesn't belong to you."

Stepping inside the apartment, he hands me a soda.

"Jenny let me borrow it," I say, pursing my lips.

"That name sounds familiar,"

"My best friend."

"Oh, well tell her I said thank you because it looks amazing on you." He kisses my cheek.

A sense of warmth spreads through my body.

"How about I make you dinner tonight?" he asks.

"What did you have in mind?"

"Ribeye steaks on the grill, asparagus, and a side of scalloped potatoes."

"That sounds amazing." My stomach is practically screaming.

"Your stomach agrees." He laughs.

"And how about I choose a movie?"

"Go at it. I'll let you know when dinner's done." He kisses my forehead and steps into the kitchen, leaving me by myself in the living room.

I've not thought much about church or God lately, but I don't feel terrible about my decision-making lately either. I used to love attending church, but lately, I've felt distant from it. Not because of my promise I've broken to God; it's more about the difference between how my dad treats his own children versus those who attend church.

I turn the TV on and surf through the chan-nels, until I come across a Marvel movie.

"How's *Spider-Man?*" I holler.

"As long as it's the original, I'm all for it!"

Ah, he must not care much for the newer ones.

I scroll through my phone, waiting for him to finish when an idea pops into my head. I place my phone down and take off my dress, which leaves me in a black lace pair of underwear and my tan strapless bra. I stuff them behind the couch pillow and cover myself up with the blanket that's resting on the top.

About thirty minutes go by—luckily, YouTube is a thing—before he steps into the living room with plates.

"Hungry?" he asks, placing them on the coffee table.

"Starving!" I put my phone down and reach my arms out forgetting about not having a dress on.

He plops himself on the couch beside me. "Didn't know you had another meal in mind?" He smirks.

"I forgot I took my dress off..."

"Eat first. I want to make sure you're not hungry later when I eat you."

My face quickly flushes, and I immediately start eating while the movie starts.

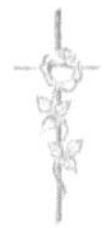

With his hand in mine, he gently guides me into the bedroom and whispers, "Princess, tell me how badly you want to be pleased." he brushes his thumb over my cheek. I can still taste the wine from dinner on my tongue, but my mouth also waters at the thought of Toby's lips on mine.

"Really bad." I say.

"Beg for it." he says as he towers over me.

"Toby, please touch me."

"Silly girl, you can do more than that." His voice is a low whisper, sending goosebumps down my arms as he speaks to me.

"I want you now."

"Now, now, what exactly is it that you want?"

The air feels charged with energy, and my heart beats rapidly in response. His words make my body erupt in goosebumps, igniting a fire within me. I take a deep breath, gathering my courage.

"I want your tongue." My words hang in the air for a moment, I can feel the tension building between us. His eyes darken.

"Is that all, my princess?" he teases, a playful smirk dancing on his lips. My cheeks flush with a mixture of embarrassment and arousal.

"I want your touch, your hands exploring every

inch of my body," I breathe, my voice trembling with need. Toby's grip tightens on my hand, pulling me closer to him. His gaze intensifies, filled with a hunger that matches my own. He lays me in the bed, hovering over me. "Tell me more," he whispers. His voice husky and filled with longing. I bite my lip, my mind racing with the explicit images that flood my thoughts.

"I want your lips on mine, kissing me passionately, leaving me breathless," I reply, my voice barely above a whisper. A surge of heat rushes through me as I speak my desires aloud. Toby's eyes darken further, his desire mirroring my own.

"Anything else, my love?" he asks, his voice dripping with anticipation. I take a moment to gather my thoughts, the intensity of the moment making it difficult to focus.

"I want you inside me," I finally confess. Toby's grip tightens on my hand, his eyes burning with desire.

"Your wish is my command, princess," he murmurs.

With each step, my breath quickens, and I'm growing hot, knowing what we're about to do. His presence is both comforting and exhilarating.

He gently caresses my face, his touch making me become more sensitive.

He leans in, kissing me, and I deepen it. I nearly rip off his shirt. I don't know what takes over me, but after about a minute of making out, I flip us over and climb on top of him.

"Oh, baby girl," he moans as I trail my fingertips down his chest and stomach and tug at his pants and boxers before sliding them off. I take my panties and bra off. I've never done this before. I'm not even sure sex can happen in such a way, but I want to be on top.

I trail kisses down his body till I reach his cock and begin to go down on him. Moans escape his lips as he gently tugs at my hair, urging me to lower my head. Just as he begins to release his grip, I seize the opportunity to stop. I line myself up and slide onto him. As I adjust to his size, I begin to slowly move up and down, finding the perfect angle to hit that sweet spot inside.

Toby begins to lose patience at the slow speed and grabs my hips to take over control. I can't help but release a loud moan as he thrusts quickly into me, causing my body to instinctively arch in pleasure. His strong hold on my hips adds an extra layer of pleasure to the sensations flowing through me.

Just as I am reaching the precipice, he lifts me and flips me onto all fours.

"You want me to fuck you, princess?" he murmurs, slapping my ass.

"Yes," I whisper.

"What was that?"

"Yes, please fuck me!" I beg loudly.

"Good girl."

With a hungry groan, Toby's tongue explores my wet pussy, his finger joining in, eliciting a loud exclamation of pleasure.

I never knew I had this wild side, but I'm glad it's revealing itself tonight. This is our second time having sex, my second time.

"You went from my sexy little princess to my dirty little angel."

I moan into the sheets as he inserts himself inside me. He holds my hips tighter, and my knees become hot from rubbing against the sheets. I can feel my entire body convulsing with pleasure as his cock brings me to an intense orgasm, causing me to scream out from how good it feels. With each thrust, the friction builds, making me increasingly sensitive, until he finally pulls out and releases onto my back.

I lie breathless on the bed, feeling my chest rise and fall with each sigh.

As he cleans me up, he chuckles lightly to himself.

"What's so funny?" I ask.

"I never knew you had such a wild side."

"Me and you both." I laugh in response.

CHAPTER TWENTY-TWO

Friday morning rolls around. The smell of bacon fills the air. Opening my eyes, I look at my phone to see it's only eight. Great. This means Dad is home. Mom doesn't cook anything in the morning as she's almost always gone before seven thirty.

I wish time stood still and money wasn't a need. I groan, not wanting to leave my bed, but kick the sheets off me anyway.

I get dressed in a blue blouse and black leggings, sliding on some cute flats before heading downstairs. I want to avoid him at all costs, but it's not like I have a choice.

"Elena! Good morning, dear," he cheers, kissing me on the forehead. "I made you a plate."

"Thanks." I sit at the table and slowly eat my breakfast.

"You're not going to believe what I heard about last night."

"No? What's that?" I ask.

"You know the Snyders two houses down?"

"Yes?"

"Well, I guess their son and his girlfriend got caught in the cornfield together a mile away from the church."

I widen my eyes. Not the words I want to hear from my dad, especially this early... or ever.

"Oh, that's interesting." I cough.

"It's a good thing you know better than that girl. Sex is only for married couples.. Before that, it's giving in to the sins of the flesh."

If he knew what I'd been doing, I'd be locked in my bedroom with bars attached to my window.

I hear stomping of feet heading into the dining room. I look back to see my mom red in the face with apartment brochures tight in her grip.

"Elena, why do you have these?"

Clearing my throat, I say, "I, uh," but no more words leave my mouth. I didn't even know she was still home.

Christian walks in, taking them from her hands. "Those are mine, Mom. I threw them in Elena's trash can because I was telling her about them last night."

Her eyes soften, and the red in her cheeks

reduce. Of course. My parents are way more accepting about him moving out.

"I'm so sorry, sweetie, you're my baby girl, and I don't want you making mistakes." She hugs me, kissing me on the forehead.

"May I be excused?" I ask.

Mom and Dad nod, and Christian follows me out the front door. It's inventory day, so I need to be at work early.

"Thanks for saving me back there."

"You've saved me many times. It's my turn to return the favor."

"Have you booked an appointment with a therapist yet?" I ask.

"No, not yet. I'm trying, but we are on our parents' insurance still. If it's not God I'm seeking help from, it's bad juju to them."

"Gosh, I wish they'd just stop being lunatics!" I get in my car and slam the door and rush to work.

The lights are already on inside the library. Walking inside the building, I see Toby organizing some papers. "What are you doing here so early?"

"Dropping some items off for Mom, but I also came by to see you."

"Oh yeah?" I flirt.

"My friend is having a big birthday party tonight. Come with me? We'll have a lot of fun together."

I purse my lips, unable to resist those blue eyes. "Okay, but I worry people will see us arrive together and think things... I'm not ready for word to spread yet."

"Bring your friends. Anyone is invited."

"Okay, I figure that'll be fine."

We lean in to kiss. "See you tonight. I'll text you the address." He gives me a few more pecks on the lips and hurries out of the library.

I grab my phone, opening a group text with my friends.

ME

Party tonight?

JENNY

Yes!

ROSE

Uh, yeah!!!

EMILY

TEXT THE DEETS

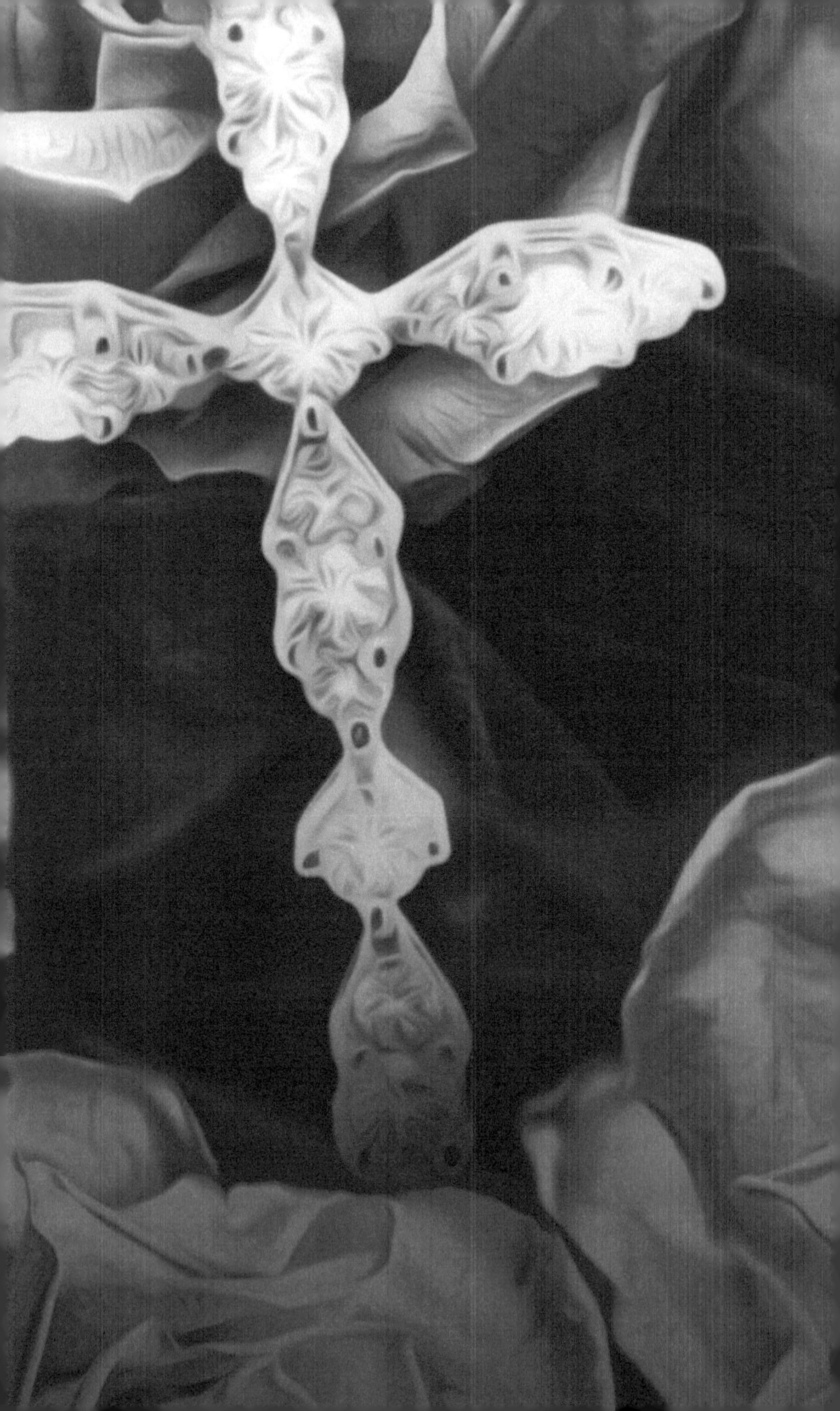

CHAPTER TWENTY-THREE

The loud music reverberated throughout the house, but I could hear it while we drove up and were still a mile away. Jenny's voice echoes through the room as she declares, "I'm going to get us some drinks." The other girls disperse, leaving me as the lone figure amid the crowd. Glancing around, I realize that I hardly recognize anyone except for a small group of old classmates; the rest of the people seem to be visitors from out of town.

A pair of strong arms wrap around me from behind, and as I glance back, I see Toby standing there. His embrace is warm and comforting, enveloping me in a sense of security. I lean into him, feeling his steady heartbeat against my back. His presence alone brings a sense of peace to my chaotic mind.

Toby's familiar scent fills my nostrils, a mix of

earthy cologne and a hint of his natural musk. It's a scent that instantly puts me at ease, reminding me of all the times we've spent together. His arms tighten around me, pulling me closer, as if he never wants to let me go.

Emily shoots me a wink and puts a finger against her lips before walking off. I am so glad she won't say anything.

"Want a sip?" he asks, holding out his cup to me.

"Sure." He hands me the red Solo cup, and I take a sip, wrinkling my nose at the bitter taste.

"What is that?"

"Straight tequila."

"Yuck!"

"If you tried it with a margarita, I'm certain you'd enjoy it." He laughs, kissing my cheek.

"Not if it tastes like that!"

"It won't in the margarita."

Being here with him and my friends makes me feel normal, like I belong. At church, I'm beginning to feel like it's a space not meant for me. I like it here. Everyone is having a good time. Toby and I are dancing to the beat, and my friends aren't too far away.

We're lost in the music when I feel Toby's grip rip off from me. A random man shoves him to the ground, punching him in the face.

"You think you can just waltz in here and act

like nothing happened?" The guy's voice trembles with a mix of anger and hurt.

Toby's eyes widen with surprise. "Jake! I never used Serena. I cared about her. I would never steal from her," he defends himself.

I can feel the stares of everyone around us, waiting to see how this confrontation will unfold.

The guy scoffs, his face contorted with disbelief. "Save it, Toby. I have proof. I found messages between you and Christian, planning to take advantage of her. Don't deny it."

My heart sinks as I watch Toby's expression turn from surprise to guilt. I can't believe what I'm hearing. How could Toby do something like this?

"What does Christian have to do with this?" I ask.

Toby's voice quivers as he tries to find the words to defend himself. "I... I made a mistake. I was desperate at the time, but I never went through with it. I realized it was wrong, and I broke things off with Serena. I'm truly sorry."

"Tell her, big guy," the man demands Toby.

"We were planning to steal some of her dead grandfather' items. I'd distract her with having sex, and Christian would take the items."

The guy's anger seems to intensify, his fists clenched tightly. "Sorry? That's all you have to say? You destroyed my sister's trust and broke her heart. Sorry doesn't cut it."

Tears well up in my eyes. The weight of the situation becomes too much to bear. I step forward, my voice shaking. "Look, I understand you're angry, but violence won't solve anything. Let's try to find a way to resolve this peacefully."

The guy glares at me, his anger still evident. "And who are you to meddle in this? You're just as guilty for being with him."

I take a deep breath, gathering my courage. "We all make mistakes, but it's how we learn from them that matters."

Finally, the guy takes a step back, his anger subsiding. "Fine," he grumbles. "But if you ever hurt anyone else, Toby, I won't hesitate to make you pay."

As the designated driver, Emily drops off our friends one by one, leaving me for last. I roll the windows down and take a deep breath in. The night air is cool, and I wrap my arms around myself, replaying the evening's events in my mind.

"Tell me about Toby," Emily says, her voice soft as she navigates the quiet streets. "You seem different lately."

I glance out the window, the streetlights casting elongated shadows. "Toby... he makes me happy. Happier than I've ever been." I hesitate, knowing I can't reveal too much. Not yet. "But I can't say anything until I move out and start living my own life."

Emily smiles knowingly. "He cares about you, Elena. I can see it."

The warmth of her words settles in my chest. Maybe Toby and I have a chance—a fragile one, but a chance, nonetheless.

When I arrive home, the house is dark except for the light streaming from under Christian's door. I tiptoe past my parents' room and pause outside his door. His room is cleaner than I've ever seen it, and the faint scent of soap lingers in the air. He's taken a shower recently, and he looks better than usual—less worn down, less haunted.

I push the door open, and Christian glances up from his desk. His eyes widen when he sees me. "Elena," he says, his voice rough. "I can smell alcohol on you."

I swallow, my guilt rising. "I'm sorry. It was just—"

"It's fine," he interrupts, surprising me. "I've been there. It'll be a struggle, but it's a battle I want to fight and overcome."

My heart swells with hope. "You applied to some jobs today?"

He nods. "Yeah. We're both rooting for each other, huh?"

My brother, flawed and determined, and me, trying to find my own path. As I slip into my room, I change my clothes and kneel by my bed—the same nightly ritual I've done for years.

"Guide us," I whisper. "Guide Christian, Toby, and me. We're all navigating uncharted waters, and I need your light to lead the way."

I believe that things are about to get complicated.

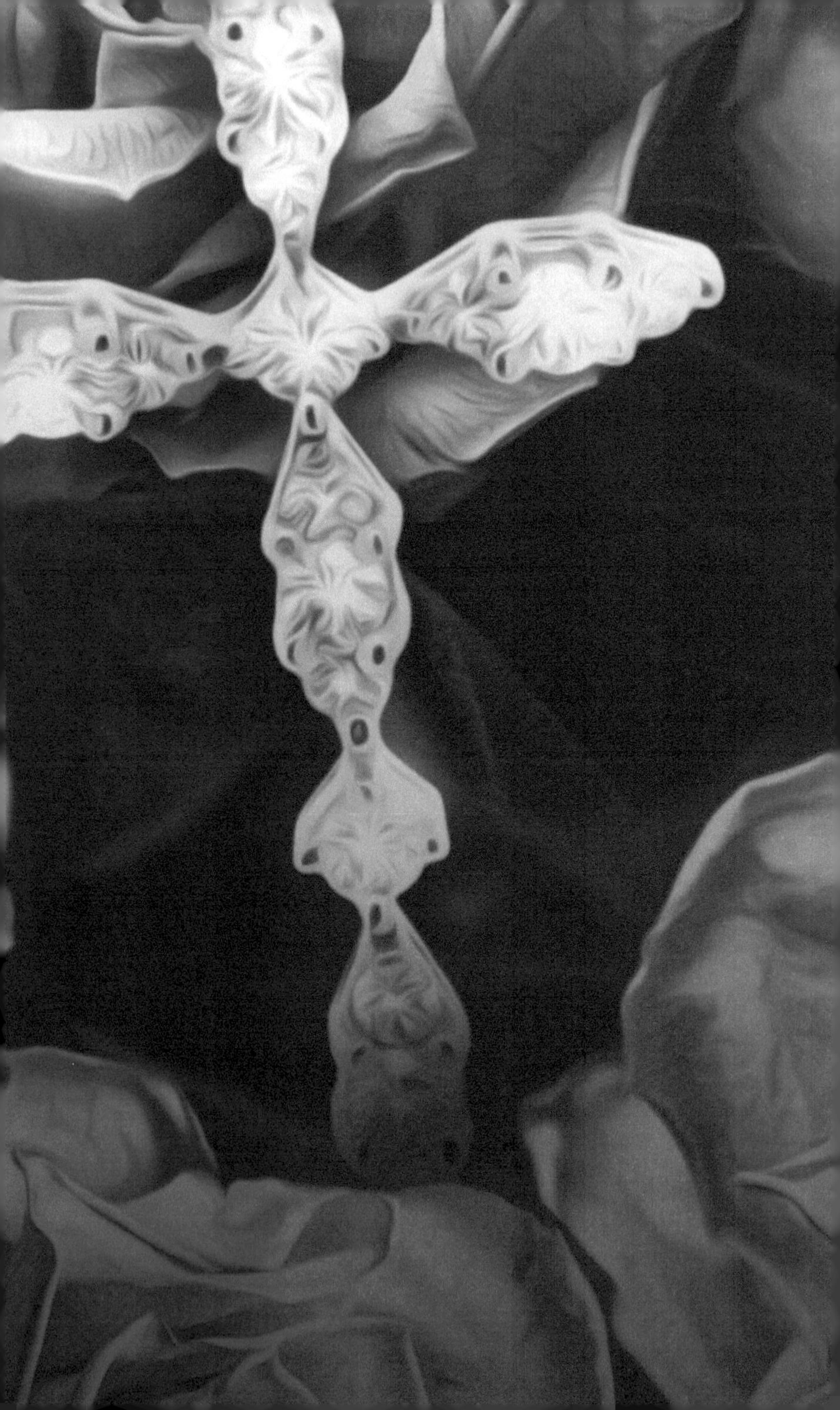

CHAPTER TWENTY-FOUR

Hours go by, and I can't sleep. While I watch a show on the TV, my phone buzzes on my bedside table, causing me to stir.

TOBY

Meet me at the park over where we had our first date.

I quietly tiptoe, making my way down the stairs, tying my hair up into a high ponytail. Looking around the house, I don't see or hear my parents so they must be asleep and I leave the house to meet him.

There he is, perched on the tailgate of his old pickup truck. My heart stutters as I exit my car, the gravel crunching under my sneakers. The scent of gasoline and freshly mowed grass lingers in the air.

"Hi, princess," he says, his voice a low rumble. He steps down, and before I can react, he lifts me into a twirl. My laughter spills out, and when he sets me down, his lips find mine.

He sits me on the tailgate, the metal cool against my thighs. "So what's up?" I ask, nudging his shoulder with mine.

"Well," he begins, his gaze steady, "you know I love kids,"

"Yes..." I prompt, my pulse quickening. What's he getting at?

Toby reaches into the truck bed, pulling out a cardboard box. "I once volunteered at the local community center," he says, his fingers brushing mine as he hands me a stack of colorful paper. "Story time for the little buggers."

I flip through the pages—dragons, castles, and knights. "This is neat!"

He nods. "Thought we could read them together."

My heart swells. "Toby," I say, my voice barely above a whisper, "You're amazing."

He leans in, his lips brushing my forehead.

"Elena," he murmurs, "I love you. No one else has ever made me feel this happy."

My throat tightens, and I taste the salt of unshed tears. "I love you too."

"I have to get home before my parents wake up. I don't need to be questioned by them when I get back," I say.

"I know you're worried about what they'll say and how they'll act, but you are your own person, and know that I'm here for you always," he hugs me, kissing my forehead.

"I know,"

I had hoped to slip inside unnoticed, but the soft glow from the living room window betrays my late-night escape. My heart races as I turn the key, the door creaking open like a guilty secret.

And there they were—my parents, sitting on the couch, their faces etched with concern. I hadn't expected them to be awake. Not after the way they'd been lately distant, preoccupied. But here they were, waiting for me.

"Elena," my mother's voice trembles, "where have you been?"

I hesitated, my mind racing for a plausible lie. "With my friends," I stammers. "We went to the diner for milkshakes."

My father's eyes narrow, face red like a tomato. "Don't lie to us," he snaps. "We know the truth."

My stomach twists into knots. How could they know? Toby and I had been careful, stealing kisses in hidden corners, being covered by friends. But secrets have a way of slipping through the cracks, like whispers carried by the wind.

Maybe this is God telling me it was a bad idea. Perhaps he is mad at me and punishing me for disobeying.

"It's not what you think," I whisper, my voice barely audible.

My mother's gaze bores into mine. "We heard it from Mrs. Wren," she says. "She saw you and Toby in town earlier. Kissing."

The room seemed to close in on me. Mrs. Lawson, our family friend—the one who bakes us cookies and attends church every Sunday. Why was *she* out so late?

His anger flares. "Toby?" He spits out his name like a curse. "That boy is trouble, Elena. A sinner."

"But Dad," I plead, "we love each other."

He scoffs. "Love? You think this is love? He's broken the commandments, Elena. Stolen, lied, and worse. And now you're entangled in his web of sin."

I want to defend Toby, to tell them that he was more than his mistakes. But my voice failed me. How could I explain the way his touch ignited my soul, the way his laughter chased away my darkness?

My mother's eyes softened. "Elena," she says gently, "we want what's best for you. Toby isn't it."

"But Mom," I whisper, "sometimes love isn't neat and tidy. Sometimes it's messy and complicated."

She shook her head. "Not this kind of love. Not with someone like him."

"It's not your place to judge people!" I scream. I can't handle their behavior any longer.

"You are not allowed to see that boy again! Do you understand me? We forbid it!" My mom points in my face. I've never seen her so angry before. I wipe the tears falling down my cheeks.

The atmosphere in the room becomes increasingly tense, making it difficult for me to breathe. As I stand before them, my parents' disapproving gazes pierce through me. Suddenly, Christian storms into the room. If he was a cartoon, smoke would be flowing out of his ears.

"Enough!" his voice echoes off the walls. "Elena has done more for me than anyone else. She also deserves to be happy. Without her, I'd still be drowning in my own misery, drowning in alcohol. She's been my lifeline."

My mouth gapes open. I cannot believe he's admitted to his alcoholism.

I saw their expressions mirroring my own

shock. For years, we've endured their selfish actions and had to deal with it but we are old enough now. To face them.

"This is unacceptable!" my mom screams. "Our daughter associating with someone like Toby—"

"And what about me?" he retorts. "I've sinned too, haven't I? But Elena didn't judge me. She stood by me, helped me seek help. She's the reason I'm on the path to recovery."

"We will talk about your disgusting sin later. But right now, that Toby kid is who we are talking about and is trouble. He's going to hurt your sister, clearly already by just being near her. You want that for her? Your sister hurt?"

"You know, out of everyone else in this town, I'm glad it's Toby. He's my best friend, and no one else would be more perfect than he is for her."

Our parents exchanged outraged glances. "Both of you," my father's voice trembled, "entangled in sin."

I couldn't bear it any longer. They weren't even listening. Just repeating their bullshit.

The weight of their expectations, their rigid beliefs—it was suffocating. I push past Christian, my resolve firm. "I'm done," I whisper. "I won't be your pawn anymore." I run up the stairs and storm into my room, packing a bag and rushing back down the stairs. My dad stands in the doorway, blocking me.

"Move."

"This is my goddamn house. I will do what I want!"

"Move, or your Sunday church buddies find out your money laundering in the back room with everyone's money."

His eyes widen, and he looks at me with a blank stare before stepping aside. I open the door with blurry eyes. "I'm right behind you," Christian says.

"If you leave, you are not allowed back here. Both of you!"

I throw Christian the keys, and we hurry out of the driveway.

"Where are we going?"

"Toby's."

After a few minutes of driving, we arrive, knocking on Toby's door. The lights turn on inside and the door opens, revealing his silhouette against the dim hallway light. He stands there, his tiredness evident on his face, as his gaze shifts back and forth between Christian and me. Our eyes meet, and in that fleeting moment, a thousand unspoken words pass between us.

Without hesitation, he steps forward, closing the gap between us. His touch is gentle yet firm as he takes my trembling hand, pulling me into an embrace. The warmth of his chest envelops me, and I bury my face against his shoulder, sobbing uncontrollably.

Christian enters behind me. The weight of everything—the secrets, the pain, the longing—presses down on me. But in Toby's arms, it feels bearable. He traces soothing circles on my back.

"We'll talk about everything tomorrow, let's get some sleep," he says.

I nod. We all camp out in the living room.

I take a seat on the couch, grabbing a blanket from the top. And cover myself. Christian lays on the opposite side and gives me a sad smile.

Toby leans down to kiss my forehead, and he puts his pillow and blanket on the living room floor. The two most important people in my life being in the same room with me brings me comfort and I drift to sleep.

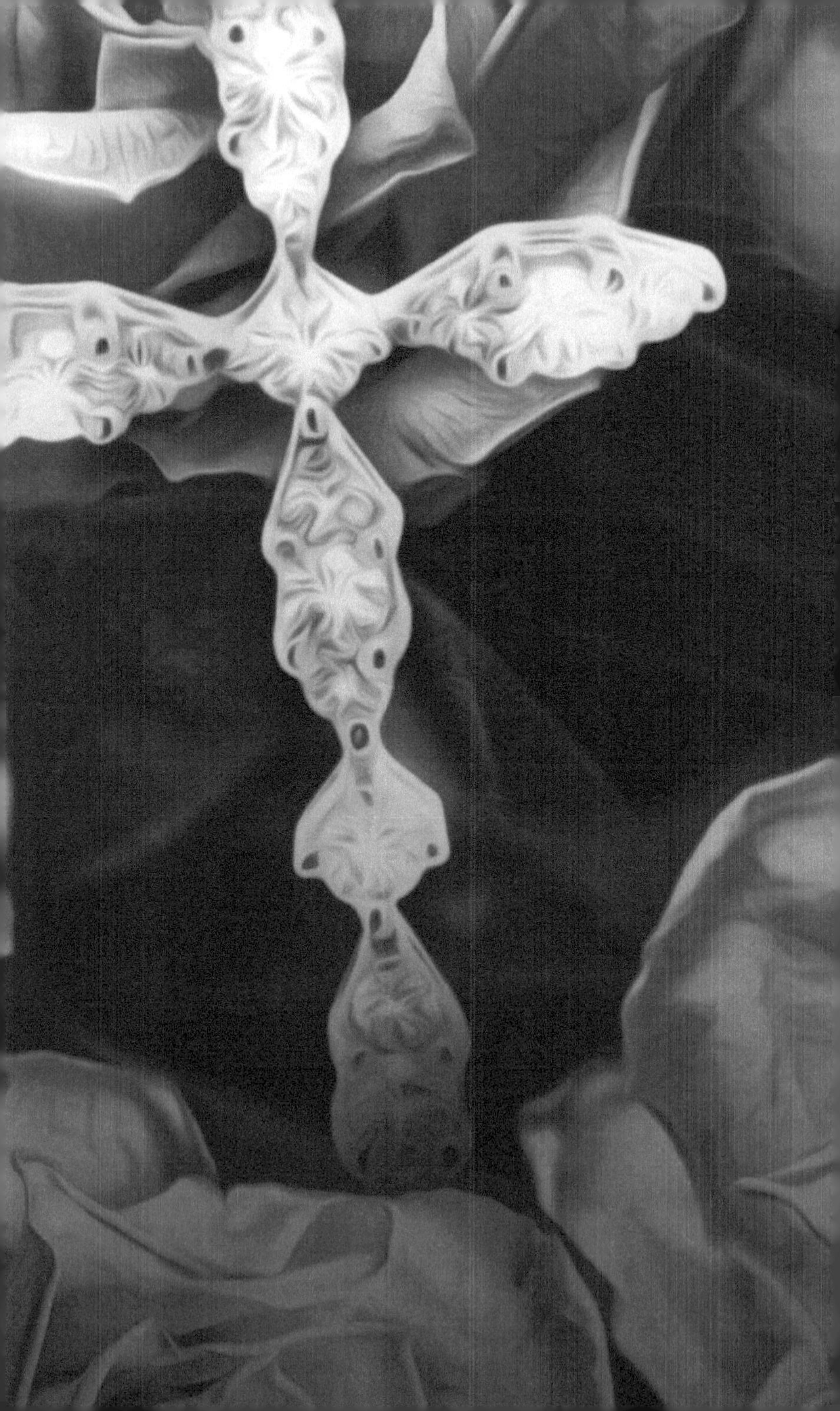

CHAPTER TWENTY-FIVE

The morning sun filters through the curtains, casting a fragile glow upon the room. I lay there, my heart shattered. The events of last night replay in my mind like a movie scene.

Disowned.

The word hung heavy in the air, suffocating me. My parents' voices echo, their disappointment deep in my soul. I had dared to defy their beliefs, to question the very foundation of their faith. And now, I lie on the precipice of an unknown future, abandoned by the only family I had ever known.

"Are you awake?" Christian asks me.

I nod.

"Want something to eat?" he asks.

"Sure."

"How about we go get breakfast?" Toby suggests.

"As long as they have pancakes, I don't care where we go." They both chuckle.

"Then let's go."

I take a few minutes to get ready before we head out the door.

Not one single text or missed call from them. It's almost like unless I don't listen or obey them, I'm not loved or important. Like I am less than nothing. I'm unsure if they meant they'd disown us, but who knows? Given their behavior last night and toward us throughout our childhood, I wouldn't be surprised.

I rub my neck, wincing.

"You okay?"

Toby asks me.

"Yeah, I must have slept on my neck wrong,"

"I have ibuprofen in the car, want me to go grab it?"

I nod. "Will you?" I ask.

He nods and stands, walking outside of the diner.

Christian taps my hand. "What are we going to do?" I can tell he's worried. We've been in a shell that has been our comfort zone for our entire lives.

And now, here we are sitting at a diner with more questions than answers. Unsure of where to begin.

"I don't know, but we'll figure it out, okay?"

I need to find an apartment. As soon as possible.

"I hope," he whispers.

Toby sits back down, handing me two ibuprofens, and I drink them down with water.

"Thanks."

He hasn't stopped looking at me since last night. He's concerned, but I feel like he wants to say more, do more.

"Okay, so how about you guys stay with me until we figure out a more permanent situation?"

"I don't know, man. Are you sure?" Christian asks.

"Yes, I am going to stay at my mom's house so it's not so awkward between us three."

Raising my brow, I say, "Toby, it's better if you stay at the apartment. Maybe we should go back."

"Absolutely not. We're not going back there," Christian growls.

Toby leans back, "Guys, it's okay, just stay at the apartment, it'll be fine—" leans forward,

"Okay, fine," Christian says and crosses his arms.

He's hurt. Pissed off. Unsure and confused. I wish I could take away our struggles with a click of a button.

"I'm going to head out to a friend's house for a couple of nights," Christian adds.

"Why?" I ask.

"Just need space from everyone I'm close to."

Normally, I'd feel hurt for something like that. But I get it. Being around people who only remind you of those who hurt you can be difficult.

The TV lights up the dark living room. Toby's in the shower, Christian is god knows where, and I'm here resting on the couch, staring at stupid commercials. I miss my bed. I miss my mom's cooking. I miss my comforter. I miss all the good before it got complicated.

Touching my cross, I glare at it as I look down. "What are you thinking about?" Toby walks in with a towel around his waist.

My chest becomes hot, and my eyes fill with tears. "I don't believe like my parents do. I don't picture God like they do." I take in a shaky breath, wiping the tears from my cheeks. "If my way is wrong, maybe I'm not a true Christian."

He sits down beside me, placing a hand on my back.

"Look, I don't know as much as you do, but the

only thing that matters is your own relationship with God."

I nod, sit up from lying on my stomach, and look up at him.

"Thank you for being there for me. For Christian. My entire life is shifting."

I'm scared. Yet excited at the same time.

"I need to contact those apartments soon and see what's available."

"I have a better idea."

"What's that?"

He grabs my hands, pulling them up to his mouth and kissing them.

"Move in with me."

My heart flutters at his words.

I enjoy being here with him, but I'm surprised by this.

"I don't know. I don't want you to offer it just because I need a place to stay. I want you to want me to move in with you."

"I do want this. I've been thinking about it for a bit, but I've not said much yet because of your parents, and I didn't want to pressure you," he admits.

"You don't think it's too fast?"

"The way I feel for you, nothing is too fast."

He places his hand on the back of my neck, pulling me into a kiss. My skin erupts into goose bumps as he slides his hands underneath my shirt, breaking the kiss for a moment to slide it off. I climb on top of him and deepen the kiss, our tongue dancing with one another. He unclips my bra with one hand easily, throwing it to the floor and grabbing my boobs, teasing my nipples causing my breath to quicken.

I stand and slip off my pants and underwear, and head into the bedroom. I can hear his footsteps behind me.

As soon as I reach the end of the bed, he grabs my hand, spinning me around to face him. His eyes were dark.

"Don't be scared, you won't break me," I whisper in his ear.

He kisses me again, grabbing my hips and laying me down on the bed to climb on me. I can feel his cock harden in his boxers. His lips hover over my neck, giving gentle kisses until he reaches my nipples again, licking and sucking slowly with his tongue. A moan escapes my lips, and I grip the sheets.

I giggle loudly as his tongue traces the V line above my pubic area.

"You like that, princess?" His breathing tickles it even more.

"Y-yes." I can't control myself. My breathing grows faster, and he lowers himself, licking my outer lips and causing me to squirm.

His touch is intoxicating, and I can't help but let out moans of pleasure.

As his tongue flicks over my clit, my body arches in response. The sensations overwhelm me, and I find myself losing control. I grip the sheets tighter, my breath coming in ragged gasps.

He looks up at me with a wicked smile, his eyes filled with desire. "You're so wet for me," he whispers huskily. His voice sends shivers down my spine, intensifying my pleasure.

I can't help but nod, unable to form words. The pleasure builds, and I can feel myself getting closer to the edge. His skilled tongue continues to work its magic, driving me wild with desire.

With one final flick of his tongue, I explode in a mind-blowing orgasm. My body trembles with pleasure. He continues to please me, prolonging my pleasure until I can't take it anymore. I moan loudly, pushing his head off me.

As I catch my breath, he climbs back up my body, his lips finding mine in a passionate kiss. We lie there, entwined in each other's arms, and I soon fall asleep.

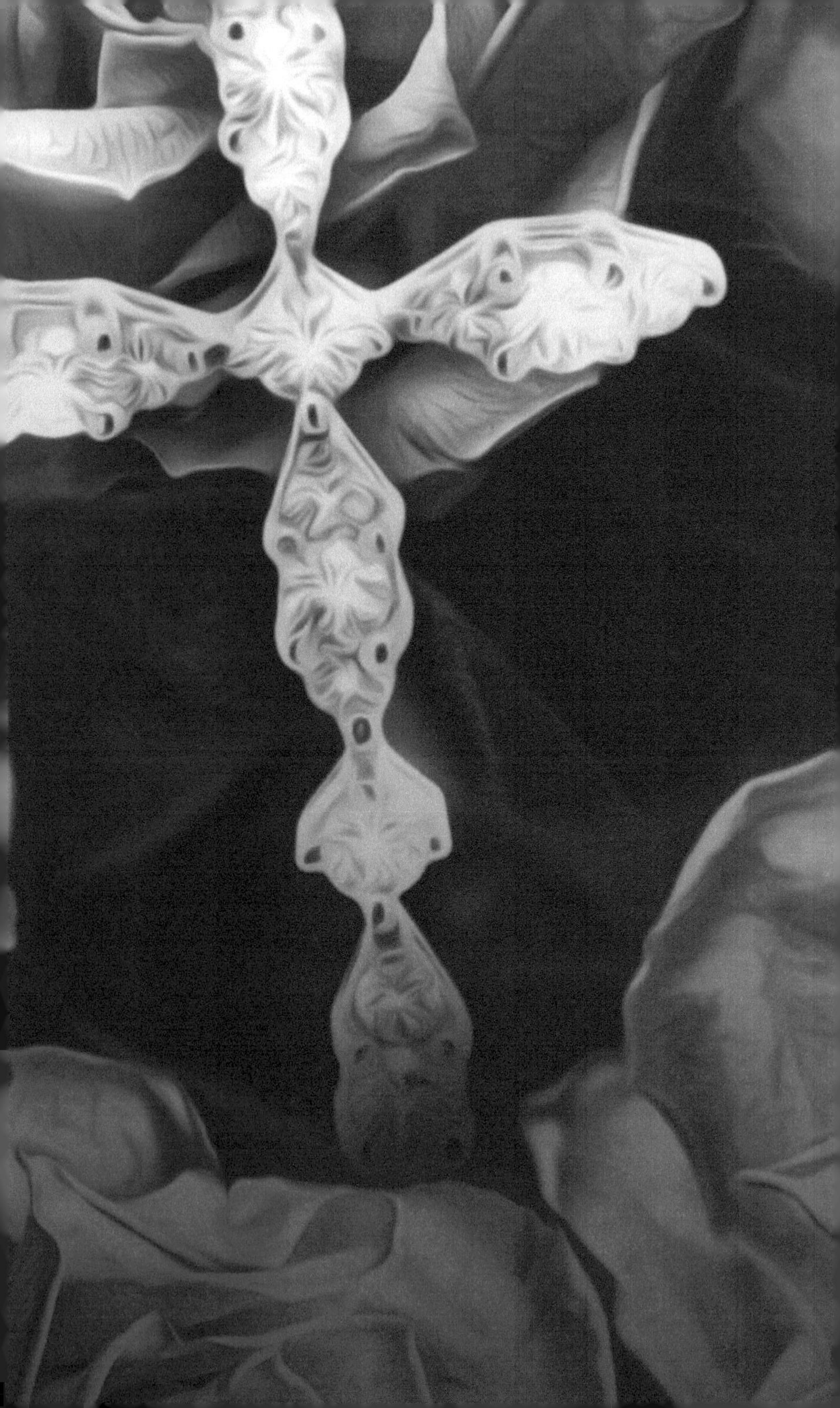

CHAPTER TWENTY-SIX

Toby offering me to live with him means a lot to me. It's not that I don't want to take the offer. I want to live with him. It does feel a little too fast, but I can't shake away my strong feelings for him. I don't believe God would have put me on this path if it wasn't meant to be. Maybe this is a lesson. To learn and grow as a human being in his image.

I take a drink of my coffee before typing up the inventory on the computer's database and hear a ping from my phone. The library is dead today, and I wish it wasn't. The busier my work life is, the less I have to think about my parents and the drama surrounding us. My phone dings and I look down at my phone,

CHRISTIAN

Meet me at our parents'. Shit is about to get real.

Clearing my throat, I hover my thumbs over the keyboard and type a reply,

ME

Okay, see you soon.

"Toby!" I holler.

"Yes?" he asks, walking around the corner.

"Can you come with me to my parents'? Christian just texted me saying to meet him there," I ask.

He glances around the library before nodding. "Yeah, let's go."

The gravel crunches beneath my sneakers as Toby and I hurry up the driveway.

Christian is standing by his car. His eyes meet mine, and in that silent exchange, I glimpse the weight of his pain. He was grabbing everything he owns.

"What's happening?" I blurts out, my voice raw.

My dad stormed out of the house, red in the face. "Disgrace!" he spits at us. "Both of you have tainted this family name."

My mom stands on the porch, tears streaming

down her cheeks. I can't even look at her. I don't know how she could ever allow this to happen.

Christian looks at our dad. "I'm not asking for your forgiveness," he says, his voice steady. "I'm just asking for a chance to heal, and I can't be around this negative family any longer."

If my dad could get any redder, it'd turn purple. "Healing?" he scoffs. "You think AA meetings will save you? You're unworthy, sinful."

I step forward, my heart pounding against my chest. "Dad, he's my brother," I say, my voice trembling. "He's hurting."

"He is a stain on our reputation, and so are you. You've become a whore!"

My face becomes hot, and I slap him hard in the face out of instinct. Not regretting a single moment.

His head turns sideways, and he looks back at me, eyes glowing with rage.

"You get the fuck off my property and never come back. Do you understand me?"

"Yes, sir," I say.

Toby and I stay back as we wait for Christian to get all of our belongings. I carry what's mine. Shaking my head in disbelief, I climb back into the car.

"I'm going to continue staying at a friend's house, someone I met through therapy. I feel I'll be better off around those who are in the same boat as I am," Christian says. We got back to Toby's a couple of hours ago. Sitting in silence on the patio outside for hours.

"Are you sure?" I ask.

He looks at me. "Yeah, I mean, it's not that far. Just a couple of blocks from here. But it's just better for me if I do."

"I understand." My voice barely audible.

"Don't worry, I am still coming to see you. You're my twin, I'm here to bug you for the rest of our lives." He laughs.

I smack his arm lightly, laughing along with him.

"Do you ever wonder if Mom regrets all of this?" I ask.

"Regrets what exactly?" He asks.

"Life with that particular man as a husband which we call dad, having kids and being a christian," I shrug.

"Sometimes, but she has a funny way of showing it."

Sighing, I look down at my hands. The world

around me is confusing. "Maybe it's more Dad, not Mom. I mean – the way things went down when we grabbed our stuff, she stayed away on the porch and let Dad handle it all."

"If that is the case, maybe one day she will open up."

"I hope so," I say.

Everything I thought I once knew, gone. My beliefs have changed, my world has changed. My life is changing. I press my lips together. "What do you want for dinner? I'll cook something."

"You? Cook? I rather eat dirt."

"Christian! I thought you liked my food!"

"Mom made me not tell you the truth."

Shaking my head, I say, "And she says we are sinners."

We both laugh.

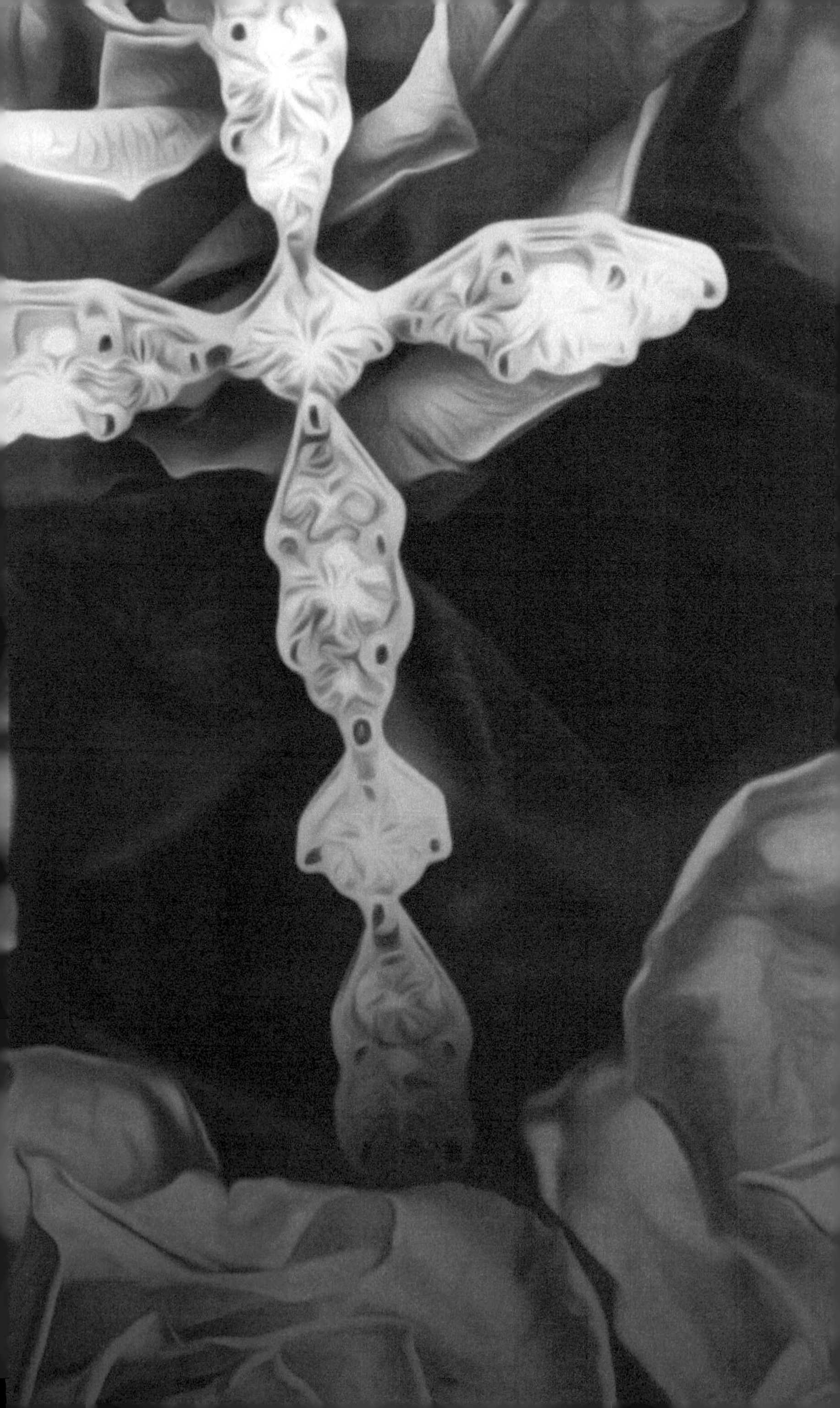

CHAPTER TWENTY-SEVEN

"Rise and shine, princess." Toby's deep morning voice is a delight to my soul.

I open my eyes, looking up at him as he hands me a cup of coffee.

"I could get used to this," I say with a smile, savoring the aroma of the freshly brewed coffee. Toby chuckles, his eyes sparkling with affection.

"Well, get used to it because I plan on spoiling you every morning," he replies, sitting down on the edge of the bed next to me.

As I take a sip of the hot beverage, warmth spreads through my body. I feel grateful for moments like these, where time seems to stand still and the worries of the world fade away.

Toby reaches out to brush a stray strand of hair behind my ear. "You deserve to be treated like a princess every day," he whispers.

I realize today is Sunday. It's the morning of church. And I'm not there. I've never missed a day unless I was sick, but even that was rare.

"We should probably get more things from my parents' house while they are at church."

"Are you sure?" he asks, "Maybe we should wait until things calm down?"

"I'm sure. I need more of my clothes, especially underwear."

He grins, pulling me into a kiss. "I could buy you new ones, or maybe just don't wear any."

"I'm sure you could buy me new ones, but ew, no, I will wear underwear thank you very much." After setting the mug down on the nightstand, I throw the blankets off me.

"I need to shower," I say, heading to the bathroom. I can feel his eyes burning in the back of my head.

Stepping inside the bath under the hot shower, my muscles relax from their tension. But before I could wash my hair, Toby steps in the shower with me. "Oh, hi," I flirt.

Toby smirks, his eyes lingering on me as the water flows over our bodies.

As I reach for the shampoo, Toby moves closer, his body pressing against mine. His touch gives me goosebumps, and I can't resist leaning into him.

His touch, his kiss, everything feels intoxicating. He kisses my neck, pinning me face-first against the shower wall.

"You are so hot, princess," he whispers in my ear.

I can hear him spitting on his fingers. He spreads my legs and slides a finger inside me, curling it slightly. A tingling sensation floods through my body as a moan escapes my lips, tipping my head back from the pleasure. He slides out, and I feel his hard cock enter inside me. He grabs my hips and holds me steady, thrusting in and out. "Oh fuck, you're so tight," he growls into my ear.

My moaning gets louder as he continues to fuck me fast, and I grow wetter. "Clench on me, princess, come for me." His saying that brings more throbbing and pulsating inside me, friction increases and I scream against the wall as orgasm, he doesn't slow down and he continues. "Oh yes, that's it, good girl, you're so good," he slides out and I let out a breath, he releases into the shower tub, and the water rinses it away.

After we wrapped up our fun-filled shower, we arrive at my parents' house fifteen minutes later.

We collect the remaining boxes from my bedroom and move them to the car. I return inside and stand in the hallway near the front door. My heart hurts thinking I won't come back.

"I know you're hurting, Elena, but I promise you things will turn out better than you think, okay?" Toby says, his voice calms my nerves every time I'm upset.

"How about we take one more stop before we head back home?"

"Home?" I ask.

"Yes, our home."

It's the first I've heard him say our home.

"Okay, where?"

"You'll see."

We pull into his mother's driveway, the place I picked up Christian a couple of times. "What are we doing here?"

"We are going to tell my mom that we are together."

I let out a nervous chuckle. "Oh, uh, Lindsay is my boss. I don't know if she will be happy about this."

"And if she isn't we'll leave."

Entering the house, Toby yells, "Mom!"

"Chaos is here!" Lindsay hollers back.

I laugh, and she walks into the living room, where the front door is, and embraces him. I wish my mother was that welcoming.

"What are you two doing here?" she asks, glancing between us both. Toby takes my hand, intertwining it with his.

"We wanted to tell you that we are officially dating."

Her eyes widen, and I squeeze his hand, bracing myself for the negative comments.

"Oh, that's wonderful to hear! I had my suspicions, and I'm glad it's true!"

My pulse slows down. It was racing moments ago out of fear, but his mom being okay with us is good.

"You had your suspicions?" Toby asks, sitting down on the couch, me following.

"Yeah, you two would be talking secretly in the library as if I couldn't see you."

My face heats. "Funny."

"Want some lunch? I have chicken baking in the oven."

"Please tell me there's potatoes and green beans inside the pan?" Toby asks.

"Of course!" She gets up to leave the room, and he looks at me and kisses my forehead.

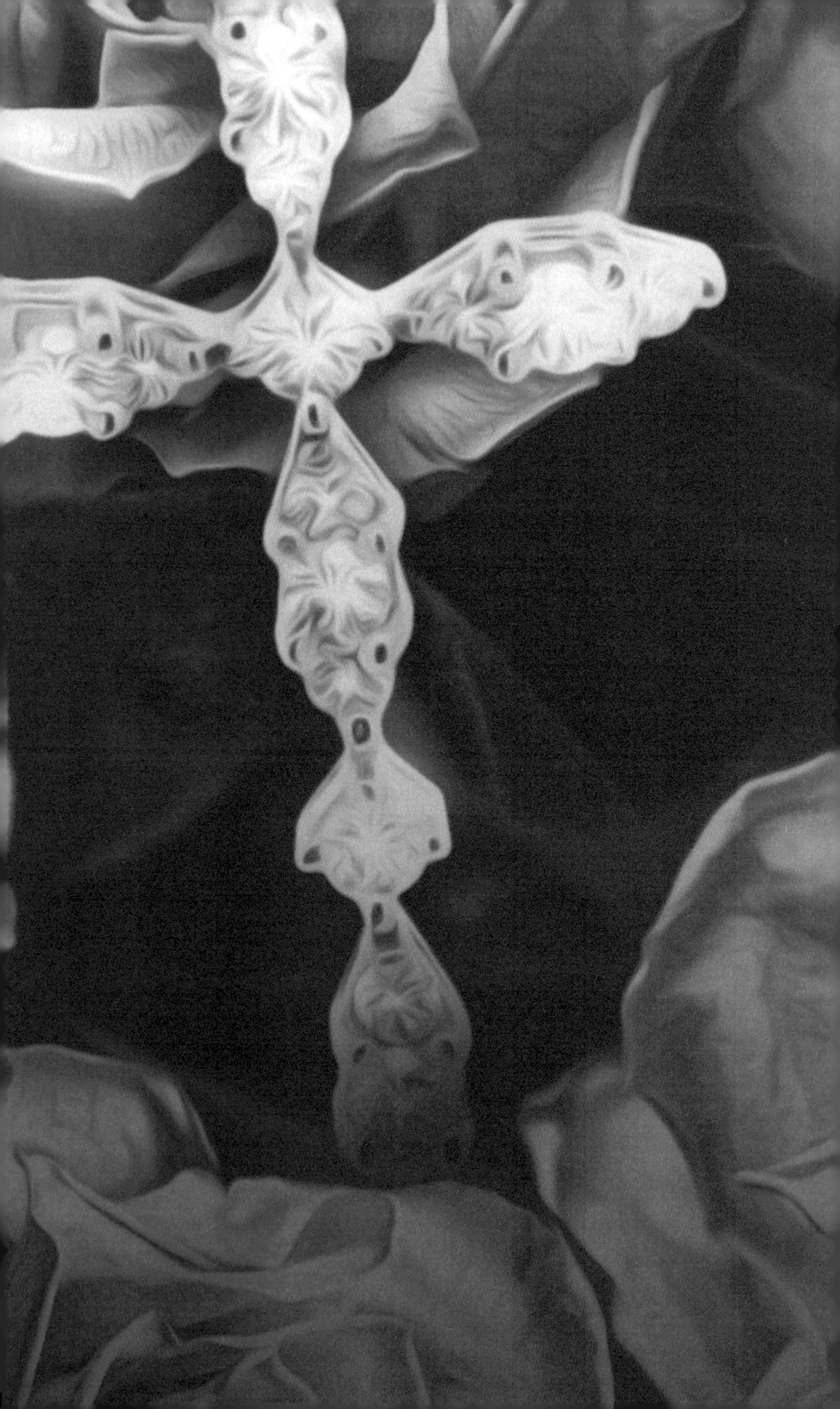

CHAPTER TWENTY-EIGHT

It's been a couple of weeks since everything shifted. The looming presence of the upcoming school year is undeniable. Kids will be running around here more often in the next few weeks, along with teachers.

There's been no word from my parents, but strangely, I no longer feel the need to dwell on their absence. I've moved on, carving out a new path for myself, one that doesn't revolve around their expectations or judgments.

Christian is doing remarkably well. He's still attending therapy, but he's officially in AA meetings, and every time I see him, I see the determination in his eyes to stay on the right track. He's found employment at a local hardware store and has plans to enroll in business classes at our community college. I couldn't be more proud of how far he's come.

As I dress for work, Toby brews us coffee, a ritual that has become second nature to us both. It's in these small, everyday moments that I find true happiness, a contentment I never thought possible.

I fasten my cross necklace around my neck. I still believe in God, and my necklace is a part of who I am. My belief just so happens to be different from my parents.

My faith has been redefined, free from my parents' oppressive beliefs. My father's words haunt me. Calling me such a name the last time I saw him broke my heart. But I let God handle it. I know one day my parents will calm down; I just don't know when.

Toby drives me to work before I step out of the car.

"Hey." He takes my hand. "I really think you should open your own bookstore in the city."

"Really?" I ask.

"Yes, it would be yours and a fresh start."

I nod. "Yeah, I mean, I'd like to own one. I just need to think on it for a bit."

"Okay princess, love you." He gives me a kiss.

"Love you."

The money I saved up for my own apartment still sits untouched in my account, and I pour into it every check I make. Seeing it grow is nice.

I make my way into the library and greet Lindsay with a smile. "Hi."

"Hey, where's Toby off to?" she asks.

"He is heading into the city to grab some stuff for the apartment."

"Let me guess, he got tired of the pull-out couch?"

"Yeah, just sitting on that thing is uncomfortable. I don't know why he didn't buy a regular couch."

She shrugs and heads back into her office.

Toby has me thinking about the future—a bookstore in the city someday. It was his idea and, though I'm not quite ready for that just yet, it's something I have found myself thinking about over and over again.

At my desk, I take a moment to browse listings for buildings for sale. Maybe it's not just a pipe dream after all. Reflecting on my journey with Toby, I realize how much he's pushed me to break free from my self-imposed limitations and embrace what's possible for me. Despite not being a

Christian, he has always been respectful and supportive of me. God put him in my life for a reason and I'm forever thankful for that.

I never anticipated falling for Toby, he was a bad boy with a reputation for breaking hearts and sleeping with many girls, but now, I can't imagine my life without him. People change. It's as though we were always meant to find each other, two souls drawn together by fate.

Toby has always insisted on taking me out—surprise dates and spontaneous adventures. It's one of the things I love about him. So when he suggests a Sunday evening outing, I don't think twice. I slip into a simple dress, checking my hair one more time before we head out.

But as we drive, I notice we're not heading to our usual spots—the cozy coffee shop or the park where we've shared countless picnics in the past month. Instead, he takes a turn down a street I'm not familiar with. I see the restaurant in sight, the one he's been talking about lately that's new in town.

"The Olive." is what it's called.

We step inside the building, and the scent of garlic and basil envelops me.

It's beautiful inside. Hardwood flooring, booth tables with candlelight in the middle, and soft classical music playing in the background.

"Hi, what can I get you two today?"

I go to speak, but Toby starts first. "She'll take a plate of your three cheese marinara spaghetti with meatballs, and I'll have a chicken alfredo, both meals with a Pepsi please."

I couldn't stop grinning ear to ear. He knows I love this type of food.

"Coming right up." The server leaves, and we sit there in silence for a moment.

"This place is so pretty. It just opened up, right?" I ask.

"Yeah, some friends have said their food is really good."

"That's awesome," I say.

After some time, our food is set out, and we start eating. The taste makes me crave more.

"Wow, this is good!" I continue digging in.

"Damn, my friends were right!" he says. I laugh.

I'm loving every moment of this. Every second I'm with him, I feel happy, safe, and alive. A small crack is in my heart because of my parents. One that may never seal up, but as long as I have him and my brother,

I think I'll be okay. I notice Toby placing his hand in his right pocket and standing up. "Follow me." He extends his arm, gesturing me to loop mine in it.

He guides me into this outdoor area in the back that has twinkling lights hanging alongside the walls and soft music playing.

"Elena," he whispers, getting down on one knee.

I can't help but cover my mouth in shock.

"I know it's only been a few months, but I love you so much, and nothing in this world matters to me without you." He pulls out a small black box. Tears well up, and I let out a shaky breath.

"You're beautiful, smart, caring, strong, and you put up with me. I'm not sure how or why, but I'm thankful for you and the love you have for me. You're everything I've ever wanted, needed, and I hope you'll do the honors by being my wife."

"Will you marry me?" As he opens the box, a stunning princess-cut diamond ring catches the light and sparkles brilliantly.

I nod my head fast. "Yes!"

He slides the ring on my finger and stands back up, pulling me into a hug, lifting and twirling me in the air. I giggle and hug him tight.

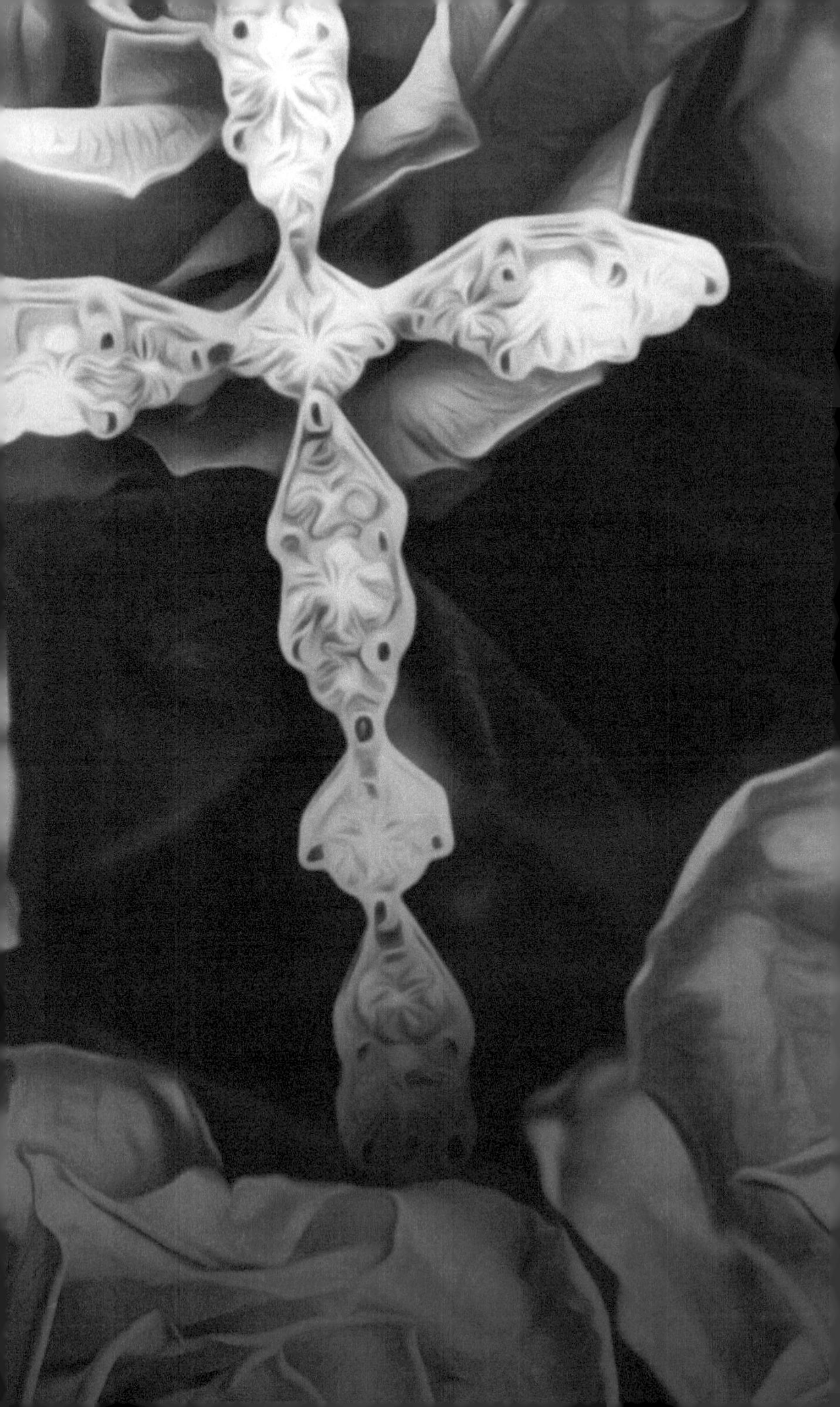

CHAPTER TWENTY-NINE

Every day, I drive past the church to head to work. It's the only way. I want to park in the small concrete parking lot, but I worry my parents won't take that lightly. Do the people who attend know of the so-called sin I've made? Or about my brother's drinking? If so, have they cast me out? Lord only knows.

As I drive by, I notice Christian's car out front. It's a Friday. Mom normally does bookkeeping on Fridays.

Without hesitation, I pull in and trudge up the stairs, counting each step to keep my heart from exploding.

As I stand there hesitating to open the door, grappling with the whirlwind of emotions swirling within me, I take in the sight of Christian's car parked outside the church. Confusion grips me—why is he here when we haven't seen Mom in months? I push open the door and walk toward the back.

"Elena baby, is that you?" her soft voice calls for me.

I step inside the doorway of her office.

I can tell by her blotchy eyes and red face she's been crying. She stands to hug me, but before she can reach me, I step back, my eyes darting to Christian, his presence reminding me as to why I came here.

"Please, don't touch me," I manage to say, my voice trembling.

Nodding, she respects my boundaries, retreating with a sigh. Turning to Christian, I can't help but feel a surge of concern. "Why are you here? Is everything okay?" I ask.

Christian meets my gaze. "I saw Mom and Dad fighting outside," he begins, "I tried to intervene, to break up the argument... and then Dad..." His voice trails off, he uses his good hand to point toward his injured hand, I see an ice pack resting on top of it. A lump forms in my throat.

Tension fills the room like a thick fog. I turn to Mom, desperation clawing at my throat. "Why were you fighting? What happened with Dad?"

Mom's eyes flicker with sadness.

"It's complicated, Elena," she mutters, her words strained. "Your father..."

I can't hold back. "No, Mom, it's not complicated! You've been avoiding us for months, and now Christian's here with a bloody hand because of your fighting! What's going on?" I shoot back, frustration bubbling up inside me.

Her frustration matches mine. "You don't understand, Elena! You don't know what it's been like, trying to keep this family together while your father..." Her voice trails off, heavy with unspoken pain.

"I don't understand? How can I when you won't even talk to us? We're your kids, Mom. We deserve to know."

She hesitates. "Your father... he's been struggling."

"Struggling with what?" I press, my heart racing with worry. "Is he sick? Is he leaving us?" Fear drives my questions, but Mom stays silent. Her avoidance fuels my frustration, but I'm trying my best to keep my cool.

"Answer me, Mom!" I plead, but she remains mute, her gaze falling to the floor. Anger surges through me as she doesn't respond, "I wish you had stood up for me and Christian when we were being kicked out! Or when our dad was being terrible to us!"

"We're getting a divorce," she yells out. Her words landed like a heavy blow.

Shock washes over me, disbelief clouding my thoughts. "What? Why?" I stammer.

Tears glisten in her eyes as she continues, her voice trembling with sadness. "Your father... he's been having an affair," she admits, her words piercing the silence like a knife.

The room spins as her confession sinks in, the reality of our shattered family hitting me like a tidal wave. I glance at Christian, his expression mirroring my own disbelief.

Mom's voice breaks the heavy silence. "I'm sorry, my loves. I wanted to shield you from this pain for as long as I could." tears stream down her cheeks. "Even though it's no excuse, it's one of the reasons why there has been a lot of fights between all of us."

My mind races, struggling to grasp the magnitude of her words. "How long has this been going on?" I ask, tucking in my upper lip.

She shakes her head, her shoulders slumping under the weight of her sorrow. "I don't know... It's been going on for a while."

"I can't believe this," I mutter.

"All those arguments about dating non-Christian boys, and he's the one who's been unfaithful?"

"Honey, I know you're upset.."

"Upset with him, yes, but Mom, you hurt me too. You disowned me, didn't want me to be with someone just because they didn't have the same beliefs as you."

"I'm so sorry..." She glances down at my hand and gasps.

"Is that what I think it is?" She rests her hand over her chest.

I look down, brows raised, realizing what she is looking at.

"Yes, Toby asked me to marry him."

"Oh, my baby's getting married!" She squeals. "That's great news to hear, especially with everything going on."

"I don't think you understand, Mom."

"Understand what?"

"You and I are in a rough spot because of everything that happened. I don't want to be around negativity right now."

"I understand." She nods.

I miss our strong mother-daughter relationship. Prior to stricter rules. Our family was happier before we moved here for his new job. The past few months, even the last ten years, have been irritating and hurtful. I don't know how to build that bond back to the way it used to be.

"I'm going to head back home, Christian. I'll see you later, okay?" I tap the door and give a small smile before walking out the door.

The oven beeps, letting me know dinner is done. Except I didn't make it. He did. I should really take cooking classes.

I walk into the kitchen, greeted by the scent of cheesy lasagna wafting through the air. Toby stands proudly by the oven, wearing a goofy grin.

"You made lasagna?" I ask, genuinely surprised.

"Yep, I figured I'd give it a shot," Toby says, his eyes sparkling with excitement.

I chuckle, unable to contain my amusement. "Well, I'm impressed. Chef Toby in the house."

He beams at the title, looking rather pleased with himself. "I even followed a recipe and everything."

I walk over to him, wrapping my arms around his waist. "Thank you."

He leans down, planting a kiss on my forehead. "Anything for my favorite taste tester."

As we sit at the table, Toby serves up slices of lasagna. With the first bite, I'm pleasantly surprised. It's actually delicious.

"This is great!"

Toby grins. "See? Who needs cooking classes when you have me?"

I laugh, shaking my head. "I guess."

"You know," Toby says, twirling his fork in his hand, "I heard lasagna is the key to a person's heart."

I raise an eyebrow, pretending to consider his statement. "Is that so? Well, consider my heart officially won over."

"Looks like my culinary skills are paying off."

"Indeed they are," I reply, matching his playful tone. "Who knew you were hiding such talent in the kitchen?"

Toby leans closer, his voice dropping to a whisper. "Maybe I'm just full of surprises."

Before I can respond, I pause, remembering something important. I hide my face into my hands, swallowing the tears threatening to break through.

Toby's expression softens. "What's wrong?" he places his arm over my shoulder and I rest my hand on his chest.

I take a deep breath. "She confessed to me about Dad's infidelity."

His eyes widen, "Wow, that explains a lot."

"Yeah," I reply, feeling a weight lifted off my shoulders. "It's been hard on her, but I don't know how to move past everything that went on between us."

Toby reaches across the table, gently squeezing my hand. "I'm sorry you had to go through that. But I'm here for you, Elena. Whatever you need."

"Thank you," I say.

"I'm gonna grab some food and ice cream, then we can watch TV when I get back,"

"Really?"

"Yes, princess," he gives me a kiss and grabs his keys and heads out.

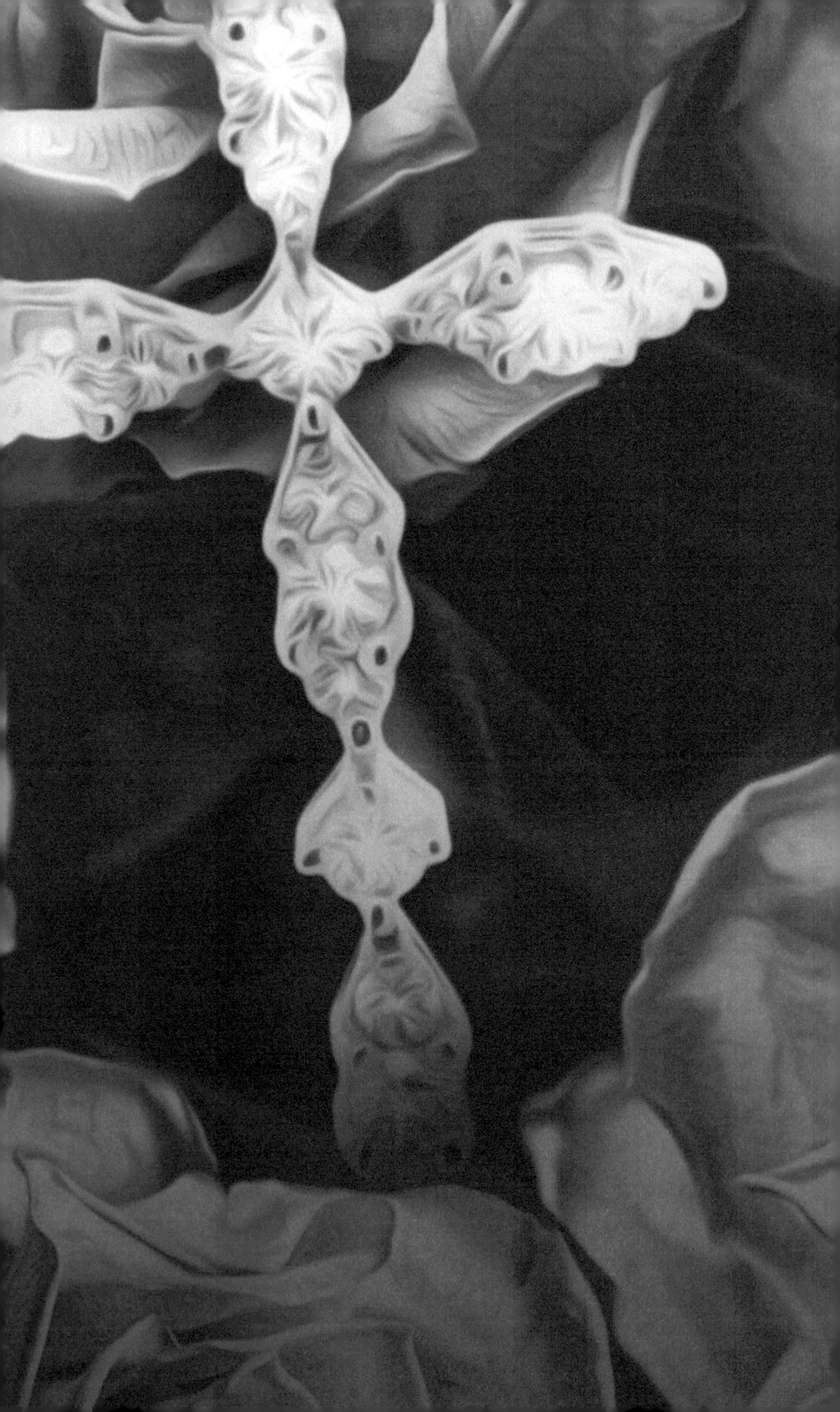

CHAPTER THIRTY

I'm standing here going through the inventory on the computer when a strong pair of arms wrap around my waist. *Oh Toby.* "Elena," he whispers. His voice is low and dangerously enticing. "You know, we're alone back here. No one would notice if we stole a kiss."

My breath hitches as I type away into the computer, it's been a couple days since I found out mom and dad are divorcing, and Toby has been doing anything and everything to keep my mind off of it. He has a way of making my knees weak.

"We're at work Toby." I bite my lip as he cups my ass.

"Like I said, no one's around." he whispers on my neck.

I glance around the room before looking at him. "Okay, backroom, now," I demand.

He pulls me into him and lifts me, carrying me to the back room.

He sits me down, kissing my lips and lowering down to the front of my jeans. I giggle as he unbuttons them. "I can't believe we're about to do this in the library."

He pulls my pants down and kisses the front of my panties, "Mmm." I let out a light moan. Gliding his fingers up both my legs only to quickly slide them off as well, throwing them to the side on top of my jeans.

He lifts me again, sitting me down on the edge of a table and moves my legs up, spreading them wide.

"Oh, someone shaved?"

I sure did. "You like?"

"So sexy, princess."

He slips his tongue over my clit, and I grip his hair in response. Every smell and touch becomes sensitive as I grow wet.

Warmth spreads through and I lean against the wall, feet in the air.

I watch as he flicks and sucks and massages my clit with his tongue and it only intensifies my desire for him.

He stops for a moment, taking off my shirt and unclipping my bra, throwing them to the side as well.

"Did you lock the door?" I ask.

He ignores my question; I don't think he did but somehow the risk of being caught turns me on. My lord he brings the wild side of me out.

One hand cupping one of my boobs, he gently licks and sucks my hard nipples.

"Oh, please, don't stop." my voice barely audible.

He sticks his index and thumb into my mouth, and I suck on them. He then places them on my other nipple. Every nerve in my body collides together erupting into an explosion

"Are you feeling good princess, do you want to get fucked baby?"

My eyes are droopy, and I nod, he then proceeds to adjust me, pulling me to my feet and bending me over the table.

"Your wish is my command."

He slides his erection inside me, and thrusts hard and deep. I moan loudly into the table.

"Shhh." he tries to quiet me down, but I can't help it, as he says, I'm a screamer.

As the waves of pleasure wash over me, I gasp for breath, my body trembling.

Toby's relentless thrusts continue, driving me to even greater heights of pleasure. I arch my back, my fingers digging into the table, unable to contain the overwhelming pleasure coursing through me.

"That's it, baby. Let go for me." His words fuel the fire within me, pushing me closer to the edge.

With each thrust, I feel myself teetering on the brink of release.

And then it happens. My body tenses, my muscles clenching around him as an electrifying climax washes over me.

"Oh, Toby," I cry out.

"Good girl." He removes himself. "Get on your knees," he sexily demands.

I bite my lip, looking up at his eyes.

He jerks himself, and I wrap my lips around his cock and swirl my tongue around it, and warm liquid rushes through. He groans, gripping my head and pushing it more toward him. I swallow every ounce until no more leaks.

We both try to catch our breath. I finish getting dressed, and so does he.

"Ready to go back to work?" He gives me a smirk.

I laugh, "Yes, but more tonight, okay?"

"I won't say no to that." He slaps my ass.

As we make our way back to our desks, I can't help but feel a sense of pride in myself.

Throughout the rest of the day, I find myself smiling and humming to myself as I work. Even the usual mundane tasks seem more enjoyable and fulfilling.

As I pull into my parents driveway, I take a deep breath and steel myself for the conversation that I know needs to happen with my mom. Although it won't be easy, I know that it's important for us to repair our relationship and move forward. I walk up to the front door and let myself in.

As I step into the living room, the soft rustle of pages turning fills the air. The warm, inviting scent of vanilla candles mingles with the faint aroma of fresh coffee. My mom is nestled into the corner of the couch, a well-worn book resting in her lap. She looks up as I enter, her eyes crinkling with a gentle smile.

"Hey there, sweetie. How was your day?" she asks, her voice warm and soothing, like a comforting blanket.

I sink into the plush cushions beside her and take her hand, feeling the familiar softness of her skin. "It was good, Mom." I pause, gathering my thoughts. "And I want to talk to you about something."

She squeezes my hand. "I'm listening," she says, her tone inviting me to open up.

Taking a deep breath, I let the words flow. "I've been thinking a lot about my faith lately," I begin.

"It's been... challenging. Sometimes I feel so connected, and other times, I feel completely lost."

Mom's brow furrows slightly, her grip on my hand tightening. "Faith isn't always a straight path, honey. There are difficulties. What exactly has been on your mind?"

"I guess it's just that I don't always feel like I'm doing enough," I admit, my voice trembling. "I see people who seem so sure, so steadfast, and I wonder if I'm missing something. And... there's something else."

She tilts her head, her eyes softening. "What is it, sweetie?"

"I feel like I've been forced to have the same beliefs as you and dad." I say, my voice breaking. "And I'm scared that if I don't, you both will hate me for it. I've been going back and forth with myself for so long, but I don't know if I can keep doing it."

A look of understanding crosses her face, and she pulls me into a hug. "Oh, Elena, I know I've been hard on you, I'm so sorry. I love you and your dad loves you no matter what. Faith should never be about fear or pretending. It's your journey, and it's okay to question and explore. I'm so sorry for making you feel so crappy about it,"

Tears well up in my eyes as I pull back to look at her. "But what if he doesn't understand? What if he thinks I'm turning my back on everything he's taught us?"

She gently wipes away a tear from my cheek. "He may not understand right away, but he loves you. Give him time and be honest with him. You're his daughter, and that bond is stronger than any disagreement about beliefs."

I nod, feeling a weight lift slightly from my shoulders. "You're right. I just want to live a life that's true to me, without feeling like I'm betraying him."

"And you are," she says firmly. "You're kind, you're thoughtful, and you're always trying to do the right thing. That's what matters."

Her words bring a sense of peace, and I lean back against the couch, feeling more at ease. "Thanks, Mom. I really needed to hear that."

She smiles, her eyes shining with pride. "Anytime, sweetie. I'm always here for you."

Standing up from the couch, I give her a small smile, "I'm going to head back."

She stands up and gives me a hug. "I love you sweetie, your dad will come around, okay?"

I nod. I want to believe her, but I'm scared that if I do, my hopes about me and my dad's relationship being good will fall and I'd hate to feel more crushed than I already am by his behavior. I walk out the door and settle back into my car. Turning on the ignition, I let out a deep sigh. A heaviness weighing on my shoulders has released.

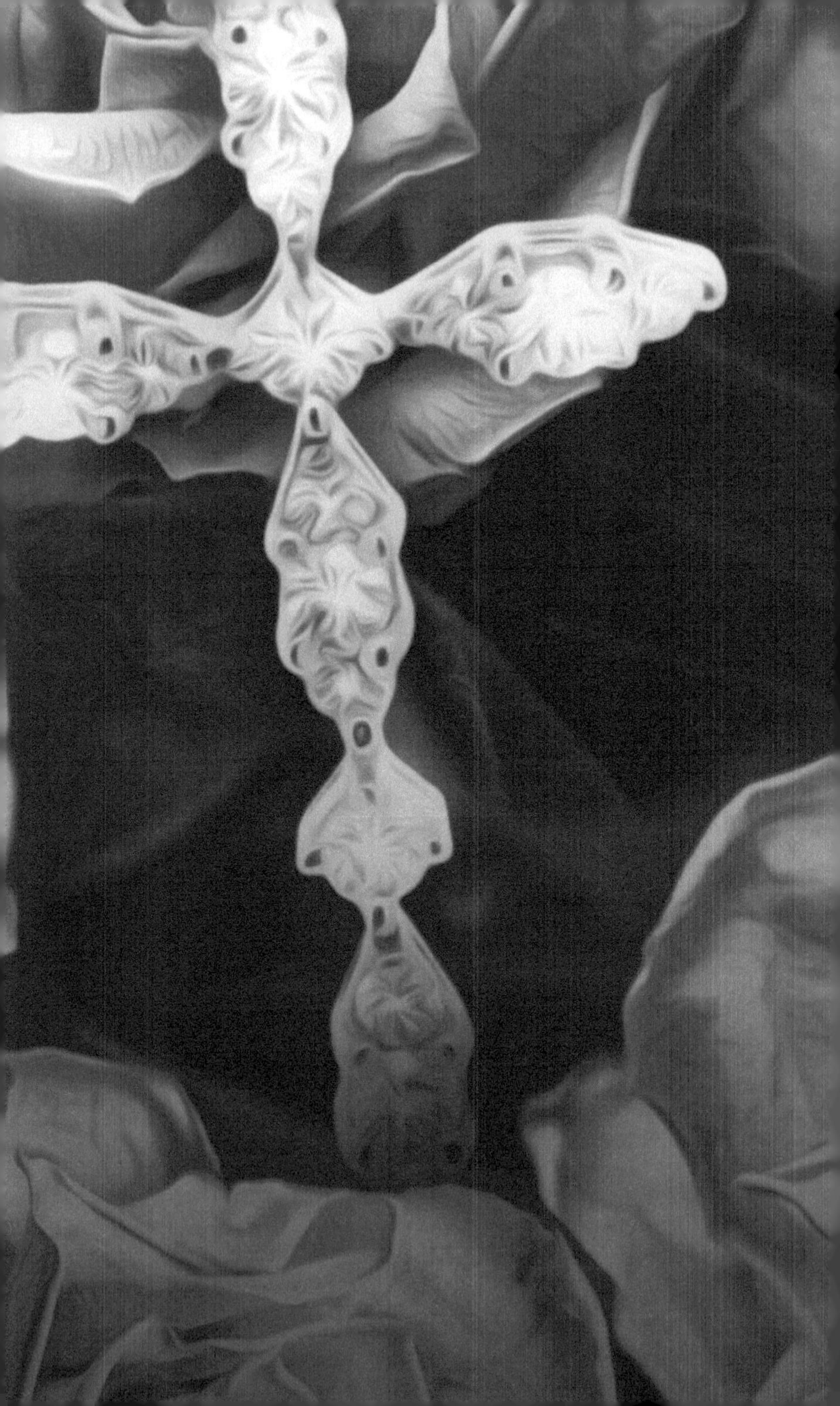

CHAPTER THIRTY-ONE

The days have been passing by in a blur, and I can barely keep track. The loud beeping of the alarm jolts me awake, reminding me it's "Church Day." After placing my phone back down, I shift to my other side and reach out my arm to find Toby but feel nothing but sheets. A heavy sigh escapes my lips.

"Toby?" I call out.

The bedroom door opens and in walks my handsome man. "Yes, princess?" Seeing him standing there shirtless in just a pair of grey sweats weakens me.

"Uh- what are you doing?" My voice comes out in a high pitch, almost squeaking.

"I'm making cinnamon rolls," he says with a smile. "What's with the high pitch?" he smirks, his voice filled with amusement as he walks over to me.

Just as I laugh and attempt to sit up, he surprises me by swiftly climbing on top of me, inching close to my face. "Is it my sweatpants?" his minty breath mingles with the scent of cinnamon, tickling my nose.

"Maybe," I stammer, feeling a rush of warmth flood my cheeks.

The scent of freshly baked cinnamon fills the air, mingling with the subtle musk of his cologne. I can hear the faint sound of sizzling in the kitchen, indicating that the cinnamon rolls are cooking to perfection.

As he hovers above me, the sensation of his warm breath on my skin sends a pleasant shiver down my spine. His playful gaze locks with mine, and he kisses my nose.

He gets up and pulls the blankets off me. "Come on, we've got breakfast to eat and church to attend."

He wants to attend church. "We?" I ask.

"Yes, we."

"Since when?"

"It's important to you, and I'd like to support you."

I cross my arms, squinting my eyes in disbelief. "You sure it has nothing to do with impressing my dad?"

He tilts his head side to side playfully. "Maybe a little."

"No, Toby, you don't go to church for personal gain."

"Actually..." he trails off, brows raised.

"I don't mind you going. Let's eat and I'll shower!"

The gravel parking lot crunches beneath my baby blue flats as Toby and I walk hand in hand toward the church doors. It's still early. People are still pulling into the parking lot. Service doesn't start for another twenty minutes.

I look at Toby. His buttoned-up blue shirt fits him well, and a white tie hangs from his collar. Very handsome. I've never seen him dressed up before.

He squeezes my hand as we walk up the steps. "Take a breather, princess," he says.

The smell of damp earth and the faint scent of blooming flowers surround us. A soft breeze rustles the leaves of the old oak trees lining the pathway. My heart races as we step inside the cool, dimly lit foyer of the church. The familiar scent of polished wood and old hymnals hits me, instantly transporting me back to countless Sundays spent here.

We find a seat near the middle, and I notice

some familiar faces nodding in our direction. Whispers of greetings and the rustling of the congregation settling in fill the air.

As we sit down, the smooth wood of the pew feels cold against my skin. Toby's presence beside me is both comforting and nerve-wracking. I glance sideways at him; he's looking around the building, seems to be curious. I don't see Christian anywhere.

I lean closer to him and whisper, "You okay?"

He nods, giving me a reassuring smile. "Yeah, just new," he coughs.

I squeeze his hand gently.

My father steps up to the pulpit, his stern gaze sweeping over the congregation. His eyes linger on us for a moment longer, and my stomach flutters in a not so good way.

As my father starts his sermon, his voice echoes through the church, commanding attention. He speaks of faith, devotion, and the importance of following the right path. He also speaks about sin like it's his best friend. But it is his best friend, he's cheating on my mom. I can't help but feel his words are directed at me, a veiled admonishment for my choices.

I glance at Toby, who listens intently, his face serious.

When the service ends, we file out with the rest of the congregation. My father stands at the exit, shaking hands and exchanging pleasantries. My heart pounds as we approach him.

"Good morning, Dad," I say, forcing a smile.

He nods, his eyes narrowing slightly. "Elena. Toby." His tone is polite but distant.

"Sir," Toby says, extending his hand. My father hesitates for a fraction of a second before shaking it.

"I hope you enjoyed the service," my father says, his gaze shifting between us.

"Yes, sir. It was very enlightening," Toby replies earnestly.

My father's eyes soften just a bit, but his expression remains guarded. "I'm glad to hear that. Church is a cornerstone of our lives, something I hope you'll come to understand."

"I'm trying, sir," Toby says, his sincerity evident.

The tension fades as we walk back to the car.

The oven timer beeps, letting me know dinner is ready. I've put together a comfort meal, not from scratch, but frozen lasagna works when hunger takes over and cooking feels like too much effort.

Sliding an oven mitt over my hand, I open the oven and pull out the lasagna, placing it on the stove. I glance at the darkening sky and wish Toby would get home soon. A storm is coming, and the sun is beginning to set. Being alone during storms, especially at night when I can't see what's happening outside, always makes me uneasy.

After making myself a plate and grabbing a glass of water, my phone buzzes, and Toby's name flashes across the screen.

"Hi babe," I answer.

"Hey princess, I'm running behind. The wind is picking up, and the rain is pouring," he says, and I can hear the whistling wind in the background.

"Yeah, I hear it," I say, taking a bite of lasagna. "Where are you exactly?"

"Near 10th Street, not too far."

"Okay, see you when you get home. Drive safe."

"Love you."

"I love you too," I say, smiling as I hang up and set my phone down.

We haven't had a good storm since spring. After finishing my plate, I head to the living room, grab the blanket from the top of the couch, and cozy up to watch a show while waiting for Toby.

The storm rages outside, wind howling and rain pelting the windows. The show on TV is barely enough to distract from the storm's fury. Cozy under the blanket, I try to focus on the characters' voices, but the drumming of the rain lulls me into a light sleep.

A loud crack of thunder jolts me awake. My heart races as I sit up, trying to shake off the remnants of my nap. Just then, the front door creaks open, and I hear the familiar sound of Toby's footsteps.

Rushing to the hallway, I see Toby standing there, drenched from head to toe, with two grocery bags in hand. Water drips from his hair and clothes, forming small puddles on the floor.

"Toby!" I exclaim, relief flooding my voice. "You're soaked!"

He gives a sheepish grin, shaking off some of the water. "Yeah, the storm caught me off guard. I didn't know it was coming."

"Let's get you dried off," I say, grabbing a towel from the linen closet.

Toby steps inside, setting the grocery bags down.

His fingers brush against mine as he takes the towel, sending a tingle up my arm.

"Come here," he says softly, his voice a soothing balm against the thunder outside. He gently takes my hand, guiding me towards the bathroom.

His touch is gentle yet firm, making me feel safe and cherished. The bathroom light casts a warm glow, and the sound of the rain fades into the background. Toby turns to face me, his eyes locking with mine.

"Are you okay?" he asks, his voice filled with concern and tenderness.

"Yeah, just... glad you're home," I reply, my voice barely a whisper. His hand reaches up, caressing my cheek, and I lean into his touch, closing my eyes for a moment.

"I made dinner," I say, opening my eyes to meet his gaze again.

He grins, a playful glint in his eyes. "But you're my dinner," he murmurs, his voice low and flirtatious.

A blush creeps up my cheeks, and I laugh softly, "Toby..."

"Shhh," he kisses me and slowly unbuttons my pajama shirt. His kissing brings me a sense of calmness.

He leans in, his forehead resting against mine. "You have no idea how much I missed you," he whispers, his breath warm against my skin.

"I missed you too," I reply, my voice trembling with emotion.

Turning on the shower, he kisses me softly

from the top of my chest all the way down, stopping just above my pubic area.

"Mmm" a moan escapes my lips and I grip his hair as he pulls my pants and underwear down kissing my lips lightly.

He stands up and steps into the shower, and I can feel the warmth radiating from the water. I pull the curtain shut, and in that moment, he grabs my hand and spins me around to face him, his touch sending a shiver down my spine. "Lean against the wall, princess," he whispers, his breath warm against my ear.

I nod, doing as he says. I love it when he touches me.

With a hungry tone, he kneels before me, "Spread your legs, princess. I need to eat." Goosebumps ripple across my skin, causing me to instinctively widen my legs.

"Good girl," he leans in and licks my inner lips, barely touching my clit as an attempt to tease me. I lean my head back and moan, every little flick of his tongue is making my body quiver from pleasure. As he licks the top of my clit, a loud moan escapes my lips. But it's that single, tantalizing flick of his tongue that ignites waves of pleasure throughout my body.

I look down at him and he looks up at me. Just as I'm about to speak he devours me into his mouth like there's no tomorrow. His little fast licks make me breath heavily and moan louder and louder. I can feel myself growing more wet and I'm shaking uncontrollably, he proceeds to lift me up to where my legs sit over his shoulders and my back is against the wall.

"I'm going to cum, Toby, don't stop!" I grip his hair and he moans into my pussy lips making it vibrate and I scream loudly as a rush of warmth leaks through and my body, my legs shaking like crazy. He sets me back down to my feet. *What a ride.*

"I'm full now," he smirks as he grabs his shampoo and washes. I giggle and he grabs the soap, washing me without being sexual, just caring. I love this man.

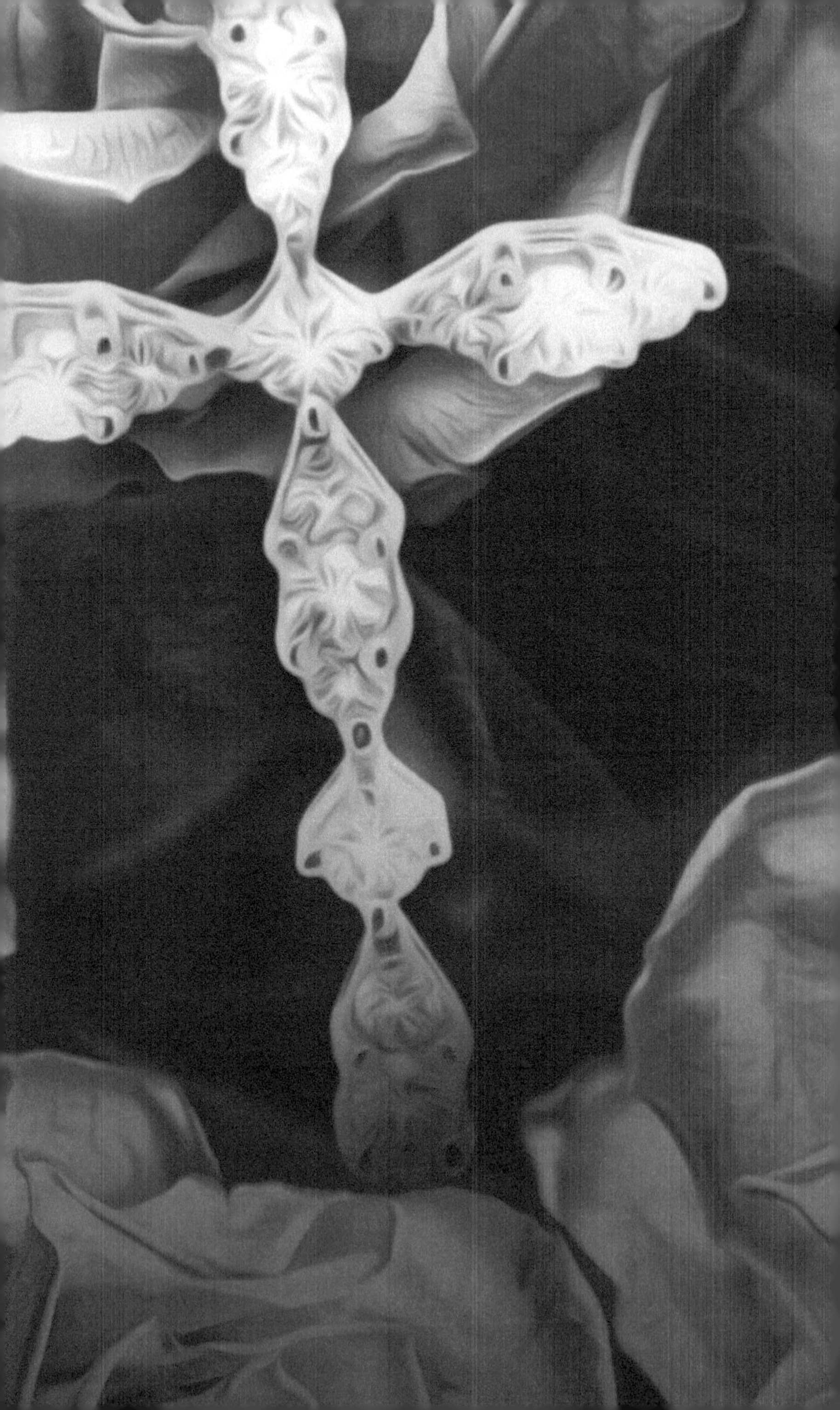

CHAPTER THIRTY-TWO

"Why won't this thing turn on!" I smack the computer in frustration and let out a deep sigh. I've only been at work for a few hours. It's not even lunch yet. Toby is at the school and here I am yelling at a computer.

"Smacking it will not help you." A familiar voice says. I look up to see Nathan.

"Nathan? I've never seen you in here before." I say as I keep pressing the power button.

"I've officially moved into town with my folks." he says. Our first date wasn't that long ago. I feel odd that he's here, though.

"Oh, well, welcome to the neighborhood!" I say with a smile.

"Do you want some help?" he asks.

"Know anything about computers?" I ask.

"Yeah, it's my job. I worked in IT back in New York city for a computer company,"

"Oh, well, have at it." I move to the side and grab my notebook from the bottom shelf and sit at a nearby table and write down all the inventory I should have finished last week but didn't. I can't even grab myself a coffee to help keep me sane, the little cafe is closed today. I open my phone to send Jenny a message.

ME

Hey, could you bring me a coffee at the library please? If you aren't busy.

I put my phone down.

Ever since yesterday at church I've felt uneasy. Toby going in with me to church was new, and my dad not being insane that we were there together was not entirely calming knowing how he is outside of church. I don't even think he knows we know he had an affair with mom.

My pencil snaps in half causing a slightly loud echo, "Shit!" I don't curse often, but when I do it's when I'm stressed to the max.

"Here," Nathan walks over with a new pencil.

"Thank you."

"Is everything okay?" He asks.

"I'll be fine, but thank you for checking on me."

"No problem, the charger from your computer

seems to be going out, I will run by my house and grab one for you."

"Oh, you don't have to do that!"

"No, really it's okay, I have spare ones for this type of computer, you'd be doing me a favor taking one from the pile of clutter."

"Thank you, appreciate it! Did you come here for a book or to fix my computer?" I joke.

With a chuckle, he casually slides his hands into his front pockets. "I'll grab the book later. I'll be back around two." he says as he walks out the front door.

I find myself staring at the not so functional computer. At least paper and pen never fail me.

Ever since Toby and I went to church together, I've been on edge. My father's reaction—or lack thereof—was unsettling.

Shaking my head to clear the thoughts, I go back and focus on the inventory list in front of me. It's mundane, but the repetitive nature of the task helps me calm down. I jot down the numbers, trying to ignore the lingering tension in my shoulders.

Just as I'm getting into a rhythm, the bell above the door jingles. I look up, expecting a customer, but it's Jenny. She's balancing two coffee cups and a bag of pastries, her face lighting up with a smile when she sees me.

"Hey! she says, placing one of the cups on my desk.

"Thank you! the cafe is closed today," I reply, pointing toward taking a grateful sip. The cold coffee soothes me, and I let out a small sigh of relief. "Thanks, Jenny. You're a lifesaver."

"Mrs. Thompson out for the day?" she asks.

"I haven't seen her here the last few times I've worked."

She sits down across from me, pulling out a pastry and taking a bite. "So, what's got you so worked up? I sense some strong feelings."

I groan, running a hand through my hair. "It's just everything. This stupid computer, my dad, Toby... I don't know, it's all piling up."

Jenny gives me a sympathetic look. "I get it. Family stuff can be a real pain, especially when they're as... intense as your dad."

"Intense is putting it lightly," I mutter, taking another sip of coffee. "And Toby... he's been amaz-ing, really. But I can't shake this feeling that some-thing's going to go wrong."

"Like what?" she asks, leaning forward.

"I don't know," I admit. "Maybe it's just me being paranoid. But ever since he came to church, I've been waiting for the other shoe to drop."

She nods, "I can see why you'd feel that way. Toby doesn't seem so bad. And your dad... well, he'll have to come around eventually."

"I hope so," I say, though my voice lacks conviction. "It's just hard to see past all the... baggage."

"Toby has a past, just like everyone else. Your dad would be a hypocrite if he doesn't accept toby because of the past."

"True."

Before Jenny can respond, the door jingles again. This time, it's a customer. I plaster on a smile and stand up, ready to help. Jenny gives me a reassuring nod before standing up, "I will see you later?"

"Yes."

The afternoon passes in a blur of activity. Customers come and go, and I manage to get through most of my inventory list.

True to his word, Nathan returns around two with a new power cord. He installs it quickly, flashing me a grin when the computer boots up without a hitch.

"See? Easy fix." he says.

"Thank you Nathan. Seriously, you saved my day." I reply.

"No problem." he says, giving me a warm smile before heading out again.

I take a moment to breathe, the hum of the now functional computer calms my nerves. With the inventory done and the computer working, I finally feel a bit of the tension easing from my shoulders. *Oh, crap he forgot to get a book. Oh well. He'll probably be back for it.*

As I settle back into my work, my phone buzzes with a message from Toby.

TOBY

How's your day going?

ME

Better now, thanks to Nathan's tech skills and Jenny's coffee delivery.

TOBY

Nathan? The lunch date Nathan?

ME

Yes, he stopped by. I guess he's moved to town.

TOBY

Uh-huh…I'm finishing up here, want to grab dinner tonight?

ME

Yes, I'll be done by 5.

TOBY

See you then, princess.

I smile at the screen, feeling a warmth spread through me. Toby has been a constant source of support, and despite my worries, I can't deny how much I care for him. He makes everything feel a little bit easier, a little bit brighter.

The rest of the afternoon goes by quickly. I help a few more customers, finish some paperwork, and organize the shelves. By the time six o'clock rolls around, I'm ready to call it a day.

I step outside into the fall evening air. Toby is waiting for me by his car, leaning against the door with a relaxed smile on his face.

"Hey," I greet him, walking over.

"Hey yourself," he replies, pulling me into a hug. "Rough day?"

"Not so bad, now that it's over," I say, leaning into him. "Where are we going for dinner?"

"I was thinking The Olive again," he suggests, opening the car door for me.

"Sounds perfect," I agree, getting in.

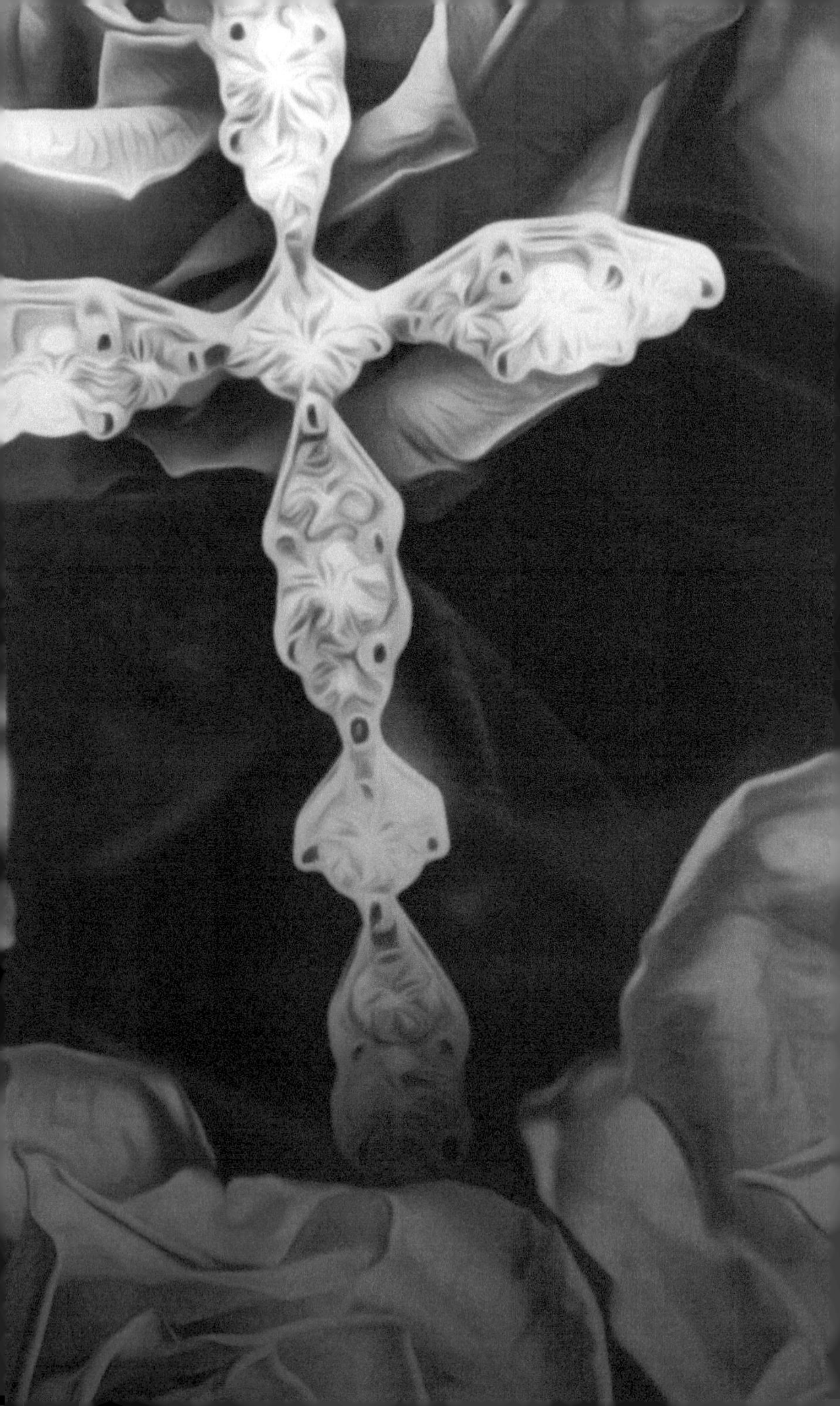

CHAPTER THIRTY-THREE

The next morning, an aroma of freshly made pancakes fills the air, gently rousing me from sleep. I stretch and smile, my heart warming at the thought of Toby in the kitchen, making breakfast. I slip out of bed and walk down the hall, the scent of butter and maple syrup growing stronger.

In the kitchen, Toby is flipping pancakes with practiced ease. He turns and smiles at me, his eyes lighting up. "Morning, beautiful. Sleep well?"

"Better than ever," I reply, wrapping my arms around him from behind and resting my head on his shoulder.

"I made your favorite," he says, gesturing to the stack of pancakes on the counter.

"You're amazing," I say, grabbing a plate and loading it with pancakes. We sit at the small kitchen table.

As we eat, I can't help but glance at the ring on my finger. The memory of Toby's proposal still feels like a dream. It was perfect, intimate, and filled with love. I know it's soon, but I don't care. He makes me feel alive.

"I need to tell the girls." I say, more to myself than to Toby.

He looks up from his plate, "Are you nervous?"

"A little," I admit. "But I can't wait to see their reactions."

I've not been wearing my ring to work in fear of losing it nor did I want to ruin the surprise to anyone. I'd like to tell them without showing it first.

I pull out my phone and open the group chat with Jenny, Rose, and Emily. My fingers hover over the keyboard for a moment before I start typing.

ME

Morning!!! Can we all meet up later today? I have something exciting to share!

I hit send and take another bite of my pancake, feeling a mix of excitement and nerves. My phone buzzes almost immediately.

JENNY

Hey! Sure, what's up?

ROSE

Absolutely, where and when?

EMILY

Can't wait to hear the news! How about in the park at noon?

ME

Perfect! See you all there!

I put my phone down. Toby reaches across the table and takes my hand, his thumb rubbing soothing circles on my skin.

"They're going to be thrilled," he says, his voice filled with certainty.

"I hope so," I reply, squeezing his hand. "I just want everything to go smoothly."

"It will," he assures me. "You've got this."

The morning passes quickly as we clean up the kitchen and get ready for the day. Before I know it, it's time to head to the park. I feel a flutter of nerves while I grab my purse and head out the door, Toby giving me a reassuring kiss before I leave.

The park is busy with activity when I arrive, families playing, joggers passing by, and the familiar laughter of children echoing through the air. I spot Jenny, Rose, and Emily sitting at our usual picnic table, their faces lighting up when they see me.

"There she is!" Jenny calls out, waving me over.

"Hey!" I greet them, my heart pounding with excitement.

"So, I have some news," I begin, my voice trembling slightly.

All three of them lean in, their eyes wide with curiosity.

"You're not pregnant are you?" Rose asks in a stern tone.

I look at her with wide eyes.

"Rose!" We all say.

"No, I'm not dork!" I laugh.

"Okay okay, continue," Rose says.

I smile, unable to contain my excitement any longer. "Toby proposed recently."

There's a moment of silence before they all burst into excited squeals, their voices overlapping as they bombard me with questions.

"Oh my god, congratulations!" Rose exclaims.

"Let me see the ring!" Jenny takes my hand, in awe of the princess cut on my finger.

"How did he do it?" Emily asks.

I laugh, holding out my hand so they can see the ring. Their eyes widen, and they gush over it, their excitement infectious.

"It was perfect," I tell them, recounting the story of Toby's proposal. "He took me to a restaurant and in the back, there were beautiful twinkling lights, soft music playing, and he had this amazing speech after getting down on one knee,"

Jenny wipes a tear from her eye, smiling

widely. "That's so romantic. I'm so happy for you, Elena."

"Thank you," I say, my heart swelling with gratitude and love for my friends.

"We need to celebrate!" Jenny declares, jumping up from her seat. "How about we head to our favorite cafe? First round of lattes and pastries is on me!"

Rose and Emily nod eagerly, their faces alight with excitement.

"Absolutely," Rose says. "This is a huge deal, Elena. We have to do something special."

I grin, feeling the joy and energy of my friends lifting my spirits even higher. "Alright, let's do it!"

We gather our things and head toward the cafe down the road from the park. As they continue talking, I can't help but wonder if my dad will be happy for me, or if he will avoid me. He puts up a façade when others are around. Will he walk me down the aisle? Or continue to be a strict person who can't handle change?

"Alright, so what's next?" Rose asks while moving her hair to the side. "Have you thought about a date for the wedding?"

I shake my head smiling. "Not yet. It's all so new, and we haven't thought that far ahead."

"We have to plan your bachelorette party," Emily teases, nudging me playfully.

"Oh, that's going to be epic," Jenny says with a grin. "We'll make sure it's a night to remember."

As the sun starts to dip lower in the sky, we finally say our goodbyes, hugging each other tightly. I walk back to my car, feeling an overwhelming sense of happiness and excitement for the future.

When I get home, Toby is waiting for me on the porch, his eyes lighting up when he sees me. I run into his arms, feeling the familiar comfort and love that he always brings.

"How did it go?" he asks, holding me close.

"They were so happy," I say, looking up at him. "We celebrated, and it was perfect."

"Good," he says, kissing my forehead. "You deserve all the happiness in the world, princess,"

"And I have it," I reply, smiling. "With you, and with them. I have everything I could ever want."

We stand there for a moment, wrapped up in each other. I love this man so much.

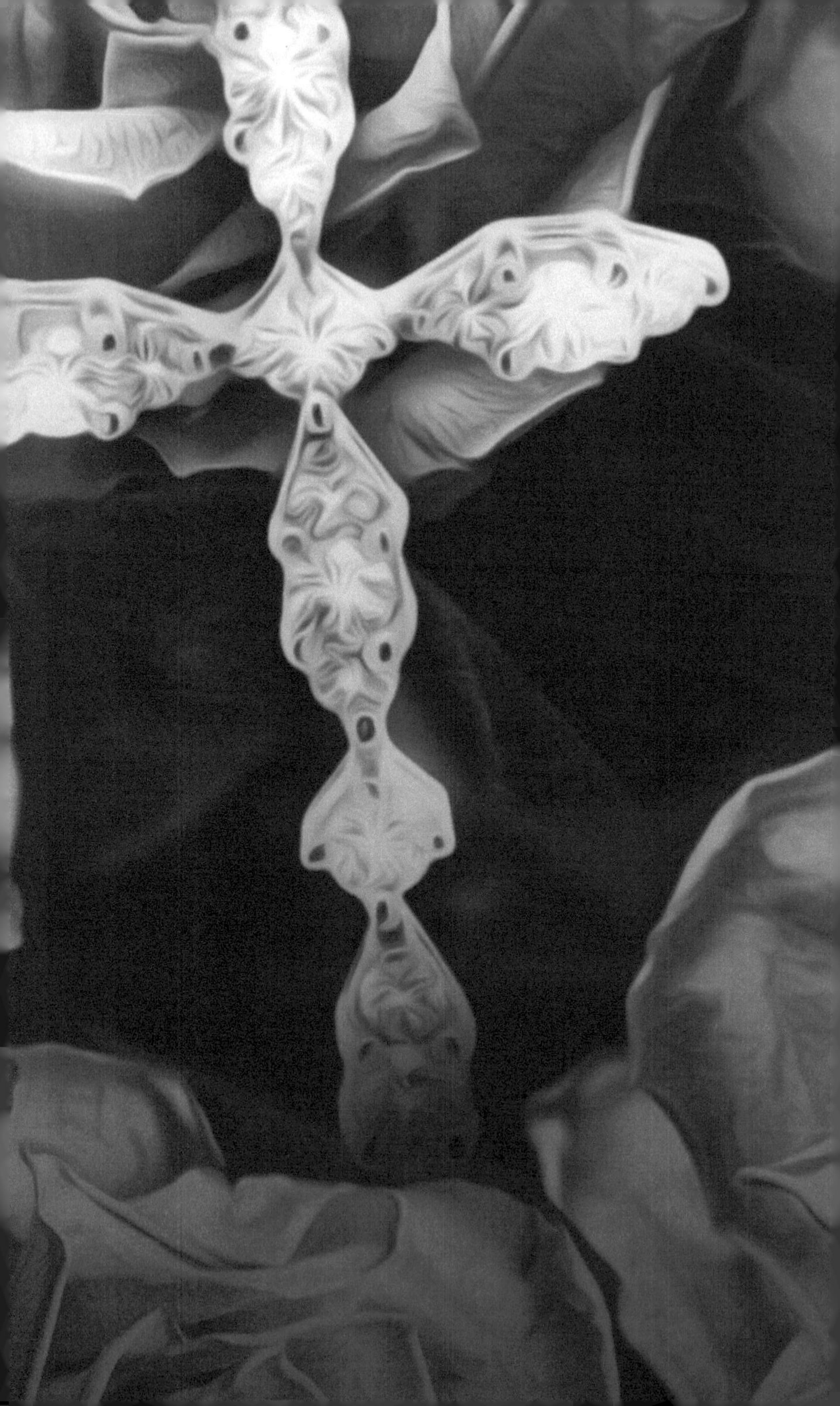

CHAPTER THIRTY-FOUR

The library is quiet around noon. Toby is beside me, shelving books with an easy efficiency that makes me grateful for his help.

"Here's another stack for you," I say, handing him a small pile of romance books.

"Got it," he replies with a smile, taking the books from me.

Toby's good with the patrons, especially the kids who come in looking for adventure stories and picture books. Watching him interact with them, I can't help but imagine our future together, maybe with kids of our own one day.

As lunchtime approaches, my stomach growls. I glance at the clock and realize it's almost noon. I'm about to suggest we take a break when the bell above the library door jingles. I look up and see my dad walking in, carrying a bag of food. My heart skips a beat—this is unexpected.

"Dad?" I say, surprised. "What are you doing here?"

"I thought I'd bring you lunch," he replies, his tone gruff but with a hint of softness. His eyes flick to Toby, and his expression tightens slightly. "Hello, Toby."

"Sir," Toby says politely, nodding.

The tension in the air is palpable.

Thank you for bringing lunch," I say, taking the bag from him. "You didn't have to."

"I wanted to," he says, his gaze softening as he looks at me. "We haven't had a chance to talk much lately."

I lead him to a table, and Toby joins us after helping a young girl find a book about dinosaurs. We sit down, and I unpack the food—sandwiches, chips, and fruit. It's a simple meal, but the gesture means a lot.

"So, how's work been?" my dad asks, trying to make conversation.

"It's been good," I reply. "Toby's been a big help today."

My dad nods, his expression still tense. "That's good to hear."

There's an awkward silence. *Someone please drag me out of here.*

"Dad, I know you're still adjusting to the idea

of Toby and me being together," I begin, choosing my words carefully. "But I hope you can see how happy he makes me. He's been so supportive and loving, and I really believe we're meant to be together."

My dad's eyes flicker with a mix of emotions—frustration, concern, and a hint of something softer. He takes a deep breath, as if steeling himself for what he's about to say.

"Elena, I just want what's best for you," he says, his voice gruff. "It's hard for me to accept that Toby doesn't share our faith. But I can see that he cares about you, and I'm trying to come to terms with that."

Toby speaks up then, his tone respectful but firm. "Sir, I understand your concerns. And I respect your faith and values. I love Elena more than anything, and I'm committed to being the best partner I can be for her. I'm also open to learning and growing, and I've going to be attending church with Elena because it's important to her. I hope you can see that I'm here for the long haul."

My dad studies Toby for a long moment, his expression unreadable. Finally, he nods, "I can see that you're sincere, And I appreciate that you're making an effort. It's not easy for me, but I'll try to keep an open mind."

Relief washes over me, and I reach across the

table to squeeze my dad's hand. "Thank you, Dad. That means a lot to me."

We finish our meal, the atmosphere lighter than before. My dad stands up, looking a bit more at ease. "I should get back to work. But we should do this again sometime."

"I'd like that," I say, giving him a hug. "Thanks for coming. And for trying."

He hugs me back, a bit awkwardly but with genuine affection. "Take care, Elena. And you too, Toby."

"Thank you, sir," Toby replies, shaking my dad's hand.

As my dad leaves, I turn to Toby, feeling a sense of hope and optimism. "That went better than I expected."

Toby smiles, wrapping an arm around my shoulders. "Yeah, it did. I think he's starting to come around."

"I hope so," I say, leaning into him. "It means a lot to me."

We spend the rest of the afternoon working, the earlier tension replaced with a sense of calm and accomplishment. By the time the library closes, I'm exhausted but happy. Toby helps me lock up, and we head home, the day's events replaying in my mind.

Any time I turn my neck slightly it hurts. "Toby, can you come here please?" I ask. I lean back on the couch waiting.

"What is it?" he looks down at me.

"I think I have a knot in my neck, can you please massage it?" '

"Let me grab the lotion, hold on," he walks out of the living room and comes back with a bottle of lavender-scented lotion. He sits beside me, placing a comforting hand on my shoulder. "Okay, just relax," he says softly, squeezing a generous amount of lotion into his palms.

I close my eyes, letting the soothing scent and Toby's gentle touch work their magic. "You know, we didn't really talk about the wedding date or the colors we want," I say, breaking the comfortable silence.

Toby pauses for a moment, his hands still. "Right, we were so caught up in everything else. What date do you have in mind?"

I think for a second. "I want a winter wedding,"

Toby nods, his fingers working the tension out of my neck. "Sounds good, princess."

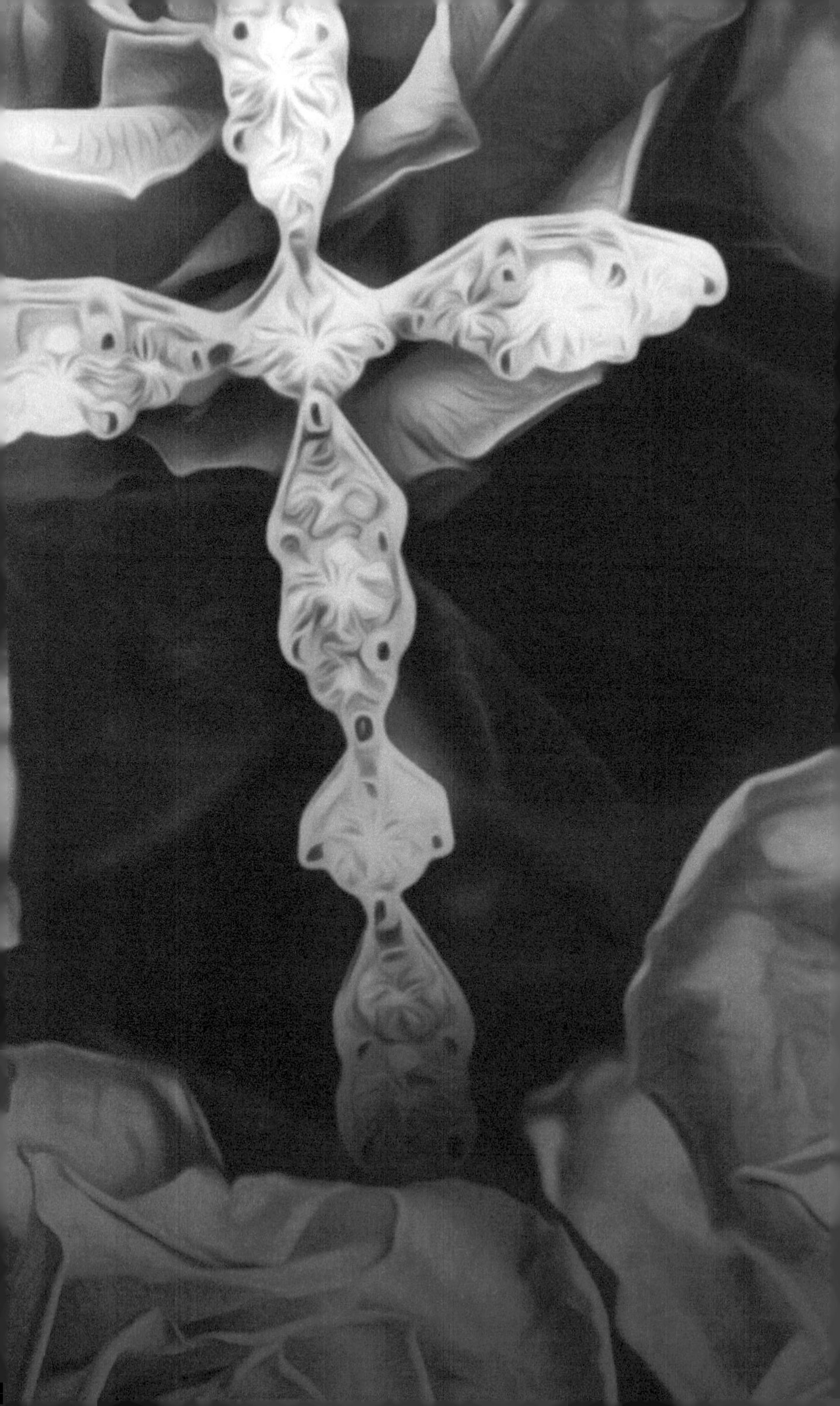

CHAPTER THIRTY-FIVE

Never in a million years did I ever think I'd fall in love so early in life. My christianity has been challenged since I met Toby, but for a little while before I began dating him, I became distant from my beliefs – well, at least I thought they were mine. All that I believed was what my dad believed, and while I still agree with most of the things he says, I know in my heart and soul that God led me on this path for a reason; to find a close relationship with him that means more than just words from another human.

This cross necklace I clasp around my neck every morning is my symbol. It's who I am. I understand I've committed sin, and I am wrong for doing so, but that is between me and God, not me and anyone on earth. My faith may have become rocky a few months ago, but now it's smooth like butter, and I'm happy. I'm happy with my relationship with God, myself, and Toby. I barely saw him growing up, but I see him now. I've overlooked his past, and I love him for who he is. I know he loves me too.

Toby is patient and kind, always willing to listen to my thoughts and concerns, even when they stem from my faith. He doesn't always understand my beliefs, but he respects them, and that means the world to me.

At church, things have changed too. Toby has decided to start coming with me more, and although it's new for him, he's embraced it with an open heart. Seeing him there, genuinely participating, brings a warmth to my soul that I can't quite put into words. It's like witnessing a miracle, a tangible sign that we're meant to be on this journey together.

My friends have noticed the change in me. Jenny, Rose, and Emily often comment on how much happier and more at peace I seem.

I pull my hair up into a high ponytail. As always, keeping myself looking neat every day. Placing my hairbrush down to pick up my phone, I scroll through my texts and send Christian a message.

ME

Hey twin, miss you, what are you doing right now?

I haven't really heard from him much after mom told us about the affair and I worry about him because of his drinking problem.

I wait anxiously for a reply, my mind racing with thoughts of how he might be coping. The seconds feel like hours as I stare at the screen, hoping to see those three little dots indicating he's typing.

Finally, my phone buzzes with a new message.

CHRISTIAN

Hey sis, I'm just out for a walk. Needed some fresh air. Miss you too. Let's catch up soon.

His reply brings a smile to my face. I put my phone into my jacket pocket and walk into the living room to grab my keys. I've not done any shopping since I moved in with Toby and I'd like to buy some new clothes.

Sipping my coffee and shifting through the clothes piece by piece, someone taps me on the shoulder. I turn around to see a woman about my age, brunette, bright red lipstick and a very pretty crop top and jeans.

Sipping my coffee and shifting through the clothes piece by piece, someone taps me on the shoulder. I turn around to see a woman about my age, brunette, bright red lipstick, and a very pretty crop top and jeans. Her eyes are intense, almost as if she's searching for something.

"Excuse me," she says, her voice steady but with a hint of urgency. "Are you... by any chance, Christian's sister?"

My heart skips a beat. How does she know Christian? And why is she asking about him? How does she know what I look like? I nod slowly, trying to keep my composure.

"Yes, I am. Do you know him?" I ask, my curiosity piqued.

She takes a deep breath, glancing around as if to make sure no one else is listening. "I'm Joanna. We met at a bar a couple nights ago. I think he might be in trouble. He mentioned something about an affair and seemed really upset. I tried to help, but he just... disappeared."

Christian never mentioned meeting anyone named Joanna. And if he's in trouble, why didn't he come to me?

"Thank you, Joanna. May I ask how you know of me?"

"I found you online while searching for his

profile. I was hoping to check in on him. Didn't think I'd run into you, so I figured I'd ask."

"Well, I'm glad you did. Christian's been going through a lot lately, and I'm really worried about him."

Her expression softens. "I could tell he was struggling."

"Thank you, I will be talking with him soon."

She nods and proceeds to walk away. That was...weird.

I grab my phone and call Christian, but it goes straight to voice mail. I hover over the keyboard and text him instead,

ME

Hey, lunch, 1pm?

CHRISTIAN

Sure, where?

ME

The Olive

Walking inside the restaurant I see my brother sitting at a booth near a window. His hair looks a mess, and his clothes are dirty.

"Christian? What is going on?" I ask as I sit in the seat across from him.

His eyes were red and bloodshot, his face streaked with tears, and his lip appeared bruised. "I have so much on my plate, I feel overwhelmed and lost."

"Please come live with me at the apartment, I want to help you."

"I can't do that Elena."

"Why? I'm your sister."

"I can't be around people that remind me of what it was like at our parents." he snaps.

The anger and rage he's feeling is valid, but I don't understand why he is ruining his life over this.

"Christian, you are so much better than this, I love you so much." I stretch out my hands towards him, and after a moment of hesitation, he reaches out and takes them in his own. "I will help you, I always will, I just need you to want it for yourself."

"I want help Elena, but I'm not living with you okay?" he says.

I give a frown and nod. "I understand."

"By the way, mom and dad invited us to dinner tonight," he says.

"What? When?" I ask.

"Last week."

"And I am hearing about it now?"

"Yes, they told me to tell you, but I wasn't sure if was going to go," he says.

"And are you?"

"I don't think so, but if I show up, I show up I guess,"

I adjust the collar of my blouse for the third time, staring nervously at my reflection in the hallway mirror. Toby's footsteps approach from behind, and he places a reassuring hand on my shoulder.

"Where are you, Christian?" I mutter under my breath, the anxiety twisting in my gut. It's been a few hours since I met with him.

"Relax, Elena," Toby says, his voice soft and soothing. He gives me a gentle smile. "It's just dinner."

"I know, but this is the first time Dad has invited us over."

He turns me around and places his finger under my chin looking into my eyes. "I love you, it'll all be okay."

I nod and take a deep breath. "Okay, let's get this over with."

As we walk to the front door of my childhood home, I take a deep breath, the familiar scent of pine trees in the evening air. I silently pray for a peaceful evening. The doorbell echoes through the quiet neighborhood, and within moments, the door swings open to reveal my father, a warm smile on his face.

"Elena, Toby, come in!" Dad greets us with enthusiasm. "It's so good to see you both."

I exchange a surprised glance with Toby before stepping inside. The familiar scent of home-cooked meals fills the air, rich and comforting, and the dining room table is set with an impressive spread of dishes.

He's never made dinner like this in my entire life.

"Wow, Dad, this looks amazing," I say, my voice tinged with genuine surprise.

"Thank you, sweetheart," Dad replies, guiding us to our seats. "I wanted tonight to be special."

"Where is Mom?" I ask, glancing around the room.

He sets a bottle of sparkling water on the table, his expression tightening slightly. "She won't be joining us tonight."

"Oh," I say, my thoughts racing. *I wonder why.* He cheats on her without any visible remorse or concern.

"Have you heard from your brother?" he asks while sitting down.

"No, I'm sorry," I say.

He breathes out a heavy sigh. "Let's say grace, shall we?" He gestures for me and Toby to grab his hands. We do, and I close my eyes.

"Dear Heavenly Father, I want to thank you for providing us this food on the table and bringing my daughter and her fiancé for dinner." His grip on my hands tightens a bit. "Father, I ask that you keep an eye on my son and my wife and make sure they are safe. Thank you, Father. Amen."

"Amen." Toby and I say.

We release hands, the echo of the prayer hanging in the air, and I take a deep breath, trying to steady my racing thoughts. What's his game? Why the sudden change in him about Toby and me?

It feels almost surreal, like I've stepped into a scene from a different life—a life where everything is normal, where the past doesn't loom over us like a dark cloud.

Toby squeezes my hand gently. His touch grounds me, and I focus on the moment. I glance at him, his blue eyes looking into mine. He's here with me, and that's all that matters.

"Let's eat," Dad says, breaking the silence. His voice is cheerful, but the tension in his posture betrays him. I take a bite of the roast chicken, its flavors rich and comforting, and for a moment, the noise of my thoughts quiet down.

"So, Elena," Dad begins, "Tell me about the wedding plans. Have you decided on a date yet?"

Mom must've told him about it.

"Uh, yes, we're thinking December thirteenth. We're thinking of an indoor ceremony. It feels right, you know, with the winter setting."

"Sounds great. Your mother and I had a winter wedding too. It was very special."

I blink, the mention of Mom catching me off guard. I push the thought aside, focusing on the present. "That's great, Dad." I wish he didn't bring it up because after what Mom has told me about him, anger is boiling in my blood.

He chuckles softly. "It was a long time ago. But I still remember it like it was yesterday."

He wipes his mouth with a paper towel. "So, toby, you're teaching huh? That's a noble profession. What made you choose that path?"

"I've always had a passion for helping others and making a difference. Working with kids and seeing them learn and grow—it's great to see."

"And your plans for the future?" he asks toby.

"Well, I'm working towards getting my teaching certification. Eventually, I'd like to teach at a high school or maybe even college level. It's a long road, but it's something I'm passionate about."

The conversation flows smoothly through the rest of dinner, with Toby and Dad exchanging stories and laughter that feels almost genuine. Despite the existing tension, the evening continues without any problems.

As the last bite is taken, I gather my thoughts and finally find the courage to speak my mind. "Thank you for dinner, Dad. It was really nice."

A subtle smile plays on his lips as he nods in agreement. "I'm glad you enjoyed it, sweetheart."

When we finish eating, Toby and I both stand up and gather our belongings together. "We should get going," I say, trying to keep my voice steady. "It's getting late."

Dad walks us to the door. "Take care, you two. Drive safe."

"Thanks, Dad," I reply, giving him a brief hug. Toby shakes his hand, and we step outside into the cool night air. The scent of pine trees and the faint scent of Dad's cooking still clings to my clothes, grounding me in the present moment even as my thoughts swirl.

In the truck, Toby starts the engine, and the low rumble vibrates through my seat. The headlights cut through the darkness, illuminating the path ahead, but my mind is lost in the evening's events.

"Are you okay?" Toby asks, glancing over at me as we pull into his apartment complex.

I nod, but he can see right through me. "Just... a lot to process."

He reaches over, taking my hand in his. The warmth of his touch contrasts with the cool leather of the seat. "I know. Let's get inside and relax, okay?"

We make our way up to his apartment, and as soon as we step inside, Toby guides me to the couch.

"Wait here," he says softly, disappearing into the bathroom.

A few minutes later, I hear the sound of running water, and he returns to the living room, a gentle smile on his face. "I ran you a hot bubble bath. I thought it might help you unwind."

He helps me to my feet and leads me to the bathroom, where the tub is filled with warm, fragrant bubbles. The scent of vanilla rises with the steam, instantly soothing my frazzled nerves. My silk pink pajamas are neatly folded on the counter, alongside fresh, fluffy towels.

"I'll give you some privacy," he says, kissing my forehead. "Take your time."

I undress myself, sink into the hot water, close my eyes and let the stress of the evening melt away. The warmth envelops me, the gentle crackle of bubbles and the heat from the vent calms me. I breathe in deeply, the scent of the bath soothing my mind, and feel the tension in my muscles begin to ease.

After my bath, I slip into the cozy pajamas and find Toby waiting for me in the living room, a cup of tea in his hands.

"Feeling better?" he asks.

"Much better," I say, taking the tea and sitting beside him. The warmth of the cup seeps into my hands, grounding me in the moment. "Thank you. For everything."

He wraps his arm around me, pulling me close. His body radiates warmth. "Always, Elena. I'm here for you, no matter what."

As Toby and I enjoy a quiet evening, wrapped in each other's arms.

I break the silence, my voice soft. "We haven't told your mom about the engagement yet. Maybe we should invite her to dinner or lunch?"

He shifts slightly, a thoughtful look crossing his face. "Yeah, I was thinking about that too. It feels like the right time. I think she'll be really happy for us."

I nod, the warmth of the tea in my hands a small comfort. "I know she will. She's always been so supportive and kind. I just want to make sure we do it in a way that feels special."

Toby smiles, his eyes softening. "How about we tell her after dinner with her? When we're all relaxed and just talking. Maybe we can make it a toast or something."

"That sounds perfect," I reply, a small smile tugging at my lips. "I love you,"

He pulls me into a kiss.

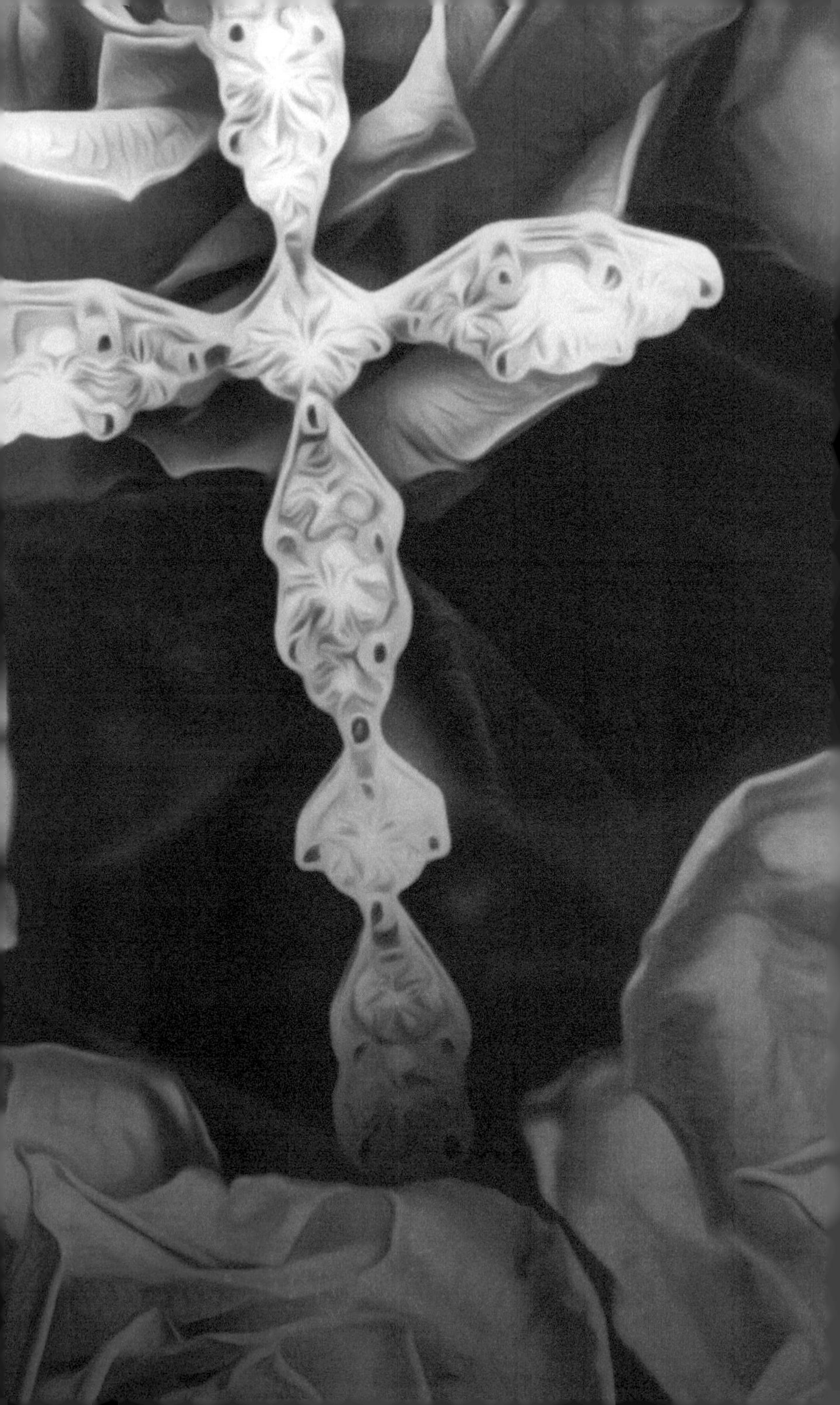

CHAPTER THIRTY-SIX

The library's been pretty chill this morning, so I've been able to handle everything on my own without getting super busy. As I'm stacking a few returned books, I spot my brother, Christian, walking in with a huge smile plastered on his face. Curiosity piqued, I wonder what made him so happy.

"Hey, Elena!" he says, striding over to me.

"Hey, what's up with you?" I ask, grinning back, but a bit confused. Just yesterday, I saw him at the Olive Restaurant looking really upset.

"I got my own place!" he announces.

"Wait, seriously? I thought you were having a rough time," I say, taken aback.

"Yeah, things turned around fast," he replies, still beaming.

"That's awesome, Christian!" I pull him into a hug, my confusion melting into happiness for him. "When do you move in?"

"Next weekend. I can't wait for you to see it," he replies, practically glowing with excitement.

"I'm so happy for you. This is huge!" I say, feeling proud of him. "But, um, how can you afford it? You don't have a job, and rent's not cheap."

Christian's grin fades a little. "Yeah, about that... Mom gave me some starting money. She didn't want Dad to know, so it's just between us."

I blink in surprise. "Seriously? I mean, I get it, but wow. That's kind of a big deal."

"Yeah, it is," he says, his smile returning. "She knew how much I needed a break, and she didn't want Dad's stuff to hold me back."

"Well, I guess that's one way to get things moving," I say, chuckling. "I'm really glad you're getting this chance."

"Thanks. It means a lot," he says, giving me another hug. "I can't wait for you to see the place. It's not much, but it's mine."

"All that matters is that you're happy."

"I'm going to head back to my buddies, I'll see you later." he says.

"See you!"

I'm so glad to see my brother happy.

I love being home. The scent of lavender detergent fills the air as I sort through the clothes, the soft hum of the washer making a comforting background noise. Toby is in the other room, lost in one of his video games. I can hear the faint sounds of gunfire and distant explosions coming from the living room. I chuckle to myself as I fold a pile of towels. The washing machine's spin cycle comes to an end, and I open the lid, taking out the clean clothes that smell like lavender after a refreshing wash.

"Do you want any snacks, honey?" I ask.

He doesn't even look up from his controller when he responds, "Sure."

Humming softly, I walk into the kitchen. I grab two bottles of soda from the door and dip from the shelf, before heading into the living room, I also grab a thing of chips.

"Here you go," I say, setting everything on the coffee table beside him before sitting on the couch next to him. The cushions softly muffle my movements as I lean against the armrest and take a sip from my soda. The cold liquid goes down smoothly as I listen to the intense action noises coming from his game. Gunshots, explosions, alarms blaring, it all melds into one big mix of sound effects. He glances at me briefly between levels but doesn't pause his game.

I can't help but admire the way his brow furrows in concentration, and the way his hands move swiftly over the controller. As I sit down next to him, I can't resist letting my hand rest on his thigh. He glances over at me, and I give him a sly smile.

Leaning in, I whisper in his ear, "Do you want to take a break from the game?" He hesitates for a moment before setting down the controller. I can feel the heat radiating off his body as he turns towards me.

He leans in to kiss me. Our tongues dance together as we deepen the kiss. I run my hands up his chest, feeling his muscles tense beneath my touch. He let out a low groan as I trace my fingers over his nipples. He pulls me closer, his hands moving to my hips, and he lifts me up onto his lap. I can feel his hardness pressed against me, and I grind down onto him and his hands move to cup my ass. He trails his fingers over the seam of my jeans, and I can feel myself getting wetter with each touch.

I reach down between us to undo his pants, freeing his hard cock. I wrap my hand around it, his cock hard and ready for me. I place my lips over him and begin bobbing my head up and down and his moans grow louder. He stops me and reaches up to undo my pants, I lift myself up slightly, allowing him to slide them down my hips.

He reaches up to pull my shirt over my head, revealing my bare breasts and leaning in to take one of my nipples in his mouth, sucking and biting gently. I arch my back, pushing myself further into his mouth. He moved his hand between my legs, sliding a finger inside me.

I can feel myself getting closer to the edge, and I move my hips in time with his hand. He moves his other hand to my clit, rubbing small circles as he continues to finger me. My breath hitches as I feel the orgasm building. I let out a cry as I came, my body convulsing around his fingers.

His strong arms wrap around my body, lifting me off the couch with ease. He carries me into our room. He lays me down on the bed, positioning himself at my entrance. I can feel the head of his thick, pulsing cock pressing against my wetness, teasing me with what's to come.

I arch my hips toward him, inviting him in. I'm already soaked at this point. He slides inside me effortlessly, filling me completely. I let out a deep moan, savoring the feeling of his hardness inside me. He starts to thrust into me, hard and fast, each stroke hitting me in just the right spot. My body responds to his movements, my hips rising to meet him. I wrap my legs around his waist, pulling him closer, desperate for more.

His hands roam my body, exploring every inch of me. He squeezes my breasts, pinching my nipples between his fingers. The pleasure is almost too much to bear.

"Oh my god, yes!" I cry out, my voice hoarse with desire.

"Clench on me, princess!" he growls, flipping me over onto all fours. He grips my hair, pulling my head back as he continues to thrust into me. I moan as waves of pleasure wash over me, leaving me feeling warm and flushed. I can feel my orgasm building, my body quivering with anticipation.

He reaches around, his fingers finding my clit. He rubs it in circles, sending shockwaves of pleasure through my body. I can feel my cum building, my pussy clenching around his hard cock.

Finally, we both reach our peak, our bodies shaking with pleasure. He pulls out, and I can feel his hot cum leaking onto my ass cheek.

He collapses beside me. I turn my head to look at him, a satisfied smile playing on my lips. He returns the smile, brushing a strand of hair away from my face.

"That was amazing." he says.

I nod in agreement, still basking in the after-glow of our lovemaking. "It certainly was."

He wraps his arm around me, pulling me close. I snuggle into his embrace, feeling safe and loved in his arms.

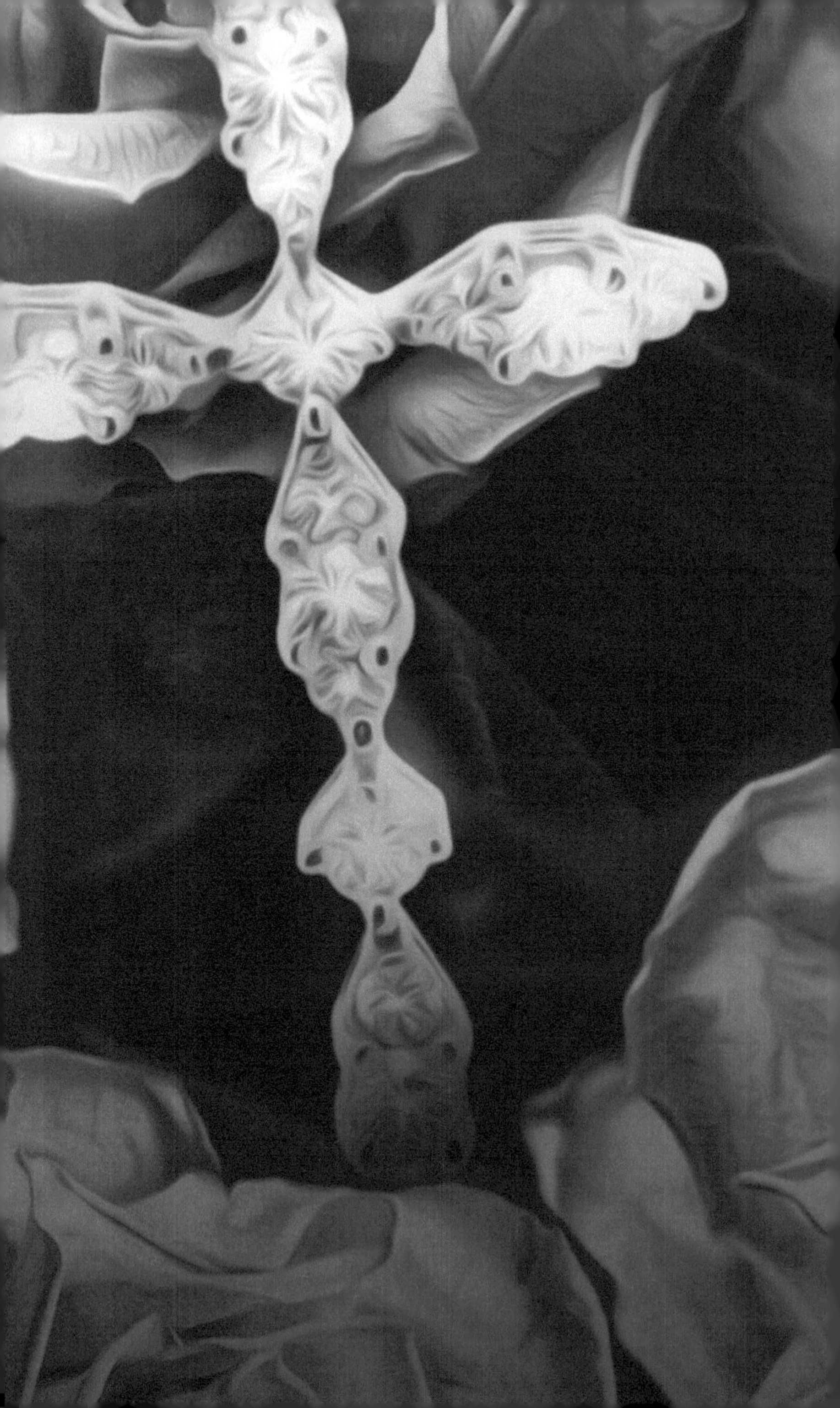

CHAPTER THIRTY-SEVEN

I walk by the little cafe and wonder why Mrs. Thompson isn't here, it's odd as I've not seen her in a while. The library is pretty busy today, which is good keeps me going. I am hoping to see Lindsay today so I can invite her over for dinner. I'm nervous telling her about me and her son's engagement, but because she was happy with us together, I don't think she'd be against us getting married.

I scan the busy room for Lindsay, and I see her sitting at a table with a stack of books. "Hey Lindsay, how are you today?"

Lindsay looks up from her book with a smile, "Oh, hello there! I'm doing well, just catching up on some reading. What's going on with you?"

"I was actually hoping to talk to you about

something," I say. "Would you be free for dinner tonight?"

Lindsay's eyes widen and a smile appears on her face as she sets her book down. "Of course, I'd love to join you for dinner!"

"Awesome, come by around 6?" I ask.

"Yes, what are you making?"

"Chicken Alfredo."

"Oh, I haven't had that in a long time!" she exclaims.

"Me either, toby is making it too!"

"Really? I've never seen the kid cook!"

I laugh and begin stocking some bookmarks.

I'm at the kitchen counter, my phone pressed between my ear and shoulder as I chop vegetables for dinner. Lindsay's excitement crackles through the phone.

"It's going to be a wonderful evening, Elena. I can't wait to see you both," she says warmly.

"We're looking forward to it too, Lindsay. See you at six," I reply, ending the call with a smile.

I set my phone down and glance at the clock. It's 5:30 PM. Toby is in the kitchen with me, stirring a pot of marinara sauce. The aroma of tomatoes, garlic, and herbs fills our small apartment, making my stomach rumble.

I move to the living room, fluffing the cushions on the couch and wiping down the coffee table. Just as I'm straightening the last cushion, the doorbell rings.

"I'll get it!" Toby calls, wiping his hands on a dish towel as he heads to the door.

I join him in the hallway as he opens the door. Lindsay stands there with a bright smile, a bottle of sparkling apple cider in one hand and a bowl of fruit salad in the other.

"Welcome, Lindsay!" I greet her with a hug. "Come in, come in."

She steps inside, her eyes twinkling as she takes in our cozy apartment. "It smells amazing in here. You two have really outdone yourselves."

"Thank you," Toby says, taking the fruit salad and cider from her. "Dinner's almost ready. Why don't you make yourself comfortable?"

I lead Lindsay to the dining table, and we chat about our week while Toby puts the finishing touches on dinner. Soon, we're all seated.

Halfway through the meal, I glance at Toby, who gives me an encouraging nod. Taking a deep breath, I turn to Lindsay.

"There's something we wanted to share with you," I begin, trying to steady my voice despite the fluttering in my chest. I show my hand with the ring on my finger, "Toby and I are engaged!"

Lindsay's eyes widen with delight, and she lets out a joyful laugh. "Oh, that's wonderful news! I'm so happy for both of you.

"Thank you mom."

"When is the wedding?" she asks.

"December thirteenth." I say.

"Winter wedding, I like it." she says taking a bite of her food. "You know, Toby was always a bit of a handful when he was younger,"

"Oh really?" I say, raising an eyebrow and looking at Toby.

"Yes," Lindsay continues, "There was this one time when he decided it would be a good idea to climb the tallest tree in our yard. He got stuck up there for hours until the fire department had to come and get him down."

I burst out laughing, picturing a younger Toby dangling from a tree branch. "That sounds about right," I say, shaking my head with a grin. "Always aiming high."

Toby rolls his eyes, but he's smiling too. "What can I say? I've always been adventurous." he winks at me.

"And remember the time you tried to make a rocket in the backyard?" Lindsay adds, her laughter is infectious. "You almost set the whole yard on fire!"

I gasp, looking at Toby with wide eyes. "A rocket? Really?"

Toby shrugs, trying to look nonchalant. "I was just a kid with big dreams. Maybe a little too big," he admits with a sheepish grin.

Lindsay and I laugh.

Lindsay leans back in her chair, a fond smile on her face. "I'm so glad Toby found someone like you, Elena. You two are perfect for each other."

My heart swells with happiness. "Thank you, Lindsay. That means a lot."

Toby reaches for my hand under the table, giving it a gentle squeeze. "I couldn't agree more," he says softly, his eyes meeting mine with a warmth that makes my heart flutter.

As the evening winds down, we clear the table together, still chatting and laughing. Lindsay helps me rinse the dishes while Toby dries them and puts them away.

"Thank you for dinner," Lindsay says, hugging me tightly. "And congratulations again."

"Thank you, Lindsay," I reply, hugging her back. "We're so glad you could come tonight."

She reaches for a hug from Toby, and he hugs her back. "I'll see you at work Monday Elena!"

"Seeya!"

After she leaves, Toby and I collapse on the couch, exhausted but happy.

"That went well," I say, leaning my head on his shoulder.

"Yeah, it did," he agrees, wrapping his arm around me. "I told you she'd be thrilled."

I smile, feeling a deep sense of contentment. "I know. I'm just so happy everything's coming together. Also, I need to text the girls, I'd like to shop for the wedding since it's in a couple of months."

Grabbing my phone to text the girls,

ME

Hey, wedding and bridesmaid dress shopping Tuesday 2pm?

We sit there for a moment, basking in the afterglow of the evening.

"You know," I say, breaking the silence, "I never did get to hear the end of that rocket story."

Toby laughs, "Well, let's just say I learned a valuable lesson about fire safety that day."

I giggle, snuggling closer to him. "I bet you did."

My phone buzzes and I see the girls texted back yes.

As the night draws to a close, we turn on a movie and curl up together on the couch and fall asleep.

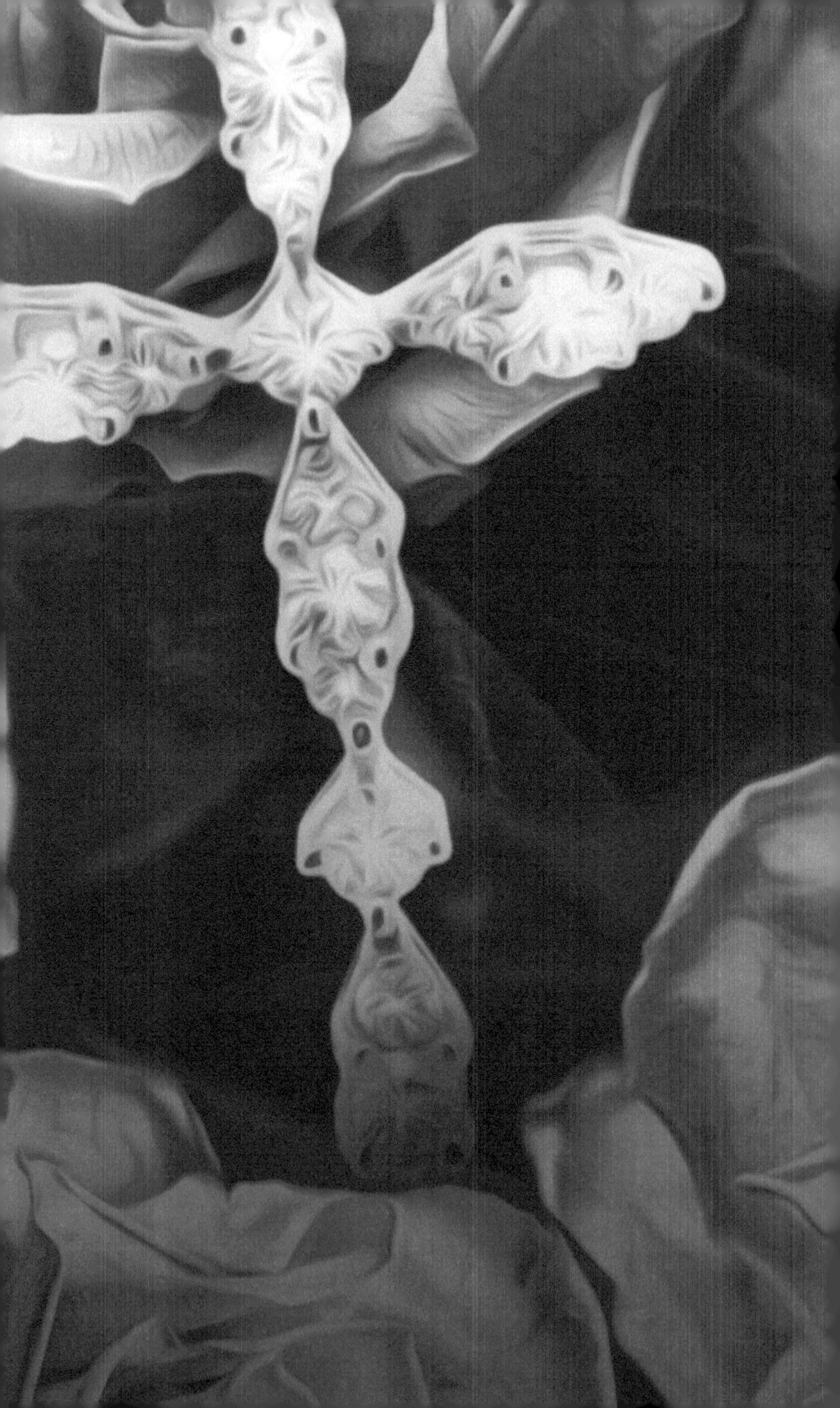

CHAPTER THIRTY-EIGHT

I push open the door to our usual café, the familiar smell of freshly brewed coffee and buttery pastries greeting me and making my mouth water. My friends are already seated at our go to corner table.

"Hey, ladies!" I call out, feeling a surge of warmth as they all look up with bright smiles.

"Hey there, bride-to-be!" Emily teases, playfully nudging me with her elbow. "Ready for some serious shopping?"

I nod, taking a seat next to Jenny. "Absolutely. But first, let's eat. I'm starving."

We place our orders and soon our table overflows with iced coffees, sandwiches, and salads.

As we finish our meals, I bring up the topic that has been on my mind all morning. "Okay girls, wedding dress shopping time! I was thinking we could start at that boutique downtown. What do you think?"

Jenny's eyes light up. "Oh yes, I've heard they have an amazing selection."

"I can't wait!" Rose exclaims, clapping her hands together. "Let's find you the perfect dress."

I step into the boutique. Soft lights hang above, casting a warm glow on racks of wedding gowns lining the walls. Each dress stuns more than the next, intricate details and elegant designs adorning them. The air fills with the sweet scent of fresh flowers, a hint of vanilla, and the pleasant scent of new fabric.

The fabric of the dresses feels soft to my touch, each delicately crafted with silky layers. The smooth, cool racks slide hangers effortlessly along them.

"Hi, I'm Hannah. Can I help you with anything?" Hannah says, her smile warm and welcoming. "Any styles you're particularly interested in?"

I take a deep breath, excitement and nerves mixing inside me. "I want something elegant, flowy, with sleeves."

Hannah nods and starts pulling dresses, each more beautiful than the last. I try on a few, each with its own charm, but none feel quite right. Then, Hannah brings out a sleeveless ball gown.

"That one is beautiful!" I say. I take it from her hands and step back into the dressing room.

My heart races and I place my hand over my chest, hovering over the front to the flowy part of the dress. The fabric shimmers under the lights, hugging my curves perfectly.

Stepping out of the fitting room, the girls' reactions are immediate.

"Oh my gosh, Elena," Emily breathes. "That's the one."

"You look stunning," Rose says, tears welling in her eyes.

"Don't cry! You'll make me cry!" I laugh. I can't stop smiling.

Turning to the mirror, my breath catches in my throat. The dress is perfect. I see myself walking down the aisle in this, marrying Toby.

"This is it," I whisper, joy rushing through me. "This is the one."

"Looks like it may need some adjustments at the bottom, but is this the one you want for sure?" Jenny asks.

"Yes. I'm positive."

"Okay!

We schedule alterations, and I can't stop

smiling as we leave the boutique. "Now onto bridesmaids dresses!"

We head to the next boutique. This store is just as charming as the first, with soft pastel walls and elegant chandeliers hanging from the ceiling. The racks are filled with dresses in every style and color imaginable. We quickly find the section of pale blue dresses and zero in on a stunning chiffon dress with a fitted bodice, V-neckline, and flowy skirt.

"Let's grab three of these and see how they look," I suggest, pulling three dresses off the rack and handing them to Emily, Jenny, and Rose.

Emily is the first to step out of the fitting room, wearing the pale blue dress. She twirls in front of the mirror, the skirt billowing around her. The soft chiffon fabric catches the light, creating an ethereal effect.

"Oh my gosh, Emily, you look like a fairy-tale princess!" I gush, clapping my hands in delight.

"Really? I feel so elegant in this," Emily says, her eyes sparkling. She runs her hands down the bodice, feeling the intricate lace details.

Jenny emerges next, the same dress hugging her curves perfectly. She strikes a pose, her confidence shining through. The pale blue color complements her complexion beautifully.

"This is so chic. I feel like I'm ready to walk the red carpet," Jenny says, laughing. She glances at herself in the mirror, smoothing down the fabric.

"You look stunning, Jenny. That dress was made for you," I say, grinning.

Rose steps out last, the dress fitting her like a glove. She smooths down the skirt, her cheeks flushing red.

"Rose, you look absolutely gorgeous," I say, my voice soft with admiration.

Rose blushes deeper, twirling to show off the dress. "Thanks, Elena. It's so comfortable too."

We stand together in front of the mirror, admiring the way the dresses look on each of them. The fitting room is a flurry of laughter and excited chatter as they discuss the dresses.

"Try walking around in it," I suggest. "See how it feels."

Emily takes a few steps, the dress flowing gracefully around her. "It's perfect. I can dance, move, and it still feels amazing."

Jenny nods in agreement. "I love how it feels. It's lightweight but looks so elegant."

Rose spins again, the skirt flaring out. "And the color is perfect for a winter wedding. It's like wearing a piece of the sky."

"This is it," I say, smiling as I look at them

standing together in the matching dresses. "You all look gorgeous."

"We love it too," Emily says, twirling one last time. "It's perfect for the wedding."

"Absolutely," Jenny agrees. "It's comfortable, stylish, and it complements your dress so well."

Rose nods, her eyes shining. "I can't wait for the big day."

I feel a surge of happiness as I hand over my card at the register. "Thank you so much, guys. I couldn't have done this without you."

"We're just glad we could be a part of it," Jenny says, hugging me tightly.

We leave the store, our arms filled with bags and our hearts filled with excitement. The sun is starting to dip in the sky, casting a warm glow over everything as we head back to the car.

By the time we reach everyone's homes, it's around 4 PM, and we're all tired but exhilarated.

"I can't believe we got so much done today," Jenny says, climbing out of the car.

"Me neither," I reply, feeling a sense of accomplishment. "Thank you all again. You're the best."

"Anytime, Elena," Rose says, waving as she heads inside. "See you soon!"

I drop off the last of the girls and head back to the apartment and sigh. Today has been perfect, and I can't wait to share everything with Toby.

I unlock the door and step into the apartment,

greeted by a glow of candlelight that fills the dimly lit space. The air carries a delicate fragrance of roses, and romantic music plays softly in the background. Rose petals are scattered on the floor, leading a path to the dining table where Toby stands, a proud smile on his face as he holds a bouquet of white flowers.

"Surprise, beautiful," he says, his eyes sparkling with affection.

I gasp, my heart swelling with love and appreciation for the effort he's put into this evening. "Toby, this is amazing. Thank you."

He steps closer, handing me the bouquet. "You deserve every bit of it." he leans in for a kiss, his soft lips touching mine.

I set the flowers in a vase I find underneath the sink, the fresh scent of the blooms filling the room. Toby leads me to the table where plates of spaghetti are waiting, steam rising in wisps from the dishes.

"I love you." I whisper.

"I love you too." he says.

We sit down together, Toby pulling out my chair like a gentleman. "I hope you're hungry."

"I am," I reply, smiling as I pick up my fork. "It smells delicious."

We eat in a comfortable silence, the only sound being made is our forks hitting the place when scooping up some noodles.

"This is beyond special," I say, breaking the silence and taking another bite of the perfectly cooked spaghetti. The rich, savory sauce bursts with flavor, complementing the tender pasta. "It's perfect."

After dinner, we move to the bedroom, the soft blankets enveloping us as we settle in to watch a movie. He wraps his arm around me, pulling me closer.

My pulse races as his hands glide over my curves, tracing my hips and caressing my breasts. He cups my them, teasing my nipples with his thumbs until a soft moan escapes my lips.

Leaning in, he captures my mouth in a searing kiss, his tongue plunging deep to explore every inch. His cock presses against me, straining against his pants. I slip my hand inside his waistband, wrapping my fingers around his rigid shaft. He lets out a low groan as I begin stroking him, teasing the sensitive tip with my thumb.

He pulls from my mouth, trailing kisses down my neck and across my collarbone before taking my nipple between his lips. He sucks and flicks until I writhe beneath him. Wetness pools between my thighs, my body aching for release.

His fingers glide inside me as he slips his hand between my legs, feather-light touches teasing my clit. I buck my hips, desperate for more, and he chuckles low and dirty, sending shivers down my spine.

He tugs off my pants, exposing my bare, soaked pussy. His blue, lustful eyes rake over me before he lowers his head, running his tongue along my slit. I cry out as pleasure washes over me. He kisses my lips, flicking my clit with his tongue, until I'm on the brink.

Curling two fingers inside me, he hits my g-spot. My body shakes as wave after wave of pleasure crashes over me.

His fingers begin to move, hitting my g-spot with each pump. The sensation is overwhelming, a tidal wave of pleasure that crashes over me, leaving me weak and trembling. I cry out, my voice hoarse and desperate as I beg for more.

He obliges, quickening his pace as he watches me squirm beneath him.

"Release for me princess," He groans in satisfaction as he feels my muscles clench around his fingers, urging him deeper.

I can feel myself building towards release, my body vibrating with anticipation. My hips buckle wildly, meeting each of his thrusts with equal fervor. He leans down to kiss me, his tongue mimicking the movements of his fingers as they worked their magic.

"Oh my god!" I come apart, my body convulses as wave after wave of pleasure washes over me. He doesn't stop, continuing to pump his fingers inside me as I ride out the orgasm.

As he teasingly licks his fingers clean, heart races as he slowly stands up, his rock-hard cock standing tall and proud. He steps back for a moment to remove his pants, revealing his throbbing shaft.

I reach out eagerly, grasping him in my hand and stroking up and down the length of his shaft. He's thick and hard, leaking pre-cum that glistens in the dim light. He stands me up to my feel with a growl, tugging me close once again, pinning me against the wall.

He kisses me deeply as he nestles between my legs, positioning his cock. With one thrust, he's inside me, filling me up completely.

He starts to move in slow sensual strokes that set fire to my insides. His hips met mine with thunderous rhythm as he drives deeper each time. I scream in pleasure, my hands pressing against the wall along with the front of my body.

His breath quickens against my ear as he nips at my lobe playfully before kissing it softly. "That's my princess," he murmurs huskily while thrusting faster, harder inside me now.

I moan into his ear in response to the pleasure coursing through my body. It feels so good having him buried within me like this - there was no other feeling quite like it in all the world.

I feel a rush of warmth spread through me, and he keeps going as I clench onto him before he pulls out and a hot liquid spills onto my thigh. I roll my eyes back, trying to catch my breath.

"You're so hot princess," he says as he wipes me clean with a hand towel.

I fall onto the bed, legs shaky.

"You wore me out." I say.

"Yeah?" he laughs cleaning himself off before laying with me.

"I love you," he whispers, placing his arm around me.

"I love you, too."

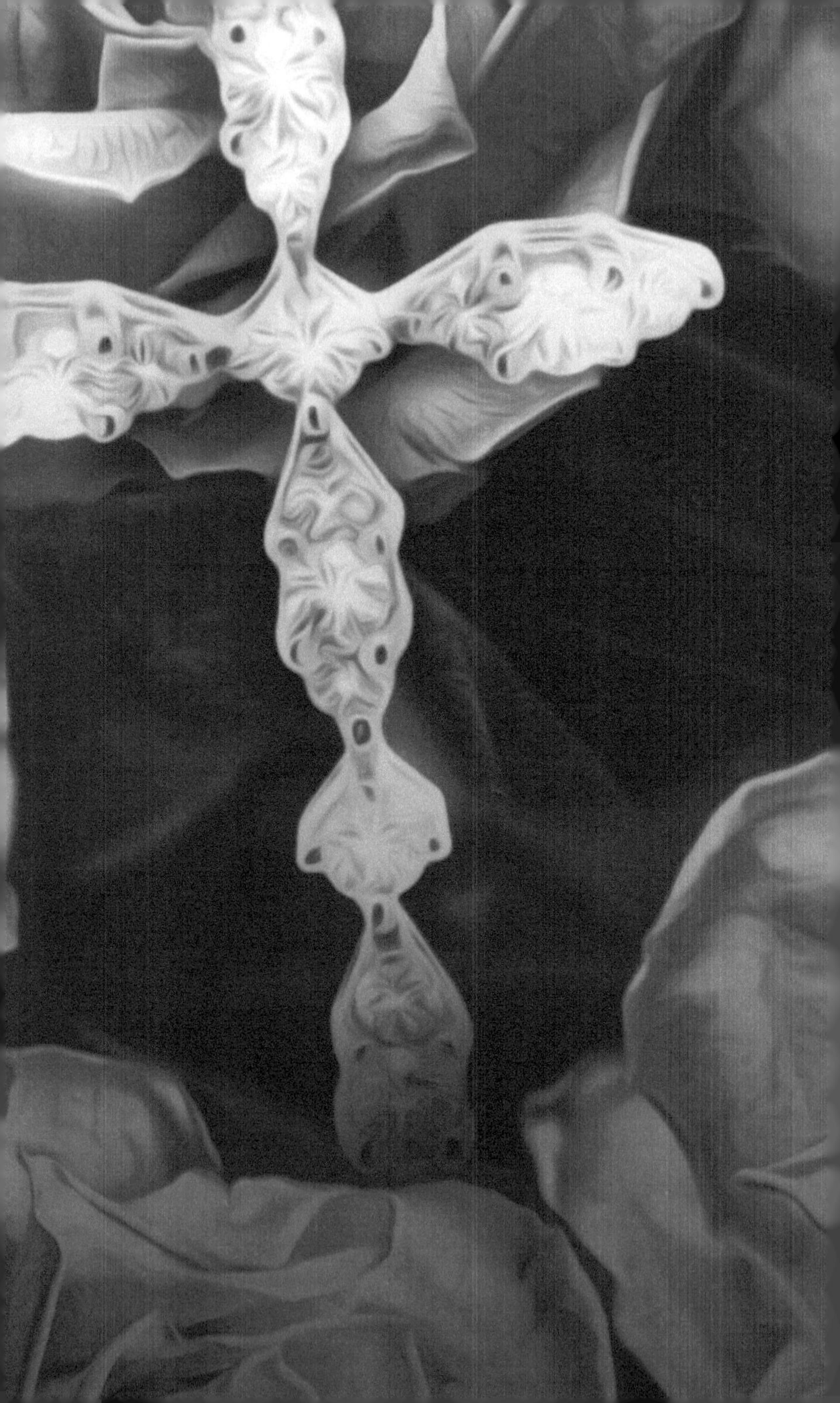

CHAPTER THIRTY-NINE

The weekend is finally here, and I'm excited to visit Christian's new place. I chop up the tomatoes, their fresh, tangy scent filling the kitchen. I place the leftovers into a container, along with the crisp lettuce, ready for our lunch. As I finish preparing, a mix of excitement and concern stirs within me. Christian's been barely sober for a week, but he's making progress. I want to support him in every way I can. Our dad still doesn't know that Mom used his old college funds to help Christian get this place—something for another day.

I grab my bag and head out, the cold air warm against my skin as I walk to my car. The drive to Christian's new apartment is short. When I arrive, I see him standing outside, waiting for me. He looks healthier than I've seen him in a long time—more himself.

"Hey, you!" I call out as I step out of the car, waving.

He grins, running a hand through his messy hair. "Hey, sis! You made it!"

I pull him into a hug, "Of course I did. I wouldn't miss this for the world."

We head inside. The apartment is small but cozy, with a few mismatched pieces of furniture and framed photos on the walls. It feels like home already.

"This place looks great, Christian," I say, genuinely impressed. "You did a good job setting it up."

He shrugs, a bit sheepishly. "Thanks. Still getting the hang of living on my own, though."

I set the container of tomatoes and lettuce, ham and cheese and a thing of mayo on the counter. "Well, you're doing a pretty good job so far. And I brought some stuff for lunch."

His eyes light up. "Perfect. I'm starving. Let's get this feast going."

"So," I spread mayo on a slice of bread, "any crazy neighbors yet?"

He laughs, filling the small kitchen with warmth. "Oh, you have no idea. There's this guy across the hall who thinks he's a rockstar. He plays his guitar at the strangest times. Midnight, three in the morning, you name it."

"I thought you just moved in?" I ask.

"I was, but they called me and said I can move in earlier in the week."

I chuckle, adding lettuce to the sandwich. "Oh well good. Also, the neighbor sounds like a blast. Maybe you should join him, start a band."

"Oh, sure," he says, rolling his eyes. "We'll call it 'The Crazy's"

I laugh, the joy of being with him filling my heart. "I'd come to every show."

He grins, "You'd be our only fan."

We finish making our sandwiches and move to the small dining table by the window. We sit, and I take a bite of my sandwich, savoring the fresh, crisp flavors.

"This is really good," Christian says through a mouthful. "Thanks for bringing lunch."

"Anytime," I reply, enjoying the simplicity of the moment. "So, how's the job hunt going? Any leads?"

He nods, swallowing his bite. "Yeah, I've got a few leads. Hoping something pans out soon."

"That's good," I say, squeezing his hand across the table. "One step at a time."

His gaze shifts, a thoughtful expression crossing his face. "Speaking of steps, how's the wedding planning going?"

I smile, feeling a warmth at the thought of Toby. "It's coming along. We've picked out the dress, and I'm excited about it."

He raises an eyebrow, a playful smirk on his face. "Toby must be thrilled. I still remember how you used to tag along with us when we were kids, because didn't come over often."

I laugh, nodding. "Yeah, those were the days. Toby's been amazing through all of this. Even with Dad being difficult."

"Yeah, Dad's really tough on you about Toby. I get it, his beliefs make it hard for him to accept Toby, but it's not fair." he says.

I nod, feeling a knot form in my stomach. "I know. Dad's always had this rigid view of how things should be. Toby doesn't fit into that mold, but I think Dad's starting to come around, slowly."

His brows furrow. "It's about time. I mean, Toby's one of the most genuine people I know. If Dad could just see that."

I glance out the window, thinking about the complexities of our family dynamics. "Dad's strict because of his Christian beliefs. He's never been easy to talk to about anything that doesn't fit into his worldview. And then there's the affair. It's like everything is tangled together."

He nods, his expression somber. "Yeah, it's a mess. Mom's been doing a lot behind the scenes to keep things together, and I know she used my college funds to help me out. It's a lot for her to manage."

"Mom's been amazing," I agree, feeling a swell of gratitude for her efforts. "She's trying to keep the peace while dealing with everything else."

He leans back, a thoughtful look on his face. "And if dad's slowly coming around about you and Toby. I guess he's seeing how much you care about him, even if he's still struggling with it."

I smile, feeling hopeful. "Yeah, it's a small step, but it's something."

"If Toby ever gives you trouble, just let me know. I've got a few ideas for how to handle him."

I laugh, feeling a wave of relief, "I'll keep that in mind."

It feels good to see Christian like this—hopeful and determined. I know there's a long road ahead, but for now, I'm just happy to be here with him, sharing a moment of normalcy and support.

"You know, I think I'm going to be okay. Maybe even better than okay."

I smile, feeling the same hope. "Yeah, I think so too." I stand up and grab my purse.

"Would you and Toby come by sometime soon?"

"Nah, we don't like you," I joke.

He rolls his eyes and stands up giving me a hug. I

And for the first time in a long time, I believe it.

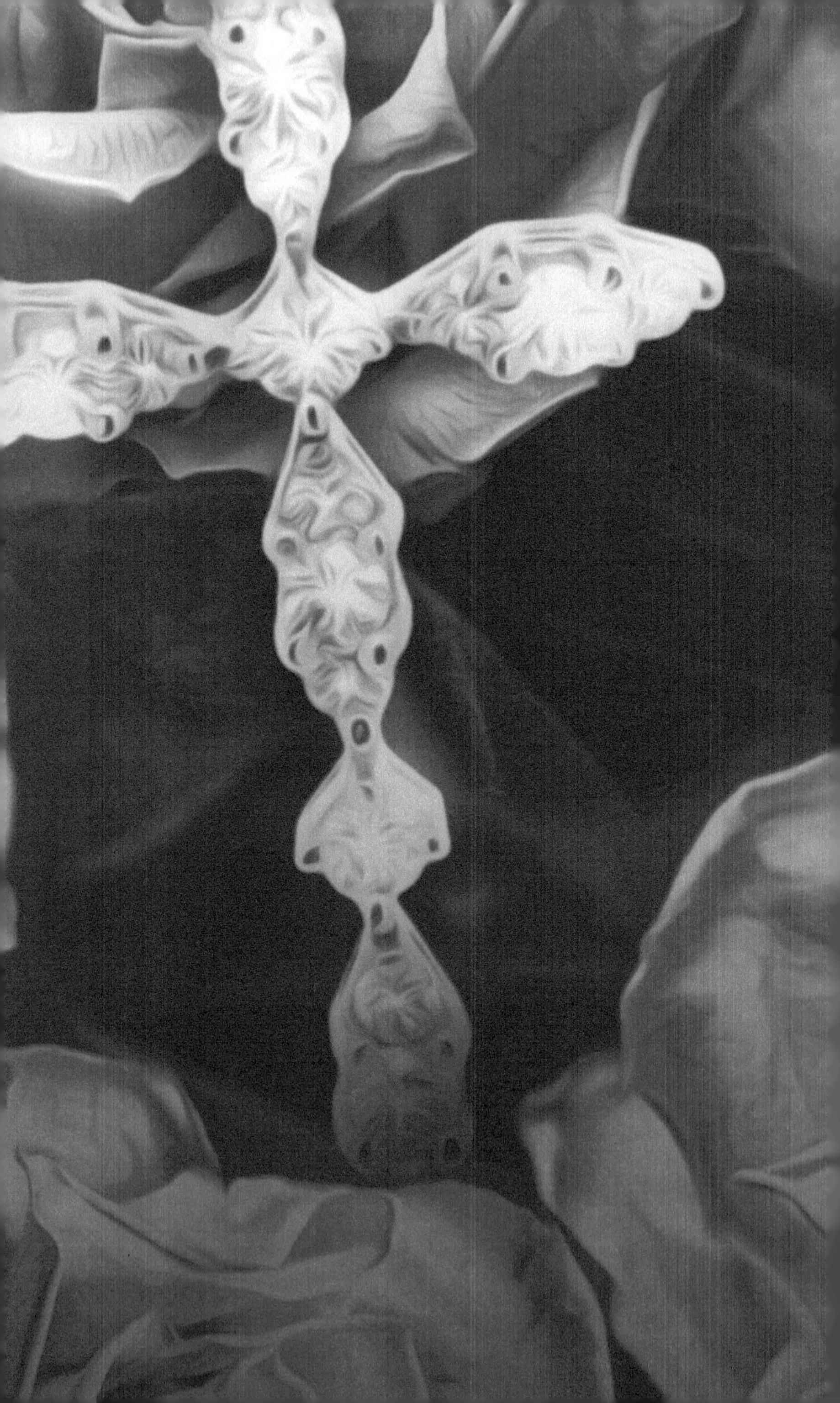

CHAPTER FORTY

It's been a week since I last saw Christian, and everything feels like it's settled into a predictable routine. The library has been quiet, and I've found some comfort in that. Toby's been grading papers at home more often, which has turned our apartment into a cozy, slightly cluttered, workspace.

Today, the sun is shining brightly as I head back to the apartment for lunch. I left my kiwi strawberry sparkling drink behind this morning, and the thought of it is the only thing keeping me going. But as I reach the door of my apartment, I spot an envelope on the doorstep. My heart skips a beat when I see my name written on it in my father's handwriting.

I bend down and pick it up, my fingers trembling as I hold it. The envelope feels heavier than usual, and I can't shake the nervous lump in my stomach. I unlock the door, the familiar click echoing through the hallway, and set my keys on the counter. My hands are shaky as I tear open the envelope.

Inside is a single sheet of paper, covered in my father's neat, but unmistakably firm handwriting. I unfold it with a sense of dread and start reading.

Dear my beautiful daughter,

I hope this letter finds you well. It is with a heavy heart that I must tell you I cannot attend your wedding. My beliefs and values have always guided my life, and it pains me to say that I cannot support a union with someone who does not share those values. I thought I could handle it and I'm sorry for misleading you.

It is not a matter of not loving you— my love for you is unconditional—but my principles will not allow me to be present at an event that goes against what I hold dear.

I am deeply sorry for any hurt this decision causes you. Please know that my absence is not a reflection of my feelings for you, but rather a consequence of my convictions. I wish you happiness and

*fulfillment in your marriage, but I cannot
be a part of it.*
> *With love,*
> *Dad*

A lump forms in my throat, and my eyes well up with tears. Each word feels like a stab to the heart. I can't believe my father is choosing his beliefs over me on such an important day. My hands start to tremble uncontrollably, and tears spill onto the letter, staining it.

I feel this crushing weight in my chest, an overwhelming mix of sadness and anger. I'm furious with him—how could he do this? How could he decide that his values are more important than being there for me? He lied. I thought he was coming around. I feel like my whole world is shifting beneath me, and I'm powerless to stop it.

I grab my phone, my fingers feeling numb as I text Lindsay.

ME

> Hi, Lindsay. I'm not feeling well today. I need to take the rest of the day off. I'll come back to work soon.

I stagger to the bathroom, the world around me feeling like a blur. I turn on the bathtub water twisting the knob hot, watching as steam begins to rise and fill the room with its gentle warmth.

I strip off my clothes and step into the tub, the hot water enveloping me like a hesitant hug. It's supposed to be comforting, but right now, it feels more like a temporary escape from the pain. I sink into the water, letting it surround me, and the tears come freely. The warmth of the bath is almost too much, as if it's trying to smother the ache in my heart.

The water swirls around me as I let my head fall back against the edge of the tub. My sobs echo softly in the bathroom, mingling with the sound of the water. I think about Toby, about how much I love him and how he's been my rock through all of this. My heart aches not just from my father's words but from the fear of what's to come.

The bathroom is quiet except for the gentle splashes and my occasional, ragged breaths. I close my eyes, trying to focus on the warmth of the bath, but it's hard to shake the feeling of rejection that clings to me. I try to remember the joy Toby brings into my life, but right now, the hurt is too raw.

As the bathwater cools around me, I sit there, feeling the weight of my father's absence and the uncertainty of the future. It's a moment of overwhelming sadness, a time to confront the reality of what it means to have my father choose his beliefs over being there for me.

And in the midst of it all, I try to find some comfort, some tiny bit of peace, even if it's just in the quiet, steam-filled space of the bathroom.

I'm jolted awake by the gentle creak of the bedroom door. The familiar sound of Toby's footsteps echoes softly as he enters the room. I feel the bed shift beside me as he sits down, his presence warm and comforting in the dim light. My eyes flutter open to find him looking at me with concern etched deeply on his face.

"Elena?" His voice is soft, filled with worry. "Are you okay?"

blink, disoriented and still clouded by sleep. I turn to face him, the weight of the day's tears making my eyes feel puffy. "Toby," I whisper, my voice barely audible. "What time is it?"

"4 o clock,"

"I didn't expect you home so soon."

He reaches out, brushing a strand of hair from my damp forehead. "I had a feeling something was wrong."

I sit up slowly, the soft rustle of the sheets around me almost too loud in the quiet of the room. The light from the bedside lamp casts soft light on

Toby's face, highlighting the lines of concern there. "It's just... my dad," I start, my voice breaking slightly. "He sent me a letter today. He's not coming to the wedding."

"What? Elena, I'm so sorry." He moves closer, pulling me into a warm embrace. His arms are strong around me, and I can feel the steady beat of his heart against my cheek. It's a comfort, a grounding force amidst the chaos.

"He said his beliefs won't allow him to support our marriage," I continue, my voice muffled against his chest. "I just... I don't understand. I thought he was slowly coming around."

He runs his fingers gently stroke my back, his touch soothing. "It's not your fault, Elena. Sometimes people cling so tightly to their beliefs that they can't see the love right in front of them. I know how much this hurts, and I wish I could make it better."

I take a shaky breath, trying to steady myself. "I just feel so alone right now. It's like he's saying that my happiness doesn't matter if it doesn't fit his ideals."

He shifts, tilting my chin up so that I meet his eyes. Toby's fingers run gently through my hair. "It's not your fault," he says softly. "Sometimes people get so caught up in their own beliefs that they can't see the love that's right in front of them. I know this hurts, but you're not alone."

I cling to him, sobbing into his chest. "But it feels like a part of me is missing. How can he choose his principles over being there for me on one of the most important days of my life?

He gently tilts my chin up, making me meet his eyes. "Because he's scared, Elena. It's easier for him to hold on to what he knows rather than embrace something that feels foreign. But that doesn't mean he's right, and it doesn't mean you have to accept this."

"I don't know what I'd do without you."

He wipes away the tears from my cheeks, his touch gentle. "You don't ever have to find out."

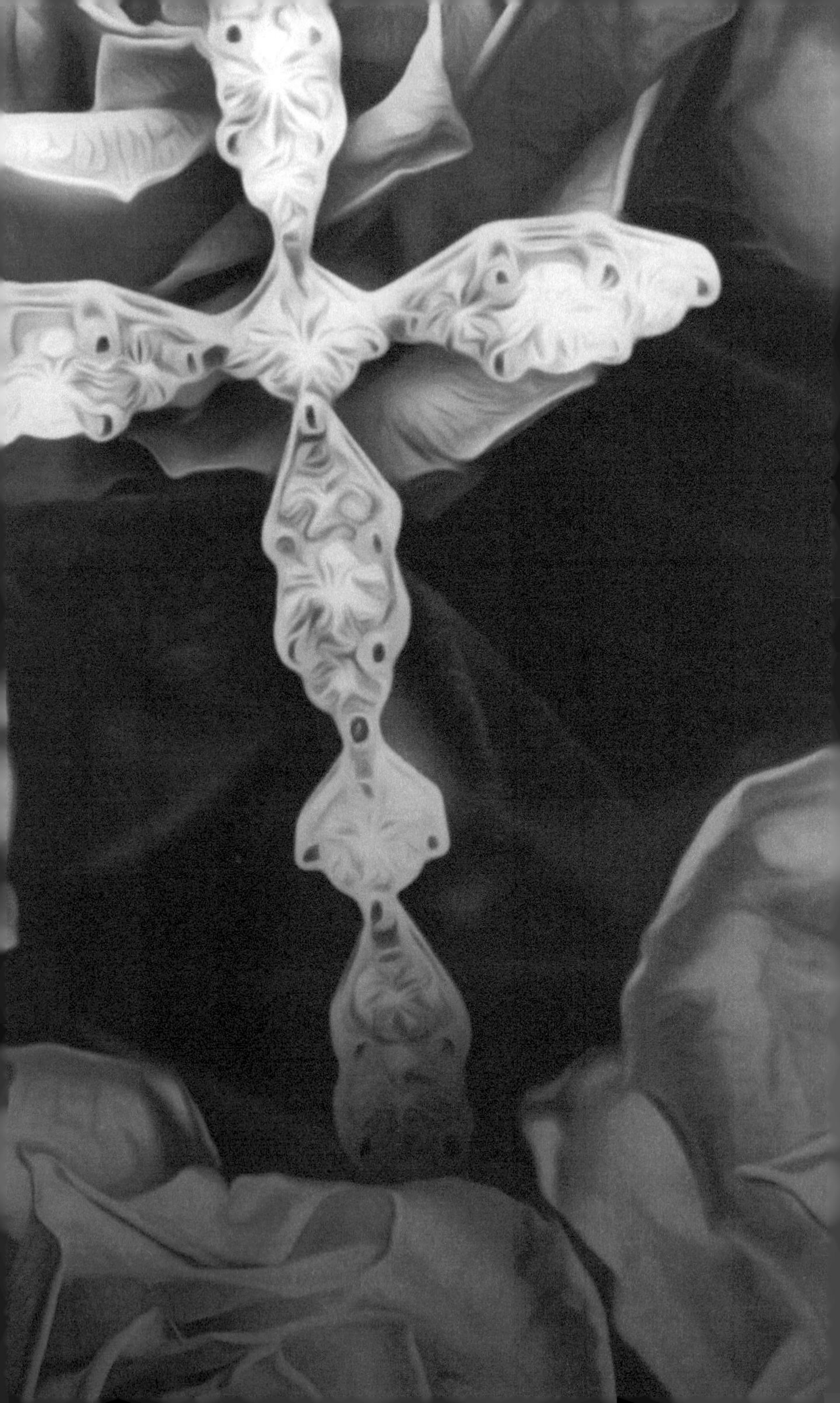

EPILOGUE

It's December. It's my wedding day and sunlight filters gently through the frosted windows, casting a soft glow over the chaos from last night's bachelorette party. I stretch and blink awake, taking in the sight of crumpled party hats, empty snack wraps, and empty bottles of sparking grape wine.

"Wow, what a night," Jenny's voice drifts over from where she's still sprawled across the couch, her hair in a messy halo of curls. "I can't believe today's finally here."

"Me neither!" Emily chimes in, her eyes still half-closed as she sits up, clutching a pillow to her chest. "Last night was amazing, but today is going to be even better."

Rose, already sitting up and pulling her robe tighter around herself, grins. "You're going to be the most beautiful bride. I can't wait to see Toby's face when he sees you."

I laugh softly, feeling a rush of warmth and gratitude for these amazing friends. "You guys were incredible last night. I couldn't have asked for a better group of people to celebrate with. And today..." I trail off.

I glance at the clock and then at my friends, still half-asleep but buzzing with excitement. "Today is our day. I can't believe it's here!"

Jenny stretches and yawns, then looks at me with a wide smile. "I bet Toby is just as excited as you are. Can you imagine him and Christian having their own bachelor party? They must've had a blast."

"I'm sure they did," I reply, laughing at the thought. "I can't wait to hear all about it. But for now, I'm just so ready for today. The dress, the vows, the whole shebang."

Emily gives me a playful nudge. "Well, let's make sure we don't keep you from your big day. We've got a lot to do, and you need to look your best. But first, let's have some breakfast and talk about how amazing today is going to be."

As we start moving around the apartment, the excitement is palpable. Jenny hops up and heads to the kitchen. "Let's have food before we get all glammed up," she suggests with a grin. "I think we all need some fuel for the day ahead."

Emily and Rose enthusiastically agree, and soon we're all rushing around, getting breakfast ready. The aroma of freshly brewed coffee fills the air, mixing with the scent of buttery pancakes and sizzling bacon.

Rose sets the table with a cheerful clatter, arranging plates and silverware.

Jenny joins us, balancing a stack of pancakes and a bowl of fresh fruit. "Today is the beginning of forever," she says, her voice warm with sincerity. "You're going to make the most stunning bride!"

We all gather around the table, digging into the food.

Emily waves a piece of bacon in front of me. "So, what do you think Toby's doing right now? Probably trying to keep himself from falling apart until he sees you."

I laugh, imagining Toby pacing around in his tuxedo, unable to wait for the moment we finally see each other. "I bet he's as excited as I am. I can't wait to hear about his night with Christian and what they've been up to."

"I am a bit down though." I admit. I just want my dad to accept me and the person I love.

"One of these days your dad is going to regret not being here." Jenny hugs me. She always knows what's going on in my head.

A tear falls from my eyes. "I better get the tears out before the makeup."

"We love you!" Rose and Emily say walking over.

"Group hug!" I say.

We all sit there for a bit hugging.

As we eat, the girls start discussing the finer details of the wedding, like the flowers, the cake, and the little touches that made everything special. Rose recounts how she and Emily managed to sneak in a few extra touches to the decorations while I was out of the apartment. "You're going to love it," she promises. "We made sure everything is just right."

Jenny finishes her coffee and stands up, clapping her hands. "Alright, ladies, time to get ready. We've got a wedding to attend!"

We all laugh and head to the bathroom to start getting glammed up.

I glance around the room, where the air is filled with the sweet scent of hairspray and the hum of blow dryers. Jenny, Emily, Rose, and I are all sprawled across the bathroom, transforming ourselves into wedding ready versions of ourselves.

Emily is in front of the mirror, carefully applying mascara.

"So, who's going to be the first to hit the dance

floor after Elena and Toby tonight?" she asks with a teasing grin. "I'm thinking it might be me, unless Rose has some surprise dance moves up her sleeve."

Rose, who's wrestling with a curling iron, laughs. "I've got a few tricks up my sleeve!"

I watch as Jenny expertly applies a touch of blush to my cheeks. "We're all so excited for you." Her voice is calm and soothing, and I feel a rush of gratitude for her steady hands and kind words.

As Jenny finishes with my makeup, Rose takes her turn, carefully pinning curls into place. "I heard the reception is going to be epic. Did you see the decorations? They're just gorgeous."

Emily nods, her eyes sparkling. "Yeah, the venue looks incredible. I can't wait to see everyone's reactions. And don't even get me started on the cake. I hear it's going to be amazing."

I sit quietly, savoring the moment.

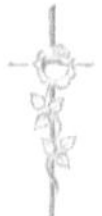

As we step out of the apartment, the crisp December air greets us with a refreshing chill. The sun is shining brightly, casting a golden hue over the snow-covered ground. We make our way to the street, where a sleek black limo is parked, its windows tinted and gleaming under the sunlight.

"Wow," I breathe, my eyes widening in awe as I take in the sight of the limo. "This is incredible. I've never been in a limo before."

Jenny, Rose, and Emily all share amused glances, their excitement palpable. "I know, right?" Jenny exclaims, grinning from ear to ear. "We wanted to make sure you felt like a princess today."

Rose opens the limo door, and I can't help but let out a squeal of delight. The interior is plush and elegant, with leather seats, sparkling glasses, and a bar stocked with sparkling water and a few non-alcoholic treats.

"This is like something out of a movie!" I gush, stepping inside and taking in the luxurious surroundings. "I feel like I'm in a scene from one of those classic romantic comedies."

Emily follows me in, her eyes wide with excitement. "And just wait until you see the sound system. We've got your favorite playlist queued up, ready to go."

Jenny and Rose are right behind, and soon we're all settled in, the limo's interior warm and inviting. I look around, feeling a mix of joy and disbelief. "This is beyond amazing. I can't believe you guys went all out like this."

As the limo starts moving, we all settle into our seats, the conversation flowing easily. Rose pops open a bottle of sparkling grape wine and we each take a glass, toasting to the day ahead.

"To Elena and Toby!" Emily says, raising her glass.

"To love, laughter, and a lifetime of happiness," Jenny adds, clinking her glass against ours.

I lift my glass with a smile, feeling the love and support of my friends surround me. "Thank you, all of you. This day has already been more incredible than I ever imagined, and it's just beginning."

The limo glides smoothly through the streets, and I gaze out the window, watching the city pass by. I can't help but feel overwhelmed with happiness and anticipation. The day ahead holds so much promise, and I'm thrilled to be starting this new chapter with Toby, surrounded by the people who mean the most to me.

The ceremony venue is a breathtaking sight. White drapes cascade from the ceiling, shimmering with silver and gold accents. Rows of white chairs are adorned with delicate floral arrangements, and soft instrumental music plays in the background.

I stand in the wings, my heart pounding with a mix of nerves and excitement. My hands tremble slightly as I clutch the bouquet of white roses, the delicate petals brushing against my fingers. My veil is perfectly placed, framing my face like a halo.

As I peer out into the crowd, my gaze searches for the familiar faces of my friends and family. My heart aches a little as I realize my dad isn't here. The empty space where he should be feels like a heavy weight on my chest. I swallow hard, pushing back the tears that threaten to spill. I remind myself of the love and support surrounding me, and I focus on the happiness of the day.

Christian, looking both nervous and excited. His blonde hair is neatly styled, and he's dressed in a sharp tuxedo. He glances at me and offers a reassuring smile. It's a smile that holds a depth of understanding and affection. I can see the small signs of his recent struggles, but today he looks determined and full of joy.

"Are you ready?" his voice is gentle but filled with warmth. He reaches out, offering his arm to me.

I nod, taking a deep breath to steady my emotions. "As ready as I'll ever be," I say, trying to keep my voice steady.

He gives me a comforting squeeze on the arm. "We're going to get through this. And you're going to be amazing. Toby's going to be blown away."

The music shifts to the opening chords of the wedding intro music and Christian gently leads me toward the aisle. As we step into view, I feel a rush of emotions. My eyes lock onto Toby, who stands at the end of the aisle, looking every bit as handsome as I imagined. His eyes meet mine, and I see a flicker of emotion—love, admiration, and a hint of nervousness. His lip quivers as a smile appears on his face.

As we walk slowly down the aisle, Christian's presence is a steadying force by my side. He gives me subtle nods and encouraging smiles, his support unwavering. The guests' faces blur into a sea of smiles and happy tears, and the soft rustling of their movements seems distant, almost muted, compared to the pounding of my own heartbeat.

With each step, I focus on the small details— the way Toby's eyes light up as he sees me, the way the sunlight catches the glimmer of the decorations, and the comforting weight of Christian's arm around mine.

I push the lingering sadness about my dad to the back of my mind, replacing it with the joy of the moment and the anticipation of what's to come.

When we finally reach the altar, Christian places a gentle kiss on my cheek and steps back, giving me one last reassuring smile. I feel a rush of gratitude for his presence and support. Toby steps forward, his eyes never leaving mine. The world seems to narrow down to just the two of us, and I'm overwhelmed by a profound sense of love and commitment.

The ceremony begins, and I allow myself to get lost in the moment, letting go of the past and embracing the beautiful future that lies ahead.

The officiant stands before us, his smile as warm as the afternoon sun filtering through the elegant decorations. The room is filled with a hush of anticipation, and I can barely contain my excitement. Toby and I are standing close, our hands entwined, ready to share our vows with each other.

The officiant's voice breaks the silence. "We're here today to celebrate the love and commitment between Toby and Elena. They've chosen to express their vows to one another now."

Toby looks at me with that familiar, loving gaze that makes my heart skip a beat. He takes a deep breath. "Elena," he begins, his voice a little shaky but full of sincerity, "from the moment we met, you've been like a bright light in my life. Your laughter, your kindness, and the way you always have my back—it's more than I ever dreamed of. I promise to stand by you, through every challenge that life throws at us, to laugh with you, to comfort you, and to love you with all that I am. You're my best friend and my soulmate, and I can't wait to spend forever with you."

His words make my heart swell, and I feel a tear roll down my cheek. I squeeze his hands tightly, trying to hold back the flood of emotions as I prepare to speak.

"Okay, um," I start, my voice trembling but filled with love, "Toby, from the day we met, I knew there was something special between us. You've been my rock, my biggest supporter, and my best friend. I promise to be there for you, to support you through everything, and to love you unconditionally. You've shown me what real love is, and I'm so grateful to have you in my life. I'm excited to start this new chapter with you and build our future together."

The officiant nods, a smile spreading across his face. "By the power vested in me, I now pronounce you husband and wife. Toby, you may kiss your bride."

His smile lights up as he leans in, and my heart races with excitement. His kiss is soft and sweet, and as we pull away, I can't help but let out a small, joyful laugh. It feels like we're the only ones in the world, wrapped up in our own little bubble of happiness.

The room erupts with applause and cheers, and I glance around at our friends and family, their smiles reflecting the joy of the moment. Christian stands nearby, his eyes shining with pride. I give him a grateful smile, knowing how much his support means to me.

Toby and I turn to face everyone, ready to begin our new journey together. As we walk down the aisle, hand in hand.

Also By Amy Rose

THE VANISHED DUOLOGY SERIES:

Vanished

Vanished: The Quantum Chronicles

BREWING LOVE & LATTES:

That's What Love Is

That's What Love Becomes

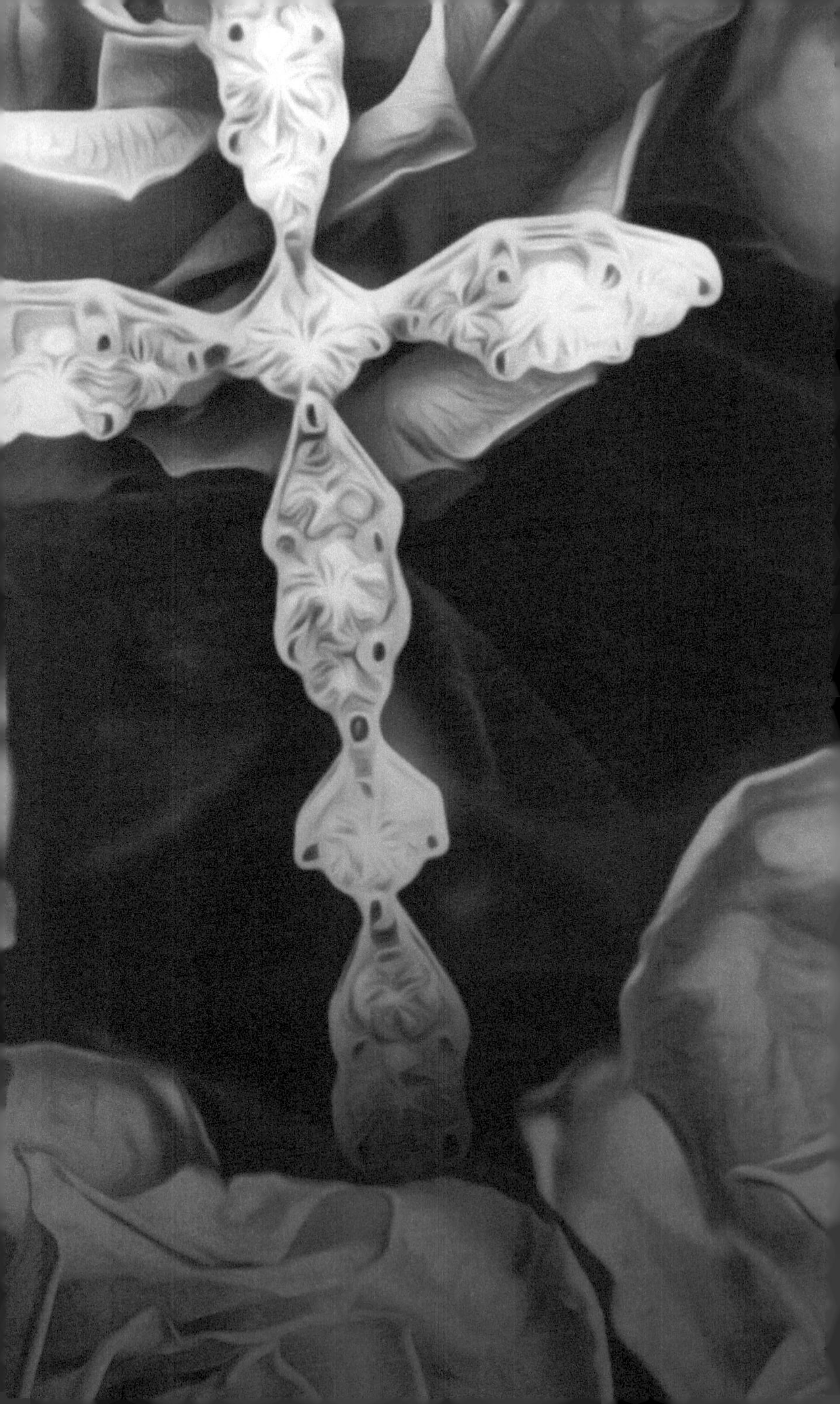

LET'S CONNECT

TikTok: @amyroseauthor
Instagram: @amyroseauthorofficial
Website: amyroseauthor.com
Email: hello@amyjudithrose.com